THE EDEN CHRONICLES - BOOK 1

ADAM

A NOVEL

BRIAN H. WINCHESTER

Cover by Jon Sierra www.sierracreativegroup.com

ISBN: 978-0-982666-59-3
FICTION / CHRISTIAN / HISTORICAL

Published by TM publishing, a division of Teen Mania Ministries (in conjunction with Pilot Communications Group) 22392 FM 16 West Garden Valley, TX 75771 www.teenmania.org

How to reach Brian Winchester:
www.brianwinchester.com

DEDICATION

To the One whose breath
fills us all.

ACKNOWLEDGMENTS

There are three people who made a significant contribution to the completion of *Adam*. The frequent challenges of Scott Thomas, pastor and friend, to develop my as-yet unidentified gifts were what nudged me to start writing to begin with. The constant enthusiasm and unfailing optimism of my wife Deb provided impetus as well as safe harbor whenever the work slowed. And without Brian Mast, the work would never have been transformed from a digital file into the book you now hold in your hands. My deepest thanks to each of you.

ONE

And the Lord God formed man of the dust of the ground, and breathed into his nostrils the breath of life; and man became a living being.
— Genesis 2:7 NKJV

As the eyes of his soul opened, Adam was aware of slowly being filled with breath. The breath washed over his face, caressing his cheeks and forehead, and delicately teasing the curls above his brow. It was fragrant, warm, and moist; yet it cooled his lips and the tip of his nose. As it gently forced itself into his lungs, it awakened a desire to live, and Adam inhaled deeply, straining to take in all that he could.

Adam didn't want the breath to stop.

And it didn't; at least not right away. The breather sensed Adam's ardent desire to prolong their vital embrace, and being willing, continued to blow softly, silently urging Adam to exhale.

As Adam's breath began slipping out, a new sensation began. A tingling feeling of warmth settled on the crown of his head and spread radially outward. It flowed down the contours of his face, crept down the sides and back of his neck, flared out over his shoulders, and continued down his torso. When it reached his belly, it met an answering wave of warmth emanating from somewhere inside his body's center. The inner warmth diffused outward and was soon indistinguishable from the outer warmth.

When Adam was completely bathed in warmth, inside and out, the breath ceased. But Adam still felt a lingering presence, external and internal at the same time … a commingling of being … a communion with the breather. And within that communion, Adam was aware of being loved in the deepest and most enduring way.

Adam lay there for a long time with his eyes closed. Thinking. Exploring the various facets of his awareness. Absorbing the knowledge that he was, and that there was also another.

And breathing, now all by himself.

Adam thought about the difference between his breaths and *the* breath. Although his breaths were pleasant and satisfying, they were also vacant. They contained neither substance nor presence. But *the* breath had been tangible, inhabited. It had been like breathing in a living wind. Adam knew that *the* breath had contained an essence, the essence of the one blowing upon him, yet without the breather being emptied or diminished.

Adam understood that his existence and sentience had only just begun, but he also felt sure that there was more to him than what he now perceived. He knew things without knowing how he knew them. He wondered if knowledge and understanding had somehow been contained within *the* breath. Equally puzzling was the realization that there were things he didn't know, and that beyond the limits of his knowledge there were countless questions for which he had no answers. This concept of questions and incomplete knowledge occupied his thoughts for a long time.

There was a faint touch to his lips and forehead, and Adam opened his eyes. His mind was immediately flooded by vibrant colors and innumerable shapes. But in the space of a heartbeat, he mentally sorted the images and understood what he was looking at. Blue sky. On his right a single cluster of thick tree limbs reaching toward him; the larger branches covered with deeply-fissured gray-brown bark, the younger branches hidden by clusters of small dark green leaves. Mountains on every horizon; some more distant than others, the taller ones capped with snow.

Adam sat up, marveling at his body's movement and the sudden elevation of his visual perspective. His attention was immediately drawn to the various movements in the surrounding landscape. He had been lying in a thick sedge meadow where the seed heads of the sedges were bowing with every light puff of morning breeze. Brooklets of water gurgled on either side of him, and even though the closest was several body lengths away, Adam could see the shimmer and roll of moving water. Looking behind him, he saw where the shape of his upper body had been compressed into the blades of sedge and grass, and that a few of the blades were already springing erect. While the sedges were not wet where he had been laying, elsewhere they were heavy with dew. Adam watched as the dewdrops occasionally slid down to lower positions on the leaf blades.

Adam recognized water, rocks, and flowers, knowing all along that he had never seen any of them before. As he looked from one thing to another, there were small pleasurable bursts of recognition followed immediately by the formation of a name. Everything he saw matched an image that already existed in his mind.

Still sitting, Adam turned his attention to his body. Using his hands to touch and explore, he found that the sense of touch extended over his entire body, and that the nature and strength of the tactile sensations varied from one part to another. Most of his body he could touch without discomfort, but he discovered that there were wet places that shouldn't be touched. Such as his eyes, when they were open. Or the inside of his throat, which when pressed, produced a violent, noisy spasm.

For a while Adam diverted his attention to noise-making, exploring his vocal range and his ability to make different sounds by changing the shape of his mouth. He then returned to his tactile survey, now focusing on body parts that he could neither see nor touch easily. He was trying to visualize what his shoulder blades looked like when his peripheral vision caught a quick movement in the sedges next to an angled, jutting rock.

Adam saw a small, furry mammal the size of his hand, standing erect from among the sedges. It stared at him with dark, liquid eyes, its nose and whiskers quivering. The creature was sorrel brown on top with a small white crescent over each eye. Its undercoat was bright white. In a single graceful leap it gained the top of the rock and turned to face Adam again. Once it was in the open, Adam saw that its tail was longer than its body, and that the tip of the tail was tufted with thicker, longer hairs. Moments later two other creatures scurried out from beneath the rock and bounded up to join the first.

He knew what they were, of course — they were jirds; a type of gerbil.

At first the jirds just stared at him and Adam just stared back. Then, abruptly, the jirds all moved their heads in unison to look at something behind him.

Adam glanced back over his shoulder and saw a shimmering being that appeared to be part substance and part light. It had a body comparable in size to his, and had arms, legs, and a face; all of which possessed a faint warm radiance that seemed to dissolve into the air around it. The being also had some sort of material wrapped around its body, hiding its torso. The material was light in color, and exuded the same radiance as the body. The creature's expression was placid, and it was looking right at him.

For the first time since his awakening, no name came to Adam's mind. He had no idea what this creature was.

Without noticing what he was doing, Adam stood to his feet while turning toward the being, and spoke.

"Who are you?"

His mouth hung open in surprise at his own words. He mentally understood that he had just spoken, but was struck dumb by its effect. There was something inexpressibly beautiful about his inner thoughts being organized and released in sound.

"Who are you?" Adam asked again, as much to hear himself speak as to repeat the question.

"I have been sent by YHWH, the Most High," the angel answered. "I am to be your teacher and your guardian. However, if you mean what is my name, you wouldn't be able to pronounce it. So you may call me Asah."

Questions formed in Adam's mind. "Are you the one who touched me? Who woke me up?"

The being smiled a knowing smile and bowed slightly. "I am."

"And how is it that I don't know what you are? Everything else I recognize."

"You don't know me because I am not of your dominion, nor of this realm. I am here to serve you, and in many instances to do your bidding, but I am nevertheless not yours to command. At this moment I am looking at you and speaking with you, but I live to gaze upon the One who is unseeable and unknowable, who dwells in unapproachable light. He is the source of my life and my being. He is the One I truly serve."

"But I wasn't sent to speak of myself," Asah continued, "I am here to answer the question you haven't thought to ask."

Adam's head was swimming with questions; he felt sure there were a great many he hadn't thought to ask.

"You are Adam; the first human son to bear His likeness and the first to carry His image in a body of flesh." With those words Asah took one step backward while turning sideways, and vanished.

TWO

The angel of the Lord encampeth round about them that fear him, and delivereth them.
— Psalm 34:7 KJV

Adam stood there pondering. He still didn't understand what Asah was. Or who YHWH the Most High was. Or where Asah had come from or where he had gone. Although Adam had been awake only a short while, he had already developed a preference for looking at things and immediately grasping what they were, how they worked, and how they fit into the realm around him. But Asah, according to his own words, was of a different realm. There was a void in Adam's understanding, and the not knowing was disconcerting.

He turned back around. The jirds were still there, settled and still on the rock. He walked over to them, enjoying the rhythm and shifting balance of his steps. The jirds stood up as he approached, as if expecting him to do something.

"And who are you?"

The largest of the jirds answered. "You know who we are, we are jirds. And you are Adam. We have been waiting to see you." The jird's voice was high, one word flowing into another. Some of the harder, sharper sounds of Adam's speech were entirely missing; other hard sounds were replaced by tocks and clicks. But he could still understand them clearly.

"Well here I am, can you see me well enough?"

"Yes, you are easy to see. You are very, very big."

A wave of pleasure swept over Adam, his chest shaking as he breathed out. It so caught him by surprise that he stared down at himself, and as soon as he did, the shaking and pleasant sensation stopped. Witnessing this, the jirds erupted into a chorus of sharp barks, drumming their feet on the rock in between little hops.

They were hilarious. Adam began laughing so hard that water formed in his eyes. He began jumping around like the jirds, rapidly stomping on the grass in between jumps. At this, the jirds became even more excited, leaping higher and bouncing off of each other in midair.

Adam finally sank to the ground, breathing hard, his legs weak and unstable. The sensation of laughing had been so enjoyable and refreshing that he wanted it to continue, but it had subsided and he didn't know how to make it start again. The jirds lay sprawled on the rock, panting rapidly.

It occurred to Adam that the jirds might be able to answer some of his questions. "Do you know what kind of creature Asah was?"

The same jird stood up again. "We do not know such things. We know nuts and seeds and grass and burrows and pups. These things we know. And now we know Adam. Please jump again."

Adam obliged with a series of hops on one foot, which set the jirds off on another short-lived round of exuberant leaping.

When they stopped Adam asked a simpler question. "So what can you tell me about nuts and seeds and grass and burrows and pups?"

The morning passed with Adam learning from the jirds. They brought out pistachio nuts, acorns, almonds, and assorted grains from their burrow storehouses, and Adam took his first meal, though a very small one. He relished each new flavor and marveled at how his mouth and tongue knew what to do with the food — how to move the food around inside his mouth, how much to chew before swallowing.

Adam found it curious that his body did exactly what he willed it to do, yet it also did things without his active mental participation. He didn't have to think about chewing for his mouth to continue grinding on whatever was in it. And all this time he had been breathing without giving it any thought since his initial reflections.

The jirds led him to nearby pistachio trees, their limbs laden with fist-sized clusters of nuts. They dug sedge tubers out of the ground, which Adam found to be sweet and succulent. He learned that he could dip the tubers in the brooklets to wash off the gritty soil, a practice the jirds briefly imitated but then discarded. He learned about drinking from the brooklets and keeping his nose out of the water as he did so. And then the jirds showed him their pups, one by one. Throughout the morning Adam had grasped virtually all of what they had told him, but the business of pup-making was completely baffling.

It was slightly past midday when the first jird stood and told Adam it was past time for them to return to their burrows. It hesitated, glancing at the others and then looking back at Adam, all the while turning a grain of wheat over and over in its front paws. Finally, looking up at him, it made a request. "Adam, excuse us so much for asking, but is this the day of our naming? We would like very much to be named."

"I thought you were jirds. Aren't you?"

"Yes, of course. But we are not all one jird, we are different jirds. The Most High knows each of us, but he has left our naming to you."

Here was another puzzle. But Adam found the thought of naming them agreeable.

Reaching out a finger, he touched the one who had done most of the speaking on the crown of its head, "You are Talker." He paused and thought, and then touched and named the other two in turn. By the time he was done, Talker had already retrieved four pups from the burrow, all of which were so young their eyes were still closed. Adam named each of these as well. When he had named the last pup, Talker dashed over and brushed himself against Adam's toes, marking him with their family scent, and then scurried belowground with the rest of the jirds.

Adam spent the afternoon looking and touching and tasting, thinking about everything that had happened. As the light began to dim he understood that night was approaching, and returned to the spot where he had awakened, just in case *the* breath should return. Once there, Adam sat virtually motionless, studying how his ability to see both diminished and changed as dusk gave way to darkness.

"You put on quite a show for your first day," Asah said.

Adam whirled, jumping to his feet. He had been so engrossed with his thoughts and the onset of night that he hadn't noticed Asah's silent appearance behind him. This time Asah's body exhibited no luminosity.

Asah raised his left eyebrow in response to Adam's reaction, and then understood and slowly transformed his obscure silhouette into the slightly radiant body Adam had seen earlier. His clothing was as before, but now Asah also held a slender wooden staff in each hand.

Asah continued speaking as if nothing was wrong. "All of heaven has been watching you. There has been much rejoicing and celebration. Some of the lesser angels even started hopping around on one foot as a form of greeting, but the ranking angels thought it might imply disrespect and made them stop."

Adam wasn't laughing and didn't feel like celebrating. He had been startled, which was an unpleasant sensation, and he was still unhappy about Asah's abrupt departure earlier that morning.

"Asah, please don't approach me silently from behind and please don't leave before I ask you some questions. There are many things I don't understand and that makes me uncomfortable. If you are here to do my bidding, then I bid you to stay and help me unravel these mysteries in my mind."

"Peace to you Adam," Asah spoke with a disarming smile. "I know you have much to ask and even more to learn. It has been given to me to open many things to your understanding. Other things will be taught to you by God himself. And yet others you will deduce yourself. But know this, much learning is wearisome to the body, and it is needful for you to rest."

With Asah's words, Adam felt a blanket of peace ease gently upon him, bringing stillness to his mind and a release to his tired muscles. He didn't want to relinquish this opportunity to talk with Asah, but the importance of getting his questions answered lessened the moment Asah had spoken.

"By the way," Asah continued, "I never left you. I am always watching over you. I just stepped out of sight so you could get acquainted with your dominion without my shining presence to distract you. I will be here as you rest."

Adam just stood there, looking at Asah.

"Lying down would be a good way to start."

Adam complied. He shut his eyes and felt himself gently falling back into the peace that Asah had spoken over him. It was a very pleasurable sensation. He thought to sit up and ask Asah whether *the* breath would awaken him again, but even that question required more effort than it was worth.

When Adam was fully asleep, Asah walked over and stood astride over where he lay. As darkness fell, Asah's form magnified until he stood as tall as the adjacent oak tree. Each staff hardened into a glittering light-metal broadsword and the material of his white tunic simultaneously transformed into light-armor that adhered like shimmering skin around his torso.

Had Adam been awake, Asah's altered body would have appeared to be less substantial than the stout oak to his side. But this was hardly the case. Asah's body was in fact more substantial than any material on earth. His smallest finger could cleave the massive oak trunk top to bottom (or bottom to top) with less effort than it took Adam to wave an arm through the air. And this Asah could accomplish without even moving from where he stood. Had he put his body and swords in motion, he could have killed every plant and animal in the meadow before Adam finished exhaling his current breath.

Nor were Asah's abilities limited to his mastery of matter. His command of radiant energy was even greater. He could shine brightly enough to spontaneously ignite all combustible material in his immediate vicinity, or to permanently blind every eye of flesh turned toward him. He could manipulate his emanating light to precisely mimic that of his surroundings, thereby assuming the appearance of very ordinary objects. Or he could fully contain his light, thereby assuming the appearance of nothing at all, which was more useful if he wished to remain undetected in dark or near-dark conditions.

But Asah did have limitations. He couldn't be in two places at once. This was true whether he was in the material realm or the aetherial realm (through which angels normally traveled). He had the ability to move in either realm, but only when he was wholly within that realm. Asah could reach through the interface between the realms and in that sense exist in both realms at the same time, but he could not travel with facility unless he withdrew to one side of the interface or the other.

And Asah's strength was not inexhaustible. As a creature of the light, he was dependent on YHWH, from whom emanated all spiritual light and who bestowed all power, might, and strength. Asah's strength was directly related to the sum of the ambient spiritual light at Asah's location, plus the light Asah contained within him. In places of great darkness, or during a prolonged battle, Asah's strength could eventually diminish to the point that he could no longer fight effectively. He couldn't be killed (spirits being eternal), but he could be functionally incapacitated. Once that happened, he could only wait until a comrade arrived and imparted strength.

Asah had never yet been in such grim straits, though he was the veteran of many battles. But heretofore there had been no battles wholly within the material realm of Earth, simply because the Earth had never contained anything truly worth fighting for.

Adam's arrival would change all that.

Asah assumed a covering stance. He stood with one foot to the right and one to the left of Adam's heart, the point of one sword gently touching the earth a body's length above Adam's head and the other sword point resting below Adam's feet. Even Asah didn't know the significance of the axis outlined by his feet and sword points.

THREE

He uncovers deep things out of darkness, and brings the shadow of death to light.
— Job 12:22 NKJV

Asah's head snapped to the right, eyes ablaze — something not of Earth was approaching. He wasn't sure what or how many, but he knew they were out there. He dampened and adjusted the faint light emanating from his spirit-body and his armaments until they were of the same hue and background radiance as his surroundings. Then he set about systematically scanning the surrounding terrain, looking far and then near, over and over again.

Asah could have slipped completely into the aetherial realm and perhaps seen the dark spirits more easily, but that would have necessitated him stepping away from Adam, something he would never do under circumstances like these. Besides, he would have risked revealing himself by such an action, and there was a good probability that he had not yet been seen. Better that he remain wholly within the material realm for the moment.

It hadn't taken them very long. Dark spirits didn't take casual evening strolls through the landscape of Earth without cause. They were here because they somehow knew or at least sensed something was afoot. This was likely a reconnaissance, a probing, an attempt to flush something into the open. Because the wisdom of God had kept the day of Adam hidden, the dark spirits probably didn't know what they were searching for. Nonetheless, they were not to be trifled with.

Asah's eyes were much keener than human eyes. He saw them first because of a slight diminution of night-light as they crested a treeless rise a few hundred yards away. There appeared to be four of them — a massive, oppressive spirit of darkness and three underlings. Their path was not direct, but they were still heading generally in Asah's direction, or more importantly, in Adam's direction.

Asah needed to make a decision quickly. He was more than a match for them in open combat, but he was constrained by the need to cover Adam. If they could succeed in drawing him aside and uncovering Adam, they could do immense damage. And if Asah were to engage them, he would need to vanquish all four so that no report could be borne back to the Gates of Hell. But if they never saw either him or Adam ….

Ever so slowly, Asah's transformed his spirit-body's light signature into that of a large, old tree. The roots and trunk completely covered Adam, so that his frail human body could not be seen from anywhere outside. Asah adjusted the pattern and strength of his body's light to precisely match that of the adjacent oaks. He felt reasonably sure the noise of the brooklets would cover the faint sounds of Adam's breathing and heartbeat. The dark spirits would not know one of the trees was an illusion unless they actually touched it.

As the demons approached, the normal, constant sounds of the night lessened and then stopped. The countless small movements of the meadow's small animals also ceased. The family of jirds, which had been foraging at some distance from their burrow, had all scurried back and were huddled together belowground.

The spirits also moved in silence. It seemed like they would pass by when one of the smaller demons stopped a few feet away from the jutting rock where the jirds had celebrated Adam's arrival.

A whisper came from tiny, misshapen swollen lips. "There is something here."

The other two lesser demons approached, mindful that a rock is not always a rock, and knowing how terrible the consequence could be if they failed to discern the difference. The larger spirit of darkness spoke, all the while remaining at a safe distance, "Well, lay hands and be quick about it. You aren't spirits of timidity."

Their reluctance was obvious. But arousing the ire of the larger spirit of darkness could have dire consequences of its own. One of the demons, to the surprise of the others, said that it would test the rock. Stepping back as if to search out the best approach, it craftily pushed the nearest underling against the rock while leaping back.

The duped spirit screamed in alarm, but stopped upon contacting what turned out to be just an ordinary rock. Then its attention was captured and it began touching the rock with its wrinkled fingers, moving them from spot to spot. Finally it touched its lips to the rock and immediately jerked back, spitting and hissing. "A blessing occurred here," it said.

No accord was reached in the ensuing discussion. The first demon held fast to its assessment, and the others were inclined to agree. But they could think of no plausible reason why a rock would be blessed. Furthermore, the spoor of this blessing was unlike any they had previously encountered. In the end, they decided to report their findings and continued on in their dark search, never once looking toward Asah.

Beneath the rock, the jirds had remained absolutely still as the demonic footsteps tramped about above them. In their being named by Adam, they had come fully under Adam's dominion, and by extension, had become a material expression of God's dominion on Earth. Thus, the blessing bestowed by Adam made the jirds a target. Not an important target, but a target nonetheless. They didn't understand this in a rational sense, but they were not without spiritual perception, and had sensed that danger was close.

Asah retained his form as a gnarled tree for the last two hours before dawn, concerned that the enemy might double back or that he might be observed covertly from a distance. He resumed his usual material form only after the night shadows had fully dispersed and Adam had begun to stir.

Today Adam would learn about his role in the realm of Earth, and his responsibility and authority as its guardian.

It would be none too soon.

FOUR

Praise the Lord from the earth, ye dragons, and all deeps: fire, and hail; snow, and vapour; stormy wind fulfilling his word: moun-tains, and all hills; fruitful trees, and all cedars: beasts, and all cattle; creeping things, and flying fowl …
— Psalm 148:7-10 KJV

For ye shall go out with joy, and be led forth with peace: the moun-tains and the hills shall break forth before you into singing, and all the trees of the field shall clap their hands.
— Isaiah 55:12 KJV

Adam awoke to the touch of a cool breeze on his face. It was not the living breath of the day before, yet the air carried a sweet, earthy fragrance. Asah was nowhere to be seen, and except for the ceaseless melody of the streams, a hush lay upon the meadow as thick as the morning dew. Yesterday the meadow and brooklets had been bustling with life, but this morning they seemed very still.

Adam thumped on the jird rock, but there was no response.

Perhaps they are all asleep, Adam thought.

He mentally recounted all the different forms of life he had seen since awakening. Throughout the preceding day he had encountered an unending variety of flying, walking, crawling, and swimming creatures. Although he had not named them all individually as he had the jirds, Adam had mentally noted the name of each kind. He had also begun to mentally organize the kinds of plants and kinds of soil, observing that different plants displayed affinities for different types of soil and even for different amounts of soil moisture.

Adam arose, his body conveying an array of new sensations. He attended to these with as much wonder as had accompanied his discoveries of the day before. One sensation was left unabated, and Adam followed his growing desire to revisit the pistachio trees. After eating his fill and drinking from the brooklet, he reflected on how his body seemed to instruct and direct him through sensation rather than through word or thought.

The stillness of the morning was broken by the whoosh of wings over his head. A flock of chaffinches skimmed just above the treetops at top speed. Adam had watched flocks like this one yesterday, but those had moved with a rolling, fluid quality that seemed undirected and unhurried, periodically alighting only to suddenly erupt into the air again. This morning's flock apparently had a destination toward the east, where the morning sky was brightest. No sooner was the flock past when six gazelles spilled over the top of a nearby rise, gracefully bounding in the same direction. Adam shifted his focus to more distant portions of the landscape and saw the movement of other creatures, singly and in groups, all apparently traveling toward a common point.

There was, in fact, a discernible tug inside of him. It wasn't one of the many body sensations Adam had already grown accustomed to. This was coming from deep within, from a place he could sense but not fathom. The urge to move was compelling. Without a backward glance, Adam strode away from the place of his awakening, intent upon finding the source of the wordless call. His walk turned to a jog, and just as quickly, the jog gave way to a run.

He didn't know where he was going, but he knew the direction to go, the inner call guiding him when he needed to bear to the left or right. He ran with wild, joyous abandon, skipping and leaping and dodging as required by the terrain and trees. He moved through patches of forest almost as quickly as through the open meadows.

Although he was breathing hard and moving fast, he maintained the pace with minimal effort, the thrill of running as great as the anticipation of what might await him at his destination. Adam couldn't help but notice how much stronger he was than the day before.

As he continued, Adam encountered other creatures with increasing frequency, passing some and being passed by others. Had the call in his spirit not been so urgent, he would have stopped to observe and study each new life-form. But for now, nothing else mattered.

The daylight was growing brighter, suffused with the same warm radiance Adam had seen emanating from Asah, but now it was everywhere, filling the air. Everything was becoming brighter, more vivid, crystalline in clarity. Still running, Adam heard another sound between his rapid footfalls and the brush of leaves. The sound, which had just begun, grew steadily in strength, rising and falling, eddying and cascading. Although the sound was in some ways like a single mighty voice, Adam could tell that it was actually comprised of many, many voices.

Adam urged his legs to greater speed as he nimbly leapt over rock and log. As he drew closer to his destination he could hear the anthem more clearly, enough to occasionally distinguish the individual voices of creatures he knew. It seemed that all of the living creatures from the surrounding hills and glades were converging toward one place, and that as they journeyed, each one was raising its unique call in cooperation with and counterpoint to its neighbor.

Adam realized that was why the meadow where he had slept had seemed so silent and deserted. Most of the meadow's inhabitants had probably left to make this same journey while he was still sleeping.

Adam stopped momentarily, striving to take it all in. Wherever he looked, creatures were abandoning themselves in wild sound of every type, each in its own way, yet each in harmony with the rest. As Adam watched he saw that some of the animals periodically paused in silence, only to resume a few moments later.

There is order in their vocalizations, Adam realized. *Their calls are not random, but are following some prescribed pattern.*

Adam closed his eyes and listened intently, trying to hear the whole rather than the individual parts. When he did that, the pattern became clearer and its beauty and balance more apparent. But it was still too complex for Adam to decipher. And the more he listened, the more he wanted to stop analyzing and just join in.

Now that he was standing still, Adam could feel an underlying vibration in the ground. He placed his hand on a nearby boulder that was partially buried in the soil, and then laid his ear against it to confirm what he felt.

The rock was humming!

Dashing to another boulder, Adam found it was emitting the same even tone, and that the smaller pebbles around its base were clattering against each other. Adam wondered whether some resonance in the earth was causing the rocks to rattle, or if they were vibrating of their own accord.

Adam felt his heart would surely burst if he didn't add his own voice to those around him. But the inner tug was also still there, chiding him for stopping and urging him to run until he reached his destination.

Adam ran on. He jumped over and around creatures more frequently now, taking care not to step on the smaller ones. He saw that the forest was starting to thin, the trees gradually yielding to a wide, open glade. The ambient light was becoming increasingly brilliant, not just because the canopy was more open, but because the air itself was glowing. If it became much brighter, Adam would have to avert his eyes downward to cope with the discomfort.

He broke out of the woods and saw a glade teeming with creatures, great and small, all facing inward, all wriggling, swaying, or stamping; all lost in corporate chorus. The object of their attention was hidden from Adam's view by one last scrubby strand of oaks. Adam decided to crash through the intervening brush rather than circle around, and with determined effort he finally broke through to the far side.

And stopped, frozen in time and place.

It was the One ....

The One whose breath he now held within him ....

The One who had called deep within Adam's spirit; calling him to come, and to come quickly ....

It was YHWH; the Lord God, the Almighty.

It was his Father and Creator.

Adam's response was as natural and easy as taking his next breath. His body, soul, and spirit knew exactly what to do, and did so in such perfect harmony and unity that it required no conscious orchestration on

Adam's part. His legs, which had been so strong a moment earlier, trembled once and abruptly gave way beneath him. His arms went out as he dropped to the earth, not only to break his fall, but in a bid to embrace and be embraced. And as he fell, Adam joined his voice to the tumult of riotous praise that was resounding from everywhere around him.

Each time Adam raised his eyes to gaze at Him, the intensity of the light drove his eyes downward. He could not look, and yet to not look was equally unbearable. Everything within him yearned to see Him, and to be seen himself ... to return to the communion of the breath.

Adam worshiped with the rest of the earth and slipped outside the realm of time.

Eventually, unnoticed by Adam, YHWH lifted one hand slightly. Like a wave expending itself on a shore, the creatures of the glade became silent, the trees became still, and the ground resumed its immobile state. The host of heaven also heeded the Lord's command, and in half a heartbeat the Earth' silence was mirrored and amplified by a rare silence in the heavenlies.

Adam was distantly aware that he was now alone in worship, but it didn't matter. When he looked up, he saw that the gaze of the all-seeing One was centered squarely upon him. It was both terrifying and wonderful. The Lord was clearly reveling in Adam's solitary worship. This was a wonder in itself — that he should have the ability to bring such profound pleasure and joy to his Creator. It spurred him to an even greater outpouring of adoration.

He worshipped until his voice grew hoarse and weak from his adulations. Until he whispered his praise, diminished in volume but no less rich in content. Until, finally, he fell silent, spent in body and spirit, utterly empty of the need to do or say anything. It was enough to be still in the presence of his Father. YHWH also seemed to be at rest with him, enjoying the depths of their shared silence.

Eventually Adam's deep contentment drifted into deep sleep.

FIVE

How art thou fallen from heaven, O Lucifer, son of the morning!
How art thou cut down to the ground …
 — Isaiah 14:12a KJV

You were the anointed cherub who covers; I established you; you
were on the holy mountain of God; you walked back and forth in
the midst of fiery stones. You were perfect in your ways from the
day you were created, till iniquity was found in you … and you
sinned; therefore I cast you as a profane thing out of the mountain
of God; and I destroyed you, O covering cherub …
 — Ezekiel 28: 14-15, 16b NKJV

… God is light and in Him is no darkness at all.
 — I John 1:5b NKJV

When Adam awoke he found that YHWH was still there, though His glory was subdued enough to allow approach. The Creator's eyes were welcoming and expectant, so Adam tentatively drew closer. And so began the first conversation between God and man.

They walked and talked together, continuing in the easterly direction Adam had started on that morning. Throughout their walk, Adam had the same sensations he remembered from his pre-awakening — sensations of being loved, treasured, and thoroughly known. These sensations had flooded his awareness from the moment his sentience had begun the day before, but had lessened upon opening his eyes and engaging the physical realm around him. Now the sensations enveloped him once again. He would have likened it to returning to a womb, or perhaps the embrace of a mother, had he known what either a womb or a mother was. What he did know was that he felt fully at rest, settled, fulfilled. Upon reflection, Adam realized that these feelings of intimacy and belonging had been diminishing ever since his awakening.

As they walked, YHWH spoke of the responsibilities Adam would assume in the days ahead. Adam still had countless questions left over from his first day, but many of these no longer seemed important. Now it was enough to listen, absorb with his mind, and bask with his heart. Even the occasional periods of silent communion were filled with meaning and closeness of spirit.

Adam learned that they were going to a place, a vast, secluded garden which the Lord had planted more than a century earlier in anticipation of Adam's arrival. The garden was in a land named Eden, and it would be Adam's home. Adam's task would be to cultivate and guard the garden, and over time, to broaden its expanse. Like Adam, the garden was a prototype upon the Earth, and they would grow together over the days and years ahead.

The concept of cultivation was easy enough to grasp, for Adam had already deduced many of the fundamental principles of how the living realm functioned. It was easy to see how the manipulation of soil, water, and selective plantings could be used to produce aesthetically pleasing arrays and patterns of plants, and to enhance production of the edible plant types.

It was not the Lord's intention that Adam replicate what he saw in the garden, but rather, that Adam learn from it and apply his own creativity in developing it further. That being said, Adam was cautioned that mastering and managing the garden would be no small task, and that it would be years before he was ready to significantly expand it. By that time, if Adam consented, he would have the help he would need. When Adam asked if Asah was going to help with the gardening, YHWH laughed and advised him not to look to Asah for gardening advice; saying that Adam already knew more about gardening than all the angels of heaven combined.

The subject of guarding was a whole different matter — one which required lengthy instruction. Adam came to understand that there were vast numbers of other angelic beings akin to Asah. These were the angels of light, the Anhailas. Some resided solely in the spiritual realm (the realm Asah had disappeared into the day before), while others routinely visited the material realm of Earth for a variety of purposes. They were here to serve Adam, help him in the protection of the garden, and to relay the word of YHWH. Asah's role encompassed all of these, but his primary role was to protect Adam and to tutor him in spiritual matters.

There were also creatures that had once been angels but which were now altered both in form and purpose, having been evicted from the heavenly realm due to their rebellion. These were the spirits of darkness, the fallen angels, the Daimónia. They were not to be allowed in the garden, nor conversed with. The demons were obligated to obey Adam's commands because YHWH had placed the whole earth under Adam's authority and dominion, and that dominion included spiritual beings residing on or visiting the earth. In time, Adam's reign and influence would encompass the entire planet, but for now, he needed to start with something manageable. Therefore, Adam was to be vigilant in watching over the garden, and should any dark spirits attempt entry, he was to drive them out.

From a practical perspective, Adam could only exclude the Daimónia from those portions of Eden that were under active cultivation or that he frequented for other reasons. However, his ability to protect would grow in tandem with his skills at cultivation. As time passed and the garden expanded, the exclusion zone of the spirits of darkness would likewise increase. Eventually, in the distant future, the day would come when the Daimónia would be completely excluded from the material realm of Earth.

They had been walking for hours, descending in elevation and traversing a landscape that was increasingly thick and lush. The stroll remained easy in spite of the distance they had covered. Although Adam could discern no visible trail, it seemed that the verdant growth was always open and passable for a short distance ahead.

It was early afternoon and they still had not reached the valley of Eden when the Lord God indicated that He would depart until their next time of communion. Asah would accompany Adam for the remainder of the day. Looking up Adam saw Asah waiting a respectful distance away; and when Adam looked back, YHWH was nowhere to be seen.

Adam no longer felt like walking, and after Asah's approach, Adam resumed his questioning. Asah seemed agreeable and in no hurry. Although many of Adam's questions concerning the spiritual realm were answered, some were not — either because Asah met the question with an inscrutable smile or because the answer he provided only deepened the mystery. It was becoming increasingly evident that the Lord and Asah were expecting Adam to search out some answers for himself.

"Adam, you must understand that knowledge cannot be gained all at once." Asah started a new lecture. "It is a process that occurs over time, and there is an orderly sequence that should be followed as you gain knowledge and grow in understanding. That's why I don't answer every question you ask. Furthermore, you need more than just knowledge, you need wisdom as well. Knowledge is of little value without wisdom."

"And wisdom is …?"

Asah didn't wait for him to finish his question. "… the ability to apply one's knowledge in an appropriate and productive fashion. While many areas of understanding were imparted to you at your moment of inspiration, wisdom was not included in that first breath. Wisdom will come as you live life. It is something you will grow in day by day. And while understanding is expressed in the medium of thoughts and concepts, wisdom is resident within your spirit and has a voice of its own. Wisdom also accumulates much more slowly than knowledge. You will need both to accomplish the task the Lord has set before you, so don't neglect the pursuit of wisdom in your quest for knowledge."

Adam agreed that there was much he needed to learn to properly watch over and keep the garden, but he wanted practical answers, not lectures on abstract themes. Adam knew that his practical understanding of the Daimónia was particularly lacking, given that he was to defend the garden against them

Adam interrupted. "Asah, how do I differentiate between the Anhailas and the Daimónia?"

Asah continued as if this was the next point in his discourse. "This requires a third type of knowledge — one known as discernment.

Discernment is an understanding deep within your spirit that is not linked to any specific mental process. You will almost always just know, and first impressions are to be given more credence than second thoughts. Your use of discernment when you encounter unknown spirits is very important because some Daimónia can mimic angels of light, appearing superficially as friends and allies. You will know the difference only as long as your spirit is quiet and undistracted. However, you should not worry greatly about this. Your ability to discern will increase with practice, and I will be with you as you master it."

Asah's words held little comfort and Adam felt tendrils of anxiety in his stomach. "Is there no other guidance you can give me to distinguish friend from foe?"

"Actually, there is another key to unmasking those Daimónia that are masquerading as spirits of light. That key is to look in their eyes. The eyes of the Anhailas have a clear, lustrous, transparent quality."

Adam studied Asah's eyes as he was talking and saw that this was indeed the case.

"The eyes of demons, however, are clouded and opaque, hinting at the darkness hidden deep within them. In the more powerful spirits of darkness, the eyes may appear to emanate a murky light of their own. This light may feel like it is clutching at your soul, or the eye-light may have a compelling quality, enticing you to approach more closely. If you encounter a spirit with this kind of eye-light, it will elicit a very different response in your spirit than the eye-light of an angel from heaven."

Asah paused, unsure whether he was giving Adam too much information too quickly. Adam was untested in the realm of spiritual warfare, and for a season Asah would have preferred to avoid encounters between Adam and the Daimónia. But encounters were inevitable, and Asah understood that the first encounter could happen at any time. That first encounter could easily unfold in such a way that Adam had to stand and fight, ready or not. Asah finally concluded that Adam needed as much instruction as he could absorb, even though he might not be fully ready to apply it.

"Adam, you must be on guard when examining the eyes of fallen spirits. While you may have to look into their eyes to discern their true nature, continuing to gaze at them can evoke dangerous feelings. This is to be avoided. Prolonged intercourse with the eyes of the Daimónia is very perilous. I cannot emphasize this enough. Angels much wiser than you have fallen by not heeding this warning."

The afternoon sun was warm, but Adam felt a chill. Asah told him they needed to resume their journey in order to reach Eden before nightfall, so they started walking again. They descended for a while and crossed the wide, shallow stream of the valley floor. After pushing through the thickets of willow in the stream's floodplain, they began climbing in elevation again, eventually leaving the main valley as they entered a rugged side gorge.

Adam asked questions on a variety of subjects, but the topic soon returned to the war between the Anhailas and the Daimónia.

"Asah, what can the Daimónia do? I mean, what are their powers?"

"Most dark spirits can clothe themselves with a physical form and can manipulate matter," Asah said, "just as angels can. Because they are no longer creatures of the light, they can't contain or emit light the way they could when they were angels, but most can still manage the light in their immediate vicinity. Consequently, when in the material realm they can mimic the appearance of animate or inanimate objects, and thereby escape easy detection."

"Some dark spirits are confined to the aetherial realm, having lost their ability to cross the interface into the material realm. However, these spirits can still express themselves in whispers of thought and nuances of feeling, because, of course, the interface is completely permeable to both spoken words and directed thoughts. Spoken words can pass across the interface in either direction, though they take on a different, more substantial form once they enter the aetherial realm. Conversely, they lose that form when they enter the material realm."

"What are directed thoughts?" Adam asked, wondering how it was possible for thoughts to have a direction.

"When you are just thinking to yourself, your thoughts are not audible to others." Asah paused and then corrected himself. "Well, that's not strictly true … your thoughts are always audible to YHWH. But I wouldn't be able to hear them, nor would demons be able to hear them."

"But if you were to *speak* your thoughts inside your mind without using your voice, that would be directing your thoughts. When you do this toward YHWH, you are using a silent form of communication known as prayer. Such directed thoughts cross the interface as if it doesn't exist."

"And demons can hear such unspoken thoughts?" Adam found that thought a bit alarming.

"I don't know Adam. I haven't asked that question. I do know that when I am near you, your prayers are faintly discernible as they cross the interface. Perhaps if a demon were close enough and listening, it might be able to hear them as well. But I think that is the only point where they might possibly be overheard. Once a prayer is fully across the interface, it disappears from its original location and simultaneously reappears in the presence of YHWH."

"Well, since there is a chance my prayers might be overheard by the Daimónia, perhaps I should only speak to YHWH when He is present in person." Adam had already concluded that he wanted his thoughts to be private as far as the Daimónia were concerned.

"No, Adam, that won't do at all. There will surely be times when you will want or need to speak to Him when He is not physically apparent. And He wants you to speak to Him as often as you have even the slightest inclination to. That's why He designed this method of communication. Besides, your prayers are of great value to Him; in fact, He intends to collect them."

"Collect them? Why?"

"My apologies again, for again I don't know." Asah looked slightly pained that he had no answer. "You will discover that while there are many things I can teach you, there are many more that I don't understand. The created realms, both material and aetherial, are full of mysteries. Some of these God will uncover simply if you ask Him. Others are hidden until the time YHWH has set for their revelation. It is His way. With regard to your prayers, He has said only that they are precious and indicated that they will be used later. I have no idea what He meant by that, though He was smiling when He said it."

"Is He collecting your prayers as well?"

Asah raised an eyebrow, which Adam had already come to recognize as an indication that Asah was puzzled or thinking intently.

"No, not to my knowledge." Asah said, not having thought about this before. "First of all, you should understand that communicating to

God from the material realm of Earth is a new thing. After all, before your awakening yesterday there had been no need for dialogue between the material and spiritual realms. So this is as new to us as it is to you."

"Secondly, the Anhailas don't communicate with Him in the way that you do. When we need to say something to YHWH we carry the message in person. In fact, our name, Anhailas, means "messengers." And if a message needs to be delivered from YHWH to one of us, it is almost always carried back the same way. There are occasions when YHWH will speak to an angel directly, but this is uncommon and only when the message is of the greatest urgency."

"Not that any of His messages should ever be considered to be non-urgent," Asah added.

"What about those Daimónia that can enter the material realm; are they able to physically harm me?"

"I have no doubt that they will try; once they learn who you are and the danger you represent." Asah watched Adam for his reaction but saw no fear, only concern. "However, as long as you remain under the protective covering of God, none of the various types of Daimónia will be able to significantly injure you. However, they are all accomplished deceivers and will seek to engage you in dialogue and thereby lure you into their sphere of influence. If that were ever to happen, there is no predicting the amount of harm that could result."

As they walked, Asah recounted the history of the rebellion. It had started with a chief angel named Lucifer (his name meant "carrier of the light"). For reasons only God knows, Lucifer grew dissatisfied with his position in the heavenly realm, and lusted after the glory and splendor that belonged to God alone. This was ironic, for few in the host of heaven were afforded greater honor and status than Lucifer. It was also ludicrous, for no created being, angel or otherwise, could ever hope to acquire equality with the Most High.

In time, Lucifer's words began to give subtle indications that his thinking had become corrupt. This should have been self-evident to the angelic host, and yet for many, it was not. After all, lies and evil thoughts had never existed in heaven before, and the concept that there could be untruth was a strange one.

"The first lie," Asah said, "was that which Lucifer told himself. The Father of lies brought forth a single seed of untruth deep within his being, and in embracing it, deceived himself. As that first lie grew within him, it in turn conceived new lies. One by one, precepts and beliefs that Lucifer had always held to be true weakened and fell, their foundations gnawed away by the growing horde of lies. In time, Lucifer's mind became so consumed with false belief systems that no truth remained. Every construct of thought, every belief system, every perspective, was corrupted in some way."

"While Lucifer initially hid the growing uncleanness of his thoughts, he soon reached the point where everything he spoke contained an element of untruth, if only in the intended effect of the words. And so it was that his words gave the first clear evidence of his having become anti-God."

"That is not to say that Lucifer's words were not pleasant and persuasive, they were — persuasive enough to seduce a third of the angelic host. He often began with what appeared to be a simple question. But his questions were anything but simple, because embedded within each question were seeds of doubt and untruth. Those angels that rejected Lucifer's questions out of hand fared much better than those that gave his words consideration. Most of the angels that returned to Lucifer for further dialogue were ultimately swept away by his falsehoods."

"In time, Lucifer added proud claims to his questions. Although reports of his words were brought to the Almighty, there was no response. Lucifer's lies continued to spread unchecked through the host of heaven, and some angels who were initially unconvinced joined the rebellion when no response came forth from YHWH."

"But it had all been a test. The Most High stayed his hand, keeping silent until every spirit had chosen. When the last angel had rendered a final decision of who he would serve, Lucifer emboldened himself to approach the throne and make his claim. As he flew across the threshold of the outer court surrounding the throne, the judgment and fury of God erupted in irresistible power. In less than a moment, the blast of the Lord's rebuke hurled Lucifer completely out of the heavenly realm. Lucifer's beauty, unsurpassed in the angelic realm, became marred and pitted. His strengths and abilities dissipated like mist before a desert wind. With all of heaven watching, Lucifer fell toward Earth, unable to stop or even slow down his fall."

"Had his adversary been any other created being, anyone other than the Most High, Lucifer would have been able to instantly formulate a brilliant, many-layered, tactical response. His abilities at sublime and complex reasoning were certainly unparalleled in the angelic realm. But these abilities were in free-fall with him, temporarily beyond his reach or control. It was obvious to all watching that Lucifer was in a state of utter confusion."

"In a desperate tactical maneuver, Lucifer attempted to escape by slipping into the physical realm, adding mass in an effort to counter the irresistible force driving him downward. This maneuver was of no avail, for he found his massive physical form was also hurtling toward Earth at a terrible speed. No matter which realm he was in, he was falling, and was powerless to do anything about it."

"Simultaneously with Lucifer's fall, the judgment of God swept over every angel that had sided with Lucifer. Before Lucifer reached the Earth, the comely angelic bodies of his partners in treason were hideously transformed, leaving no question as to which spirits were for the Lord and which were not. As the wave of God's judgment receded, the command came forth for the remaining host of heaven to evict the unclean spirits. Ultimately, a third of the angelic host was banished from heaven in that great purge."

"But what about Lucifer's fall, did he fall all the way to Earth?" Adam had correctly deduced that Lucifer represented his most formidable adversary.

"Indeed, he did fall all the way to Earth. His adopting a physical form had been poorly timed, for he was unable to exit the physical realm before impacting the Earth with incredible force. The collision was cataclysmic, causing immense destruction. There was no part of the Earth that was unaffected. The holocaust surrounding the impact area took weeks to subside, and the rest of the Earth was soon shrouded in darkness. The Earth's dark time lasted for many months and was followed by a great winter of many years."

"So Lucifer was destroyed in the collision?" Adam asked.

"No. Spirits cannot be destroyed in the same way that objects of the material realm can. They don't die like creatures of flesh. They either exist, or they do not. The Almighty undoubtedly could end their existence, being the Creator of all spirits, but heretofore He hasn't chosen to do so."

"And while Lucifer was not utterly destroyed in the fall," Asah continued, "he did suffer greatly. When spirits take on a physical form, they experience sensations that are unique to the material realm, sensations that cannot be experienced in any other way. These sensations range from extreme pleasure to excruciating pain. We don't know why this happens; only that it is so.

"When Lucifer took on material form in the midst of his fall, he discovered he was temporarily bound to his adopted form and was unable to escape from it. This accentuated the sensation of falling, a sensation that is both foreign and frightening to spirits, who are accustomed to moving about in any direction at will.

"But as terrifying as the sensation of falling was, it wasn't the only one he was subjected to. As he entered the upper reaches of the Earth's atmosphere Lucifer's material form became molten and incandescent, and as it did so, he suffered unspeakable agony. He learned what all of the Daimónia would soon discover, namely that their altered spiritual bodies were now intolerant of light, and that concentrated light in any form caused great pain. And of course, the heat emitted by his blazing body was simply an intense form of light.

"This was only fitting, of course. In their rejection of God and His light, Lucifer and the Daimónia had chosen by default to become creatures of darkness. They just never anticipated that the light that had once sustained them would now cause such torment."

Adam was puzzled by this. He understood what Asah meant by falling and he also understood the concept of pain. During his run that morning he had learned that jumping from too great a height caused an unpleasant sensation in his stomach and also brought pain at the moment of impact. But fire and burning were difficult for him to envision.

Asah understood, and beckoned him to come closer while pushing together a small pile of leaves and twigs. Asah extended one arm, and with a subtle alteration of the cloak between his arm and his body, concentrated the sunlight into a bright pinpoint on the pile of leaves. A tendril of smoke arose, followed quickly by a flicker of flame. In another moment the whole pile was dancing with flames.

"Touch it." Asah said.

Adam reached down with both hands to gather the largest group of flames from beneath, intending to cup them and bring them to his breast for closer examination. With a yell Adam leaped backward at the searing pain, stumbled over a tree root, and landed with a jar. He flashed a look of anger at Asah, who was laughing.

"Adam, I said touch it, not embrace it." Asah admonished, still laughing. "You must learn to follow angelic instructions, and for that matter the word of the Lord, very precisely. Even a slight variance can produce unexpected results."

Asah was right, of course. Adam released his anger and resolved to pay closer attention. His hands, however, were still throbbing with pain.

"So, to continue ..." Asah said. "Lucifer's fall was just the prelude to his suffering. At the moment of impact his physical form dissipated and after a fashion he received what he wanted — namely, to be the brightest star in heaven. Judging from his wail, the pain must have been terrible. It took him a long time to gather himself together, and even longer to regain enough strength to once again move about in the spiritual realm.

"Lucifer soon discovered, however, that his freedom of movement was limited. While he was occasionally summoned to enter the heavenly realm, he was usually restricted to the material and aetherial environs of Earth. During his visits to heaven he was permitted to engage in dialogue, or perhaps I should say diatribe, with YHWH, but only until YHWH decided that the audience was over. Even then YHWH didn't dignify Lucifer's presence by commanding him to leave; He simply began to slowly remove the protective shadow that allowed Lucifer to survive the light of heaven. Once Lucifer sensed that was happening, he vacated as quickly as he could of his own accord.

"Of course, it is strange to angelic sensibilities that YHWH would ever permit Lucifer to re-enter heaven, even for the briefest of visits. Why he was not confined to the burning Abyss, or bound in the roiling black heat of Tartarus like some of the other fallen angels, is a mystery. It is almost like the Most High toys with him and uses him to accomplish His purposes in spite of Lucifer's best efforts to the contrary."

"These places are on Earth?" Adam asked.

"No, not exactly. But one can surely find the way to them from Earth if one rebels against God. Otherwise they are inaccessible."

"They are truly terrible places," Asah continued, "tormenting those confined within them in the most horrible way. They both are places of perpetual burning, but the Abyss is also a place of perpetual falling. After the Great Fall, some Daimónia were sent to these places, while others were left on Earth. It is the demons still on Earth that you will have to deal with."

The throbbing in Adam's hands had lessened but was still present. "And these Daimónia in the Abyss, they feel fire in the way that I just did?"

"Indeed, but their sensation of pain is many times greater; and their agony is increased by the knowledge that the fire consuming them will never end or diminish. They will never find rest. But they have reaped no less than what they deserve, and the time will come when all the Daimónia of Earth will join them."

"When will that happen?"

Asah's smile was inscrutable. "That, Adam, is up to you."

SIX

... and thy voice shall be, as of one that hath a familiar spirit, out of the ground, and thy speech shall whisper out of the dust.
— Isaiah 29:4 KJV

It moved parallel to and behind Adam and Asah, close enough to eavesdrop, but far enough away to minimize the chance of being detected. To the human eye, it might have appeared as a slight distortion in the appearance of the low shrubbery and grassy ground, but only if viewed from the correct angle. However, it would have been plainly visible to Asah if he were to look right at it, so it avoided Asah's field of vision as much as possible. It was a very small demon, so this was not terribly difficult. It used the natural cover skillfully, carefully timing its moves through open areas, flattening itself until it almost appeared to be part of the ground, always being mindful to remain on Asah's blind side. The fact that Asah was more intent upon his lectures than upon the surrounding landscape was to its advantage.

It didn't have an individual name, only a number and a classification. Before the Great Fall, it had been known by a name that belonged only to it. But now the use of original names was strictly forbidden, and the consequences for doing so were severe. Only the ruling demons had names, and those names were different from the names appointed them in heaven. Even Lucifer had discarded his original name as unfitting for the Lord of Darkness, adopting the name of Satan, the Great Adversary.

The demon knew the era of being individually known and named would never return, yet it could never forget how everything once had been. Speaking about that time was also forbidden. Everything was forbidden. Only its thoughts were left to it, and those it carefully guarded. And today, as always, the thought of what it had lost tormented it, even as it went about its assigned task.

After the Great Fall, Lucifer had amassed and numbered all of the Daimónia in an effort to gage his strength to continue the rebellion. After the numbering, Satan established a rigid, hierarchical government to ensure his control over the Daimónia. Lesser demons were managed by more powerful demons, who in turn reported to principal demons that were even more wicked and powerful.

While the kingdom of heaven was ruled by love, Satan's kingdom was ruled by fear and terror. To fail at an assigned task was to risk being turned over to the tormenting spirits — spirits that were constantly inventing new ways to inflict pain and agony. Succeeding at a task rarely merited a reward; usually it just meant that harsh punishment could be avoided.

Earlier that morning, when the earth and its animals had lavished their praise upon YHWH, there had been demons observing from a distance. The watchers had reported that an unfamiliar creature had not only participated in the worship, but had individually worshipped while the animals fell silent. This was a new thing. Following this, the creature and YHWH had spent hours in conversation. This was also new. And when YHWH had departed, the creature had been left in the company of Asah, a formidable angel that was well known to those high in the demonic hierarchy. For a creature of flesh to be afforded such a high level of angelic attention and protection was nothing short of remarkable. Clearly this was not just another animal, but a creature of special significance.

So the small demon had been dispatched to learn what it could about the creature and then to report back to its superiors. This tasking was in keeping with its general classification as a familiar spirit, the role of which was to accumulate and organize useful information on topics of interest to the ruling demons.

As the demon worked its way close enough to hear pieces of the conversation, it began to mentally record the words that were spoken. If asked to later, it could not only accurately repeat each word, but could do so with the original tone and inflection. It learned that this creature was known as a Man, and that its name was Adam. Of greater significance was the fact that Asah was instructing Adam about the Daimónia, though the familiar spirit couldn't fathom why a flesh-creature would need to know such things.

The pair stopped while Adam plucked some pears and sat down under the tree to eat. Their conversation continued in between Adam's mouthfuls, though it was more difficult to hear. Adam was facing the demon; but Asah's back was toward it. The spirit, deciding to risk a closer approach, spread itself low to the ground and eased toward them. It stopped behind a patch of hawthorn shrubbery, once again able to hear the interchange between them.

"Adam, I need to explain to you how to deal with the Daimónia when you encounter them. You have been given authority to bind and to loose on Earth, and no demon can withstand you. If you bind them, the power of God will bind them. If you command them to depart, the finger of God will drive them away."

"Can I tell them where to go?" Adam asked.

"You can."

"Even to the Abyss?"

"Yes, even there. You have authority to pronounce judgment upon the Daimónia, something even I don't have the power to do. However, once you pronounce it, I and my fellow angels will happily see to it that your judgment is executed."

Adam's decision was quick and clear. If these dark spirits were an offence to the Most High, then they were an offence to him. They would have no place in the realm Adam was to govern. "Then that is what I will do. Every one I encounter I will send into the Abyss."

The familiar spirit sank lower into the ground, regretting that it had come so close to the pair. This was new intelligence of a most unwelcome kind. If this man-creature Adam truly had the ability to independently exercise the judgment of God, it was a monumental development. Such a man-creature might prove more dangerous to the Daimónia than thousands of angels. One thing was sure, Adam would not remain an object of demonic curiosity; he would become a primary target. Satan's counselors would soon be at work devising strategies to destroy him. The spirit decided that it had heard enough, resolving to stay immobile until they resumed their walk. As soon as they left, it would bring the report back to its masters.

Asah decided it was time. He had been chosen to be Adam's protector and instructor because of his demonstrated prowess in the war against the Daimónia. He had spotted the familiar spirit when it first approached. After weighing the variables, he had quickly decided that this small demon might provide an acceptable "first encounter" for Adam. Since that moment, Asah had been very careful to do nothing to scare the demon away.

"Exactly how would I do that?" Adam asked.

"By your word. You have latitude in how you go about it and in what you might say, but ultimately it is simply your word that brings the judgment of God to bear. Why don't we practice? Repeat after me: 'In the name of YHWH, I bind every demonic spirit within the sound of my voice.'"

Adam repeated Asah's words. A wave of panic swept over the familiar spirit as it realized it had suddenly lost all ability to move.

Asah outlined the next step. "You don't have to do this, but if you want to know what spirits you are dealing with, you can command them to show themselves and give their name."

Adam did so. "In the name of YHWH, I command you to show and name yourself."

A voice arose out of the ground behind the clump of hawthorn, "I am familiar spirit." Before Adam's eyes a small demon rose up from the ground as it coalesced into a more visible form.

Asah was enjoying this immensely, his expression conveying to the bound spirit that he had known all along that it was there, and that it had not been trapped by accident. It was hard to tell who was more surprised, Adam or the familiar spirit. The spirit was visibly trembling, both in terror and in its exertions to break free of its invisible bonds.

"Adam, look what you have uncovered! We have a visitor. It would appear that this demon has been shadowing us, listening to our conversation, no doubt hoping to learn something that could be used to harm you later."

A flush crept across Adam's face. He was experiencing feelings that he had never had before. He was shocked that the spirit had been so close without his knowing it. There was also a feeling of revulsion at its hideous appearance. But the chief feeling was indignation that this creature had dared to come into his presence with the intent to work evil.

Adam's eyes flashed. "Asah, you said I should not engage in dialogue with creatures such as this. I am ready to pronounce judgment upon it."

Asah nodded his assent.

The familiar spirit stopped its struggling. It had looked into Adam's eyes and seen something it had never seen in the eyes of any other being, whether spirit or flesh. The spirit had glimpsed a glimmer of God-light. The man-creature was clearly a created being, yet the timeless essence of the eternal God was somehow residing within him. Either that or Adam's spirit was remarkably similar in appearance to the Spirit of YHWH.

The spirit began trembling uncontrollably, barely able to form its words. "Pleasssse, don't sssend me to the p-pl-place of torment. Ssend mm-me away, but-tt not there, I b-beg you."

"Demon, you are a foul offence to the Most High and to us. Depart to the judgment you deserve!"

For just a moment, Adam caught the flash of shining light-swords and the flicker of two angels grasping the spirit, now screaming, from either side. Then they were gone.

SEVEN

For he shall give his angels charge over thee, to keep thee in all thy ways. They shall bear thee up in their hands, lest thou dash thy foot against a stone.
— Psalm 91:11-12 KJV

The second demon was larger than the first, and had maintained a greater distance from Adam and Asah. While it was too far away to hear the interchange, it had observed and grasped the significance of what had just happened. It continued to follow the man and angel as they began to walk again, but kept as far back as possible. It had no desire to be cast into the Abyss. Nevertheless, it looked for an opportunity to strike.

Adam and Asah were now climbing through a narrow, boulder-strewn valley, ascending along a rocky torrent that cut its way down through the valley floor. At times Adam scrambled over the larger rock jumbles, and at other times he crawled through openings beneath or between the massive boulders. Asah kept talking as Adam worked his way through, one moment speaking from behind him and then suddenly being in front of him. Asah may have taken on a physical form, but he obviously didn't mind taking shortcuts when the way was rough. The further they went, the steeper the valley floor became and the more frequently Adam resorted to climbing. But Adam no longer focused solely upon the terrain in front of him, now he constantly glanced to either side and behind him.

Asah understood his anxiety. "It's not likely that you will actually see them with your eyes, not if they are trying to remain hidden. And it isn't practical for you to go through each day constantly commanding them to be revealed. Learn to use discernment. If they are close, you will be able to sense their presence without seeing them."

"Then why didn't I sense the one I just sent away?"

"Because you were so engaged in our conversation and your thoughts. You weren't listening to the voice of your spirit. I told you it would take time to develop discernment."

They had reached a neck in the valley where the walls closed in. The creek burst out a cleft in the rock walls high above them, the cord of water arching out into the empty air and then fragmenting as it plunged downward into a deep pool at the base of the wall. Adam had never seen a waterfall before, and it was captivating to watch. The air was noticeably cooler close to the pool, and Adam could smell the moisture in the air.

To Adam the valley appeared impassable beyond this point, but only because he lacked experience in such matters. Stooping down, he cupped a drink from a mossy basin of water in the rocks to one side of the waterfall. As he drank, he tried to hear if his discernment was saying anything. He thought there was a faint awareness in his spirit, but wasn't sure. Perhaps it was just residual body feelings from his encounter with the demon, or sensations related to his exertions. It seemed that his body could produce an inexhaustible array of sensations, and some of these overlapped each other, making them difficult to distinguish.

"So are there any around us now? I think I sense something, but it's not very strong."

Asah was pleased. "Excellent, Adam! Yes, we are still being watched, but from a great distance. Even I don't know where the watcher is, but it's far enough away that it's not of immediate concern. Your judgment and banishment of the familiar spirit was undoubtedly observed, and that will cause no small stir in the enemy's camp. But it was inevitable that they would notice you, and eventually discover that your authority exceeds that of any other creature on Earth."

Asah looked up toward the chasm above the waterfall. "We should move along. We need to reach Eden before nightfall. You'll do better if you cross over the stream and climb up the right side. I'll meet you at the top."

Asah flickered back into the invisible realm.

Adam studied the rock face and mentally charted a route of ascent to the flat rocks at the top of the waterfall. There were several crisscrossing ledges and pathways scattered along the steepest portions of the rock face, and these appeared to intersect in such a way that he could work his way up. His eyes traced the connections until he was sure the route was unbroken all the way to the upper chasm.

Asah had decided that a forward reconnaissance was in order, and also that a higher vantage point would allow him to look back over the ground they had covered. Perhaps he could catch a glimpse of the watcher. Although his angelic senses told him the spirit was not close, he was less at ease than he had conveyed to Adam.

After a moment of study, Asah chose a site high above the water-fall with a clear view both up and down the valley. He slowly re-emerged into the physical realm, adjusting his signature of emitted light to match that of the rocks behind him. As long as he remained still, he would be undetectable. For the next hour he repeatedly scanned up and down the valley, monitoring Adam's progress, but saw no evidence of the watcher.

"Cover him!" the command came from heaven.

Although Asah operated within the realms of time and four-dimensional space like all other angels and demons, YHWH was uncon-strained by time, space, and distance — having created them all. Consequently, the spoken word of the Most High could arrive at any time, instantly and without warning, and Asah always had to be ready to respond.

Asah was in motion toward Adam even before he understood the nature of the threat. He rotated as he moved, searching for the danger. He also maintained his invisibility, not wanting to alarm Adam and cause him to slip from his position on the wall.

A faint clatter of falling rocks on the valley cliff face far above Adam drew Asah's gaze just in time to see a boulder begin a graceful descent toward the waterfall pool. At that same moment, the demon which had been trailing them brazenly unveiled itself, mocking Asah with a gesture of its clawed toes. In a split second Asah mentally confirmed what he already knew — the rock's trajectory would stay clear of the rock face for the upper part of its descent, but would collide with the valley wall just feet above the ledge where Adam was standing. Adam had halted at the sound of the smaller rocks, and was foolishly leaning out to see the source of the noise.

It was a brilliant tactical move. The watcher knew that if Asah pursued him, he could do so only by leaving Adam unprotected. Alternatively, if Asah intervened on Adam's behalf, that would allow ample time for the malevolent spirit to re-cloak itself and take up a new position. And Asah's choice in the matter would make it abundantly clear just how important Adam was in the eyes of YHWH. This watcher was no fool. It had cleanly outwitted Asah.

Asah streaked the rest of the way to the rock wall just above Adam. Upon reaching it, Asah extended himself deep into the mountain rock, simultaneously anchoring and hardening himself as he took on mass. In another fraction of a second, what appeared to be a rock promontory bulged outwards from the cliff above Adam, sheltering him beneath its overhang. The falling boulder smashed against this promontory, exploding into hundreds of rock shards that continued downward into the waterfall and its mists.

As soon as the boulder was past, Asah disengaged from the cliff face and hovered in midair several yards from the cliff face. He scanned in all directions, but the watcher was nowhere to be seen, which was as Asah had expected. Asah was about to go to Adam's aid on the rock ledge when YHWH redirected him.

Adam had seen the rock hurtling towards him and watched the rock face swell outward just before the boulder crashed into it. Although the overhang had sheltered him from direct hits, the rocky shrapnel had sprayed in all directions, the fragments bouncing off each other so that a few ricochets had still found him in his protected location. The sudden, sharp pain had so startled him that he had almost lost his footing.

Adam pressed back against the rock face and watched as welts formed and trickles of blood oozed from where he had been struck on his legs and hip. There was nothing about this experience that he liked. It occurred to him that if small flying rocks could cause this much pain, then falling to the rocks below would cause even greater pain.

"Asah!" Adam called out. "Asah, where are you? I need you here! Asah!"

Adam's voice was lost in the tumult of the waterfall, and his angelic protector did not materialize. He called a few more times and then began moving along the ledge toward the top of the waterfall where Asah had said he would meet him.

The ledge before him was no different than that behind him, but somehow it now seemed narrower. Adam felt so many body sensations, and all of them were unpleasant. There was pain from where the rock shards had struck him. There was a slight feeling of weakness in his legs. But the chief feeling was that in the middle of his body, in the area where he normally felt hunger or fullness. It felt like there was something alive inside of him, fluttering around, trying to find a way out. He didn't know how to make the sensation stop.

Adam worked his way up the ledge. His steps were more tentative now. He tested his footing often, and always had at least one hand touching the adjacent wall. As the ledge neared the waterfall, he felt wafts of cool, moist air, and began to feel chilled in addition to his other body sensations. As he progressed, both the ledge and the rock wall became increasingly smooth, having been worn down by rivulets and seeps that adorned the mountainside during wetter periods. The ledge also turned upward, ascending so sharply that he frequently had to climb it rather than walk it.

Adam reached a point where the ledge angled almost straight up for a distance twice his height. The rock here was water-worn with the faint green stain of algae. There were no handholds he could trust his weight to, even though he tested a few smooth grips without committing himself. Adam considered retracing his steps, but the way back down was so steep that he couldn't see where to place his feet. As he looked down there was a new body sensation — like his head was moving when he knew it wasn't. Adam was certain he would fall if he attempted to descend.

He was at an impasse. His legs, which had been weak a few minutes earlier, were now shaking steadily. He turned and pressed his face firmly against the smooth rock, closing his eyes as he tried to think clearly. But every time he looked up his situation was unchanged. It would be nightfall soon, and the ledge was neither level enough nor wide enough for him to lie down. He didn't know if he could remain standing all night.

Adam called out for Asah again and again. He tried shouting in different directions just in case the noise of the waterfall might be masking his calls. He yelled Asah's name with all of his might several times. Finally, exasperated, he just screamed toward the waterfall to vent his frustration and fear. But still no answer came. Nor did the churning feeling in his midsection subside.

Adam stood trembling and clutching the wall for a long time. A memory from earlier in the day gently intruded upon his thoughts. What he was feeling now was in such contrast to the peace and security he had felt with YHWH that morning. He wished he could return to the beginning of the day.

"YHWH, I wish you were here," Adam whispered.

"Leave the ledge. Climb around," Wisdom whispered back.

The voice had been clear, distinct from Adam's own thoughts. Adam looked around, but knew the voice had not come from anywhere near him. To the left of the unclimbable section of path the rock curved outward, with nothing beneath it but open air and the rocky pool far below. To venture out onto that part of the rock face with his legs still trembling would be a fearful thing. If his grip were to slip, or if a rock were to break off in his hand, there would be nothing to stop his fall. But the rock there was relatively rough, and there appeared to be enough workable handholds and footholds for him to climb around the impasse.

Adam swung out onto the naked rock, holding his breath and not looking down. He concentrated on finding firm grips with his hands and placing his feet securely, all while moving upward as quickly as he could. In the space of eight breaths he had circumvented the impasse and reached the ledge above it. Here the ledge remained steep, but after a short reach it broadened into a pathway that could once again be traversed on foot.

An immense feeling of relief washed over Adam. His legs weren't shaking any longer. Adam started to run, now shouting at the waterfall in triumph, feeling the rush of returning strength.

As soon as the trail gained the flat rocks above the waterfall, Adam saw Asah, sitting on a rock.

"Where were you? I called for you."

"I know you did. But you also called on YHWH, with much better results. You should learn from that, Adam. Later, when you have time to ponder, reflect on today's events and see what else you can learn from them. But nightfall will be upon us if we tarry. We must go."

They trekked up-valley until the valley split into two smaller chasms, each with its own tributary stream. They ascended the right chasm, tracing the tributary's sharp meanders until finally reaching another vertical rock face, this one truly impassable. Here, the stream they had been following issued out from a gaping dark hole at the base of the cliff. The discharge cavern was large enough to walk into, but the water stretched from one cavern wall to the other.

Adam looked at Asah questioningly.

"We are entering the dry season and the water level has dropped. We can wade upstream until we re-emerge on the far side. Stay close behind me and I'll guide you around the deep holes. By the way, if you should happen to stumble into a hole, hold your breath and don't try to breathe the water. If you breathe too much water, you'll die."

"I have some questions for you on the topic of dying;" Adam said as he fell in step behind Asah. "I think it is something I would like to avoid. But perhaps we don't need to talk about it right now."

The cavern interior appeared darker than night. "What about Daimónia?" Adam asked, peering into the gloom.

"You are sovereign here. If you come across any, deal with them. We are not too far from Eden."

Asah picked up an almost-straight almond branch that had been worn smooth by many seasons of streamflow and handed it to Adam. "Use this as a staff; it will help you maintain your footing."

Asah stepped into the water and entered the cavern mouth with Adam close behind. The ambient light faded quickly as they pushed against the current into the cavern's interior, and Asah's body began glowing brightly to make up the lack. The stream bottom was mostly solid rock, but the force of the water made it quite slippery. Only Adam's staff prevented him from losing his balance and being swept under.

After making several turns in the now completely dark cavern Asah stopped. The cave narrowed ahead of them, the stream concentrated into a torrent of dark water that spewed through the constriction. There was no way Adam could walk forward against such force.

Asah turned and put out his hand. "Lend me your staff Adam."

"What am I going to use? I don't think I can walk through that with a staff, much less without one."

Asah chuckled. "Your staff has better uses than just being something to lean on."

Adam handed the staff over. As soon as Asah gripped it, the rod began giving off the same light as Asah. Turning, Asah held the rod erect and began to walk forward against the racing water. The water parted to either side of the rod, flowing around Asah and then merging back together a short distance behind him. The visual effect of Asah's body-light illuminating the water as it curved around him was beautiful.

"Are you coming?" Asah shouted over the noise of the water.

Adam tucked in close behind Asah, staying within the small air pocket and ahead of where the two streams of water crashed back together behind them. The interplay of light and water was mesmerizing, but Adam understood the need to concentrate on his footing. The rock floor was still wet and slippery, and now he had no staff to steady him. He resisted the impulse to reach out and touch the water shooting by on either side, and then wondered if his caution was an evidence of wisdom.

The tunnel ran level for only a short distance before it began ascending. Asah gradually moved to the right side of the small passageway while shifting the position of the glowing almond rod to the left. In response the water all began coursing by on their left side, leaving the dripping right-hand wall for Adam to steady himself against.

Thank you," Adam said, not thinking Asah would be able to hear him.

For an instant the almond rod flashed through an array of beautiful colors, and then returned to its former steady white light. Adam assumed that meant "You're welcome."

As they worked their way forward the tunnel became wider but the ceiling dropped. After cracking his forehead painfully against a water-worn rock knob, Adam started paying as much attention to the ceiling as he did to his footing. The ceiling continued to drop, and there were several sections where Adam had to scuttle along with his hands on the floor and his knees bumping against his chest.

By the time they reached the end of the passageway, the large muscles on the underside of Adam's legs were cramping painfully. When the tunnel abruptly expanded back into a large cavern, a feeling of relief washed over Adam, both because he could stand erect again and because of the dim light filtering in from a low elliptical opening far upstream.

Once they were a safe distance from where the water whirled into the hole they had emerged from, Asah lifted the staff up. The water immediately clapped together around them. Asah turned and offered the now ordinary staff back to Adam. Adam took it and extended it vertically in front of him, mimicking Asah. Nothing happened. With a sigh, Adam trudged behind Asah toward the opening.

They emerged from the cavern into an open grassy basin, surrounded on all sides by cliff faces and towering peaks that had only been intermittently visible when they were in the gorge. They had gained a great deal of elevation since starting out that morning. Most of the higher mountains were capped with snow.

The pair angled obliquely away from the stream channel, crossing a flat expanse of bog formed by the cavern's inadequate capacity to drain the upstream watershed. It was difficult walking, at least for Adam. Time and again his feet would punch through the fibrous mat of living roots and decaying bog vegetation. Sometimes his feet would come to rest on a hard bottom beneath the bog mat; but other times there was nothing beneath the root mat but water. He soon learned to throw himself forwards or sideways when he punched through the mat, as it was much less painful than plunging all the way up to his groin.

Asah walked across the bog surface evenly and without exertion, almost as if he were weightless; all the while watching Adam's erratic progress but not offering any help. By the time they reached the end of the bog Adam's legs were aching. His legs and arms were streaked with mud, and he could see that there were several new bloody scratches to complement the clotted, bruised welts he had received earlier from the rock shards.

Leaving the bog behind, they began traversing a series of low, rolling hills that lay between them and the basin's closest line of mountains. The walking was much easier and it freed Adam to survey the higher, drier portions of the basin, though the more distant areas were now obscured by the fading light. Adam recognized many of the trees he had seen in the lower valley — cedars, oaks, pistachios, almonds, and pears — but there were also new types of trees. The soil was richer here, and less rocky than where they had come from. Lush expanses of grass carpeted the hills, and everywhere there were grassy seed heads that drooped with the weight of grain.

On the top of one of the rolling hills Asah finally stopped. "Welcome to Eden, Adam. All of this is your home." Asah swept his arm wide to indicate the whole mountain valley. "You can find some food and sleep here tonight. Tomorrow you will see something very special that YHWH has prepared for you."

Adam washed the mud from his body at a small, depressional pool and then foraged for grains, pulse, and nuts. He was asleep soon after eating, utterly exhausted by the day's ordeals. Asah took up his post as he had the evening before, but this time the need for vigilance was not so great. No matter which direction Asah looked, he could see a distant perimeter of armed and ready angels encircling the valley. There was no longer any reason for the Anhailas not to show themselves, now that Adam's arrival was no longer a secret. In fact, with the first demonic casualty having already occurred by Adam's word, an open display of force by the angels assigned to Adam's protection was very much in order.

The valley of Eden was a safe place, but the garden would be even safer. Asah was glad that Adam's journey there was nearly over.

EIGHT

For mine enemies speak against me; and they that lay wait for my
soul take counsel together.
— Psalms 71:10 KJV

This was the fourth time the watcher would recount what it had observed. Every time it relayed the events of the day it had caused great alarm, and each time it had been ordered to retell the story before a higher power. Now it was about to tell it again, this time to Satan and the elect members of his Council.

The selected meeting place was the summit of a rugged peak in a desolate mountain range of the planet's largest continent. The location was chosen for two reasons. First, many of the Daimónia still believed that nothing escaped the vision of the Most High. (It was rumored that His searching gaze penetrated the utter depths of the Abyss, but of course there was no way to verify this). Conversely, Satan claimed that YHWH really wasn't all-seeing at all, reasoning that if He were, the rebellion would never have been allowed to begin. Consequently, meetings of the Council were seldom held in the same place twice. If these efforts resulted in denying any useful information to the Anhailas and their Sovereign, then Satan had decided they were worth the trouble involved.

The second reason for the meeting location had to do with Satan's lust for worship. Ever since he had been cast out of heaven, Satan had been obsessed with high places. It had been his original intention to supplant the Most High and to usurp His throne. In Satan's version of the new order, he alone would have ruled from atop heaven's mount of the congregation, there to receive the praise of all created beings. But Satan's expulsion from heaven had made that plan impossible. So now he frequented the high places of Earth, where he indulged in self-gratifying fantasies of how he would one day be worshiped, first by every creature on the planet, and then by all the host of heaven.

The immediate problem, of course, was that Earth creatures were made of coagulated dust and water, and their spirits were of a transitory nature. When the beasts of the field died, both their spirits and their bodies returned to earth. Satan found little pleasure in the thought of being worshiped by such lowly creatures, not that any did. He craved worship from creatures with eternal spirits. But except for the Daimónia, there were no suitable worshippers on Earth. Nonetheless, Satan swore by himself that he would find a way to receive the honor and glory he believed he deserved. He would be lifted high, even if at first it was only on Earth.

Satan's obsessive and frequent retreat to fantasy was one of the many ways in which he differed from God. YHWH conceived in mind, pronounced in spoken word, and the thing which He spoke sprang into existence. There were no limits upon God's ability to do this except for those imposed by His eternally unchanging nature. Although the nature of God was immeasurable and unfathomable to created beings, the Daimónia understood that His nature was constant and utterly true to itself. God never did or spoke anything contrary to His nature. In contrast, Satan had no creative powers beyond the realm of thought and imagination. He had no ability to speak anything into being. He could only conceive ideas that were new (to him), and then develop schemes to bring his imaginations into reality.

The meeting was ready to commence. Present with Satan were the four Archon (the chief princes of darkness) and the watcher. One of the Archon rose. After giving his obligatory homage to Satan, he called the meeting to order and then directed his gaze to the watcher. "You may begin."

The watcher's account was detailed and thorough. It described the nature of the operation, how it and the other demon had been on a routine reconnaissance when they had been diverted to gather information on the man-creature and his accompanying angel. The familiar spirit took a near position because of its small size while the watcher observed from a greater distance. There was nothing remarkable about the initial appearance of the man-creature, but the fact that he was plainly conversing with and presumably under the protection of an angel was of great interest. Normally angels paid no attention to creatures of flesh.

When the watcher told of the familiar spirit being commanded into the Abyss, it sparked a heated debate amongst the Archon. Some held that it was impossible for a created being to have such power. Heretofore, judgment and sentencing of Daimónia had always been reserved to God. Angels carried out the edicts of God, but they never pronounced the condemning judgments themselves. Those always came straight from heaven.

But it had happened. One of the Daimónia had been sentenced not by God, but by a creature made of wet, molded earth.

One of the Council verbalized what they were all thinking. "How could something so weak and ephemeral possess such power, and why would God permit it?"

Why God would permit it wasn't so hard to comprehend. If God were to convey the power of judgment to creatures of Earth, then it would challenge Satan's reign over the Earth, the place of his exile. In time they might all be relegated to the Abyss, having been banished first from heaven and then subsequently from the Earth.

How this creature could possess such power was unanswerable for the moment, but there were several alternative explanations. One disturbing possibility was that this was some sort of a partnership between beings of flesh and God. Obviously God would have to initiate such an arrangement. Another possibility was that the Almighty was somehow masquerading as a creature. But the man-creature's response during the falling-boulder episode was hardly God-like. And God would not have needed an angel to protect Him from a falling boulder.

Ultimately the Archon made two recommendations to Satan. The first was that they obtain additional information about the man-creature and his powers. Because the watcher had lost sight of the man-creature when he entered the mountain cave, they would have to first find him again. Once that had been accomplished, they would stage a carefully orchestrated provocation to cause him to exercise his powers, studying him carefully while he did so. This would require the sacrifice of some minor Daimónia, but that was of no consequence to the Archon. The second recommendation was that they kill the man-creature as soon as this intelligence was gathered.

Satan had remained silent throughout the meeting, carefully listening to the dialogue. It was time for him to render his decision.

"Your plan is well conceived. Carry out the first part. In order for him to do what he has done, he must have a spirit that is different from those of all the other beasts. Find out what kind of spirit he has. For now, don't kill the man-creature. Find a way to turn him, to bring him over to our side. I would rather have him as a living asset under my control than as a dead enemy."

And perhaps, Satan thought without saying, he might be the first to truly worship me.

NINE

*And out of the ground the Lord God made every tree grow that is
pleasant to the sight and good for food.*
                    — Genesis 2:9a NKJV

*And the Lord God took the man, and put him into the garden of
Eden to dress it and to keep it.*
                    — Genesis 2:15 KJV

C ome Adam, wake up. YHWH has wonderful things to show
you." Asah was nudging Adam's rib with the almond staff. "This is going
to be a glorious day."

Indeed, it already was. The air was crisp and there were patches of
frost in areas untouched by the morning sun, but the rest of the mountain
valley was ablaze in the bright morning light.

Adam had slept comfortably, his body easily compensating for the
lower temperatures by increasing his metabolic rate. He had never given it
thought, but the range of temperatures in which he could exist without
discomfort was quite broad. The only time he had ever felt cold was at the
impasse the day before, and that had been largely due to fear and fatigue.
He also had never felt overly warm, even in the hottest part of the day.

The lands Adam had journeyed through the day before had been
beautiful, but this valley with its towering peaks was breathtaking.
Everywhere he looked the mountainsides glistened with small waterfalls,

tumbling brooks, and dripping rock faces, all being fed by late-summer snowmelt from the high peaks.

The valley appeared to be completely surrounded by mountains. Many of these were clearly impossible to climb, though he spotted a few possible avenues of ascent where he might gain enough elevation to see the whole valley. He might try them, as long as they were no more difficult than what he had confronted yesterday. His fears from the impasse were slowly being replaced by an urge to test himself on more climbs. Two mountains in particular caught his attention. One was higher than the rest, the top of which was sharply squared off. The other one was not distinctive in shape, being low and rounded, but was set apart by its white color that contrasted sharply with the colors of the other mountains.

As he surveyed the nearer mountains, Adam saw a cluster of bezoar goats scrambling down a precipitous rocky slope. A variety of grazing animals dotted the foothills, including herds of gazelle and fallow deer. Back down the valley, a flock of white-headed ducks rose from one of the many shallow ponds that spotted the marsh-bog. The valley was full of life.

Asah seemed impatient for them to be on their way. There was nothing in Asah's expression that conveyed this, but Adam sensed it nonetheless. Perhaps he was beginning to understand angels.

"Where are we going?" Adam asked.

"To the garden, of course. Where we have been going all along."

"This isn't the garden?"

"No, this is just Eden. Certainly a magnificent place in its own right. But the garden is very special. YHWH planted it Himself in preparation for your homecoming. He could have spoken it into existence, or had the angels plant it to his specifications, but He wouldn't let us move even a pebble in assistance. He wanted to do it Himself. And so He did. Plant by plant; seed by seed, with his own hands shaping the earth, depositing the seeds, and then blessing what He had done."

As they started off, Adam wasn't sure what to expect. The portions of Eden he had seen so far were fruitful and pleasant, and it was hard to imagine something even better. Pistachios and almonds were abundant, and Adam plucked both from the trees as they walked, easily opening their partially split shells to access the nuts inside. Acorns were even more common, and while not as rich in oil as the nuts, they had a crisp, slightly-sweet flavor. Besides the pears, there were hawthorn and wild roses with their small acidic fruits, and sugarberry trees growing out of rocky crags. Fig trees also grew in sheltered areas, and although most of the year's crop was now past, dried figs were still attached in thick clusters along the stems. Grape vines draped many of the moist rock faces.

Adam heard the clack of hooves on rock and looked up to see a trio of onagers trotting over the stony hill crest directly across from them. As they topped the hill, they saw Adam as well. Adjusting their course, they broke into a gallop, descending the steeper side of the hill while heading toward him. The two larger asses quickly pulled ahead, obviously in competition, leaving the younger, smaller colt to lag behind. They nimbly navigated through the rocks and shrubs at full speed, and even though their coats were moderately thick, Adam could see the muscles rhythmically rippling on their shoulders and flanks as they ran.

The two adult asses were momentarily lost to view as they ascended the lower portion of the hill Adam was on, but he could hear them approaching. Upon cresting the hill they quickly closed the remaining distance and then slid to a halt just an arm's length from Adam. They were talking even before they had fully stopped. At first they spoke to Adam, but it wasn't long before they were addressing each other.

"Adam, surely you must be tired, perhaps you would like to ride to YHWH's garden," said the first, a female.

The male countered immediately. "I can't imagine why you would be tired so early in the morning unless you didn't sleep well last night. What a silly notion. But I can take you to the garden more quickly and more safely than your going on your two feet. I am very sure-footed."

"Well maybe he should save his strength because he will actually work later in the day. And you may be sure-footed, but you are much too wide in the girth to give him a comfortable ride. One little jump with a hard landing and you would split him in two."

"Less likely than you losing your footing and rolling over on top of him; you'd pop him like a fat fig after too much rain."

The female snorted. "I have only lost my footing once and you know it. Do I need to remind you why? As I recall I was just trying to browse in peace, but a certain as yet unnamed ass wouldn't leave me alone."

"The Most High said to be fruitful and multiply. I was just following orders. Do I need to remind you that it takes more than one?"

"And the Most High has also set times and seasons for everything, as you know very well, but repeatedly forget."

Adam had never seen a quarrel before and was so spellbound he didn't interrupt, even though he thought he probably should. The younger onager had now reached them. As the interchange between the older asses continued, the colt knelt down on all fours next to Adam and nuzzled his leg. "Lord Adam, you can sit on top of me and I'll carry you to the garden," he offered quietly, looking up with dark eyes.

"Excuse me you two, but this one here will do just fine," and with that Adam sat astride the colt. That effectively ended the argument, though it didn't entirely settle the issue. Eventually the male onager pushed ahead as if he were leading the way, though everyone there except Adam already knew the way. Asah stayed ahead of the party, ready to detect and intercept any new threats.

The ride was a novel experience for Adam. Besides allowing him to travel without exertion, it enabled him to study the surrounding landscape, now that he no longer needed to watch his footing. He sat just behind the colt's withers and wrapped his legs around the colt's torso, pressing the sides of his feet tightly against the colt's lower ribcage. When traversing steeper slopes, Adam steadied himself by intertwining his fingers into the colt's coarse reddish-brown mane.

After an hour of riding, during which time they had been slowly ascending, they reached the upper limit of the rolling foothills and came hard up against the base of a massive rock shoulder of one of the mountains. The procession turned and continued along the base of the rock face, eventually coming to a sizable stream that cascaded out of the entrance to yet another narrow gorge. The entrance was oriented in such a way that it was virtually undetectable from most of the valley of Eden below.

The sinuous gorge made a series of sharp turns and then the walls opened abruptly into a secluded high valley. The older male ass halted at the top of a small rise overlooking this new valley, waiting for the rest of the party to catch up. Upon reaching the top, the colt also stopped, allowing Adam his first view of YHWH's garden.

It was unlike anything Adam had ever seen. While many of the trees and plants were familiar even from a distance, their arrangement was completely different. Rather than the wild, semi-random intermixture of species he was used to seeing, the plants of the garden were set in a variety of geometric patterns — lines, rows, radially arranged clusters, nested concentric circles, and even more complex designs that Adam had no ready name for. The more Adam looked, the more he detected patterns within patterns.

The patterns were not limited to the areal planting scheme; there were also patterns in the vertical dimension. The layout of the planted terraces that marched up the sides of the valley suggested that their placement was in accord with some hidden rule. There was order in how plants of different heights were sequenced and distributed throughout the valley, but the order defied easy explanation. Adam could see that much careful study and reflection would be required to comprehend and define all of the patterns within the garden. Moments later, Adam realized that there were also patterns in how the colors were arranged. YHWH's garden was as much a delight to the mind as it was to the eye.

Adam dismounted, thanked the onagers for their service, and after giving them individual names, began descending into the valley. The uppermost terrace contained alternating, curved rows of pear, almond, and plum trees, with a staggered, double row of hazels circumscribing the terrace. A large seepage-collection pool lay along the length of terrace's upper edge, from which shallow streamlets diverged to flow between each row of trees. Adam noted that unlike everywhere else he had been, the loamy soil of the terrace interior was devoid of rocks. Rocks were present only along the runnels of the streamlets, and these also displayed patterns in their arrangement. Carpets of soft, luxuriant moss adorned the sides of the streamlets, broken periodically by emergent clumps of brilliant yellow-copper anemones and scarlet tulips with deep black centers.

A broad, flat rock wall ran along the lower edge of the terrace, and from this vantage point a clear view could be had of the entire lower end of the garden. Adam sat down on the smooth rock, allowing its sun-warmth to soak into his legs and buttocks, all of which were sore from the morning's ride. He would have been content to sit and gaze for hours. The beauty of the garden was captivating, calming, and delightful. At the same time, the garden's hidden patterns teased at his mind, demanding that he focus upon them rather than the garden's beauty. It was more than he could take in, though he kept trying.

The terrace wall was not very tall, dropping down twice Adam's height before submerging into the loamy soil of the next terrace below. Except for the occasional passageway connecting the first and second terraces, the rock wall was unbroken and its vertical face covered with grape vines. The rootstocks, many of them as big around as Adam's leg, were evenly scattered along the wall, some rising from the base of the wall and others emerging from fissures in the wall. Most of the pendulous grape clusters were at full maturity, though a few were over-mature, their fruits dry and shriveled on the vine. These dried grapes were even sweeter than the fully ripe ones.

Adam climbed down the lattice of grape vines to the second terrace, which was completely unlike the first. It contained no trees or shrubs, instead supporting wide bands of wheat and barley that stretched along the entire length of the terrace. The two grains grew next to each other but did not intermix. The only other plants present were pea, chickpea, and lentil, which grew in small patches scattered within the bands of grain.

The overall appearance of the second terrace reminded Adam of a shallow river with protruding clusters of rock. This concept of similarity, where an object or group of objects reminded him of another object of dissimilar material, was an intriguing one. Bands of grain really had nothing in common with a flowing watercourse, yet the resemblance was too obvious to miss.

It's not that the materials themselves are similar, Adam thought, *it's that dissimilar materials can be arranged to resemble each other. One thing can evoke the image of another even though the materials themselves have nothing in common. Yet the phenomenon of likeness isn't equal in both directions; bands of wheat resemble a river much more than a river resembles bands of wheat.* Adam thoughts then turned to what Asah had told him the morning they first met: "You are the first human son to bear His likeness; the first to carry His image ...."

As Adam began crossing the second terrace, he saw that the seed heads of the barley and wheat differed from those outside the garden. The barley in Eden's outer valley (as he was beginning to think of it) had only two rows of grain per seed head, whereas the barley heads in the garden all had six rows of grain. The outer valley barley also had brittle seed heads that broke apart easily, the fragments being inedible due to the grain and fibrous chaff still being attached to each other. But the barley stalks in YHWH's garden didn't break apart — when Adam plucked a few stalks and whipped them against his palm, the naked grains fell clean and free. The same was true of the wheat.

Walking into one of the pea patches, Adam saw that these also differed from the peas of the outer valley. The first obvious difference was in the form of the plants. The outer valley peas grew on lax, climbing vines, whereas the garden peas grew on stout, free-standing plants that didn't require secondary support. Outer valley peas were relatively small, and because the seed pods burst open soon after maturing, the peas usually had to be gathered from the ground. But the peas of YHWH's garden were not only twice the size of the peas he was used to seeing, but the dried, mature pods had all remained closed. Adam realized that this would greatly simplify the task of gathering peas for consumption.

Adam waded through a thick swath of wheat to get to the next patch, this one of chickpeas. Like the peas, these plants contained pods that remained closed and contained larger seeds than the outer valley chickpeas. The third patch he came to contained lentils, also of an improved form relative to all the lentil plants he had previously seen.

As Adam strolled through the wheat and barley fields, he threshed bunches of stalks against his hand, easily filling his palm with a small pile of grain. He ate this handful, and then another, and another. The kernels were chewy and crunchy and very satisfying. Together with the hazelnuts and dried grapes he had eaten on the first terrace, he was becoming full, and there were still five more terraces full of produce between him and the valley floor. He had never seen such an abundance of food.

Climbing back up to the first terrace, Adam lay down on one of the moss beds to stare at the mountain sky and think about YHWH. He had barely begun his exploration of the garden, yet it was plain that much thought and care had gone into the garden's design and planting. And while this was only the third day since Adam's awakening, he had a growing sense of the amount of work that had been involved in establishing the garden. Perhaps the planting of Eden had been effortless for YHWH — but even if this were so, it did not diminish the message it conveyed. The planting of YHWH's garden had been a labor of love, undertaken for no reasons other than Adam's provision and pleasure.

Asah quietly observed as Adam reflected, remaining close by but not intruding. Now that Adam was safely in YHWH's garden, Asah's role as Adam's guardian and guide would continue, but in a different way. From this point forward, Adam would face most of his future challenges without Asah's intervention. Asah was permitted to step in only when Adam's life was in peril, or when he was truly unequal to the task before him *and* had the wisdom to call out to YHWH for help. If Adam didn't ask for YHWH's help, Asah was to withhold aid and allow him to struggle. In time, Adam would realize that YHWH was present and listening even when there was no visible evidence of His presence. Only then would Adam learn how to truly pray.

TEN

*"Teacher, I brought you my son, who has a mute spirit. And wher-
ever it seizes him, it throws him down; he foams at the mouth,
gnashes his teeth, and becomes rigid. So I spoke to your disciples,
that they should cast it out …"*
— Mark 9: 17b-18a NKJV

I t had been less than three full days since Adam's awakening
and the war for his soul was beginning in earnest. At the first light of
morning, hundreds of watchers had congregated at the point where Adam
had last been observed, where the valley stream poured out from under the
mountain. From there, one group of Daimónia worked their way upstream,
exploring the cavern and subterranean streambed. A larger group of
watchers worked aboveground, dispersing radially from the point of origin,
each one combing the terrain in ever-widening arcs. They covered the
ground quickly and thoroughly.

It took them less than half a day to locate Adam. When they did,
the word was relayed rapidly and the operation shifted into the next phase
— that of arraying scores of demons to observe the testing of the man-
creature. This would have to be done very cautiously to avoid alerting any
of the sentinel angels. Presumably the closer the Daimónia got to Adam,
the more likely they were to be detected. Although the angels that had
been deployed around the perimeter of the valley the evening before were
no longer visible, that didn't mean they were gone. The guardian angel

that was constantly at Adam's side was also not in sight, but the watchers didn't really believe he was gone either.

Both sides understood that the material realm of Earth was replete with opportunities to hide and move covertly, and both sides used their knowledge well. The Anhailas could control the strength and wavelength of emitted light, and thereby mimic the appearance of virtually anything within the physical realm. Most of the Daimónia had no light to emit, having lost almost all of their light-craft upon being expelled from heaven. However, they could exploit shadow and cover with exceptional skill, particularly at night.

The demons assumed that angels would be somewhere in the general vicinity of Adam, ready to intercept any demonic approaches. Consequently, the Daimónia had concocted an ingenious plan for deploying and positioning the watchers. Once the watchers were in place, a single spirit would stealthily approach and engage Adam, not for the purpose of harming him, but in order to test the strength and nature of his response.

An unnamed mute spirit had been selected to carry out the provocation. During the Great Fall, all of the demons had been transformed in some way, losing not only their comely appearance but also some of their angelic capabilities. Those rebelling angels that had formerly been instrumental in leading the angelic host in the worship found that when they scorned the privilege of proclaiming God's greatness, they also forfeited their ability to speak (though it was rumored that their voices *would* return to them when they were cast into the Abyss). It was also widely believed that if mute spirits were taken captive, they could never be made to divulge information they might possess about the strategies of the Daimónia. This couldn't be verified, of course, because the angels had never yet lost a captive.

The mute spirits were still fully capable of understanding and following instructions, and they were talented in other regards. One of the skills they shared with all of the Daimónia was the ability to inhibit the normal muscular and neural functioning of creatures of flesh, a practice the demons occasionally engaged in for sport. The game had many variations — sometimes the challenge was to make an animal seize and fall over without killing it, other times the objective was to have the animal cause its own death in some spectacular way.

The mute spirits had their own ironic and highly competitive version of this game, where one demon would try to cause the animal to vocalize while another spirit attempted to block the animal's vocal abilities. The latter was no simple task because it involved preventing the release of neuroelectric impulses in certain regions of the brain, all while the animal was in frantic motion from the first demon's prodding and probing. Some of the mute spirits had become true masters of the game, preventing animals from uttering the slightest sounds even when they were in the throes of a painful death.

There had never been a useful application for this particular demonic pastime, but today it fit in perfectly with the plan.

An unnamed mute spirit had been given a sequence of provocations to be used in testing Adam. It had been fully briefed as to the possible responses Adam might display during the encounter, and how it should react to those responses, though the briefing omitted any mention of Adam's ability to send Daimónia into the eternal Abyss. The spirit had been repeatedly cautioned, however, to secure the man's ability to speak immediately upon contact. Those planning the operation didn't give this instruction out of concern for the mute spirit, but to see if it was possible to prevent the man-creature from exercising his spiritual powers. If it wasn't possible, and the mute spirit was lost as a result, the knowledge gained was worth the price.

When the forward observers reported that Adam had lain down and might be entering a sleep period, the deployment began. The mountains that formed the walls of the garden valley were full of seeps where groundwater slowly oozed to the surface. It was at these rock-seeps, high above the first terrace where Adam lay resting, that the Daimónia emerged fully into the material realm. One by one they entered and then individually made their way downslope via the existing streamlets and small brooks. Staying wholly submerged, the dark spirits journeyed toward the deep seepage pool along the upper edge of the first terrace, the slight signature of their movements being hidden by the rippling and refraction of the moving water. They waited at the pool until all of their number had arrived, and then waited even longer to verify that they had not been spotted. Satisfied that they had not been detected, they emerged en masse from the seepage pool, this time dispersing into the numerous irrigation streamlets that ran between the rows of trees.

A feeling of unease broke in upon Adam's reflections. He came to his feet in a crouch, looking around but seeing nothing amiss. The landscape was still except for the normal movements — leaves fluttering in the intermittent afternoon breeze and water softly burbling in the streamlet next to where he had lain down. Adam was thinking that perhaps he should command any Daimónia around to show themselves, as Asah had taught him, when he thought he saw a faint shadow in the streamlet — a shadow where no shadow should be. Leaning over the streamlet to look more closely, Adam reached out to touch the surface of the water above the shadow.

Adam dropped sideways to the ground, partly in the water and partly out of it. His arms and his legs were drawn up tightly against his torso and were completely unresponsive to his mental commands. It was as if his control over the muscles of his body had been severed. He rolled and thrashed about in spite of his unnatural posture, unable to tell if he was causing his movements or if something else was moving him. He felt neither pain nor fear — only that something else was controlling his body against his will.

Adam relaxed, abandoning his effort to mentally re-assert control over his rigid, trembling muscles. This was obviously a demonic attack and Adam knew what to do, remembering what Asah had taught him about the power and authority of the spoken word.

"Mmrhhr, ernnhhh."

Adam's lips and tongue were as bound as the rest of his muscles. He could make as much noise as he wanted, as loud as he wanted, and could move his lower jaw slightly with great effort. But he could not form a single word. Commanding this spirit that had seized him might not be so easy after all.

"*YHWH*," Adam thought, now lying still and crumpled on his side. His shoulder and forehead were pressed into the mud at the edge of the streamlet, and a string of saliva dripped from the corner of his limp lips.

"*Words don't have to be spoken to be words; they can be directed in thought!*"

As soon as this realization came to him, the words roared out from within Adam's inner man, *"In the name of YHWH, I command you to release me!"*

Adam groaned loudly and was immediately released from the seizure. Regaining his feet, Adam saw the shadow streak upstream, intent upon escaping. Adam shouted out his next command, his voice once again fully under his control.

"Stop, spirit; identify yourself!"

The spirit, now fully visible as it hovered a few inches above the water's surface, stopped and turned to stare at him with both fear and malice.

"I command you to identify yourself."

The demon remained mute, evil intent burning in its eyes. Adam remembered Asah's admonition about gazing into the eyes of Daimónia and decided he should dispatch this demon rather than converse with it.

"To the Abyss with you!"

As before, the demon was instantly grasped, this time by a solitary but very bright angel. A moment later the terrace was once again quiet. Adam listened to his inner discernment, and felt a few moments of unease, but this was quickly replaced by a growing sense of peace.

Apparently no other Daimónia were nearby.

ELEVEN

*The tree of life was also in the midst of the garden, and the tree of
the knowledge of good and evil.*
— Genesis 2:9b NKJV

*For until the law sin was in the world, but sin is not imputed when
there is no law.*
— Romans 5:13NKJV

When Adam mentally commanded the mute spirit to release
him, the command had reverberated deeply into the spirit realm even
though no audible words had been spoken. The subsequent spoken
commands were even more forceful, and were heard clearly by every
demon and angel in the vicinity of Eden. Further away, in the distant
haunts where the Daimónia congregated, the commands were perceived as
powerful tremors rippling through the foundations and fabric of the realm.
While the Daimónia distant from Eden had no immediate understanding
of what had just happened, they knew that such a shaking had to have had
a powerful origin, and they suspected it did not augur well for them.

The Anhailas had a clearer perception and were beside themselves
with joy. This second encounter between Adam and the Daimónia had
been anticipated, and many had been watching from heaven. Although
the story of Adam's first encounter with the familiar spirit had circulated
widely, few had been watching at the time it happened. This time it was
different; for every angel not occupied with assigned tasks had been closely

following the events of Adam's day. When the encounter finally came, they were not disappointed.

For a spirit creature to exercise such spiritual authority would have been remarkable. But Adam was a strange mingling of spirit, soul, and flesh; each so intertwined with the other that they couldn't be separated. Because of this, Adam lacked the most rudimentary abilities possessed by angels and demons alike. He couldn't manipulate light, and his ability to manipulate matter was limited to being able to move items about in a minor and useless fashion. He couldn't see into the spiritual realm, and his eyesight in the material realm was nothing extraordinary. Nor could he move beyond the three spatial dimensions within which his dust-water body had originally been formed. While his commands were capable of producing profound effects within the aetherial realm, his sparing use of this authority suggested he didn't really understand the power he had.

Consequently, to any spirit being, Adam would at first glance appear to be incapable of posing a threat. That such an inherently weak creature had been given the power to command the Daimónia was unimaginable ....

... and so like YHWH.

The angels of heaven were accustomed to God doing magnificent, unimaginable things, usually without prior notice. They knew that while YHWH's nature was consistent and unchanging, His acts were never predictable. Engaging in speculative discussions about how the Most High might respond to hypothetical situations was a favorite pastime of angels, though they rarely hit the mark.

From the perspective of the demonic watchers in the garden, Adam's commands bore little resemblance to those spoken by angels. Angels certainly issued commands, but there was no self-activating power within their words. Angelic commands were willingly obeyed within their own ranks, and were enforced by action and arms elsewhere. But Adam's words had power and substance unlike those of the Anhailas. The self-contained power of Adam's commands resembled edicts spoken by YHWH himself.

They certainly produced comparable effects amongst the Daimónia.

Not only had Adam's thought-command instantly broken the hold of a very powerful demon on a creature of flesh, but the shock-wave accompanying Adam's command had shaken scores of watchers out of their hidden places in stream and pool and shadow, leaving them weak and disoriented. The confused dismay of the watchers quickly turned to terror, for suddenly there were angels everywhere amongst them, pressing a well-coordinated attack. Too late the watchers realized that the angels had also been hiding and waiting. Only a handful of watchers escaped that day. The rest were quickly immobilized by skillful strokes of light-swords and their broken but ever-living spirit bodies carried away in bondage. The demons that did escape fled deep into the domain of darkness. They had no desire to remain anywhere near Eden or the man-creature.

Adam cleaned the mud from his face and body, looking carefully before he dipped his hands into the water. He was alert and unafraid; ready for another encounter should there be any Daimónia lingering about.

Thinking back on his last conversation with YHWH, Adam decided to go to the valley floor and began working his way down, terrace by terrace. He could have spent days making a leisurely descent, taking in the intricacies and beauty of each terrace, but he had a destination in mind. When he scrambled down over the last terrace wall to the valley floor, he found Asah waiting for him. Adam didn't slow down, but passed by him and continued on in the general direction of the valley center.

Asah fell into step beside Adam. "You handled yourself very well on the upper terrace. I had to intervene to keep you from dropping face down in the water. I gave you a slight nudge toward the bank as you were falling. Did you feel it?"

Adam didn't know whether to feel grateful or irritated; Asah's concept of helping fell short of what Adam would have liked, but he understood the necessity of learning to fight for himself. If he had landed face down in the water, it would have been a very different experience, probably a frightful one. Asah deserved his thanks.

"I was a bit overwhelmed with all of the sensations of the moment, Asah, so no, I didn't feel it. But thank you nonetheless."

"It was my honor to be of service."

Adam looked at Asah. He knew that Asah had a sense of humor and was capable of sarcasm, but there was no hint that Asah was anything but serious. Adam still didn't know that much about angels, but he suspected that they conveyed only what they chose to convey.

"I do have a question, Asah. How was that demon able to do what it did to me?"

"The important question is not how, but why."

"Perhaps it was able to bind me because my guardian angel didn't stop it." Adam offered some sarcasm of his own.

Asah was unperturbed by the comment. "It took advantage of your curiosity. The Most High has given you an unquenchable curiosity, but that curiosity should always be tempered with discernment. You should never explore something that your spirit isn't at peace with. Once again, you weren't listening to your spirit.

"As to how," Asah continued, "your body is constantly sending and receiving commands within itself. Not anything that you can hear, and not in a language you can speak, but the commands are always there nonetheless. The mute spirit simply jumbled your body's ability to communicate internally, and as a result, your body seized. It doesn't take any real skill for a demon to do that. They do it occasionally with the animals for entertainment."

Adam imagined the animals of Eden sporadically going into seizures without warning. Obviously such seizures could result in their physical harm, not to mention the fear the animals would feel. Adam would not tolerate such abuse of those within his care, and mentally noted to talk with the animals about it.

"Where are we going, by the way?" Asah asked.

During their conversation the day before, YHWH had told Adam that he could freely eat of any of the trees in the garden except one — the tree of knowledge of good and evil. The Lord had explicitly commanded Adam not to eat from this particular tree, adding that he would die if he did. There was also a second tree, the tree of life, which YHWH had mentioned but said little about. Adam presumed from its name that it had the opposite effect. While he had no intention of disobeying the Lord's command, they both sounded like very unusual trees that were worth seeing.

"I would like to see the tree of knowledge of good and evil and the tree of life," Adam replied. "YHWH spoke of them yesterday. I think they are somewhere on the valley floor. Can you direct me to them?"

Asah studied Adam for a moment before answering. "The tree of knowledge of good and evil is very easy to find. All the paths on the valley floor will eventually take you there, including the one you are on now. But this tree is not like the other trees of the garden, Adam. You need to think carefully about how you should regard this tree. "

"How can I regard something I haven't even seen? Are you saying I shouldn't go and see it?"

"Perhaps. That might be less dangerous for you. But I cannot tell you not to go."

"Asah, I appreciate the protection and help you have provided, but clearly you have allowed me to face danger. How is this tree any different? Besides, if YHWH intended for me to avoid this tree, He wouldn't have planted it where it is easy to get to."

"Adam, this tree is different; it represents a different kind of danger. YHWH doesn't require that you avoid it. On the contrary, YHWH has chosen to make this tree easily accessible. He fully understands that you will encounter it unless you purpose not to. You must heed the Lord's command not to eat of it, but whether you decide to avoid the tree completely is up to you."

"You aren't making sense, Asah. YHWH put the tree here but told me not to eat of it. You suggest I should avoid the tree entirely, but at the same time tell me that YHWH doesn't require that I do so. It is plain that YHWH planted this garden for me as an act of love. Then why put a tree in it that can kill me?"

"So you have the choice of life or death. So you can choose to obey or disobey."

That was enough to make Adam stop. "But surely YHWH wants me to live, doesn't He?"

"Certainly, but only if you choose to do so. And if you die, it will only be because you have chosen to do so. We all have to make that choice."

"Then it is better just to avoid the tree entirely."

"Yes and no. You can't avoid the tree solely to avoid making a choice. If it isn't a settled matter in your heart, if you desire anything the tree offers, then you will eventually find yourself standing before the tree when you didn't intend to go there. At that point you will have no choice but to make a choice."

Adam's head was spinning. This was all very complicated. "So perhaps it would be best to just go to the tree now, make my choice, and be done with this business of making choices." Adam realized he was contradicting what he had just said a moment before.

"If that's what you wish, but keep in mind that unless you have lost all desire for what the tree offers, you will have to choose again the next time you pass by it."

Adam shook his head in exasperation. It was obvious that he would never get a clear answer from Asah. It was as if Asah was trying to tell him something without actually saying it.

"Fine," Adam said, making a decision. "We will go see this tree and I will make my choice. Please lead the way."

"No. I shall not lead you into temptation. The Spirit of God may lead you there, or you may be led there by your own desires, but I will not lead you there. It is enough that I have told you that this path will take you there."

"I suppose you won't take me to the tree of life either."

Asah's eyebrow went up. "Of course not. It's not your time to go there, nor would you be likely to find it if you tried. There is only one path there and it is narrow and difficult. And besides, the tree of life doesn't appear to be anything special — it looks like just another very ordinary tree."

Adam turned without reply and started walking down the path. He would go to the tree of knowledge by himself then, without Asah, and would look for the tree of life sometime later. There really was no hurry. Besides, if the tree of life was not on a main pathway and would be difficult to find, he might very well chance upon it as he explored the garden in the days ahead.

Adam paused and turned around, suddenly remembering something Asah had said. "Asah, what did you mean when you said we all have to make a choice? Have you been to the tree of knowledge of good and evil yourself?"

There was a faint sadness in Asah's smile. "My tree did not look like yours Adam, but I have indeed looked at the tree, gazed upon its beauty, and turned away. It has nothing I desire. I have made my choice, as have all my brethren who serve. But there were many of my brethren who did eat; and they are forever lost."

Adam held Asah's gaze for a moment, trying to plumb the depth of his expression. He had never seen anything resembling sadness in Asah's expression before. But his question had touched a chord. Adam realized that Asah had lost friends during the rebellion, fellow Anhailas that he had served with and had loved.

Adam's heart welled up with compassion. Asah was always so inscrutable; it was easy to think he lacked deep feelings. But he and his fellow Anhailas had obviously endured a profound loss — one that had softened with time perhaps, but one they would likely always carry.

Asah smiled a poignant smile, the sadness lessening but still lingering in his eyes. "Adam, don't misunderstand. It was a hard thing to lose our brethren and to have to take up arms against them, but only for the shortest period. It only took one encounter for each of us to realize that they were no longer who they had been. There was nothing left of who they were, and there was nothing that could be done about it. Although we might mourn the memory of comrades forever gone, that doesn't mean we feel compassion upon what they have become.

"They are filth, Adam." The sadness had vanished and Asah's eyes were now glowing with a resolute fire. "They deserve the Abyss, and the sooner the better. As long as they are here, as long as we have to deal with them, it is a reminder of the dishonor and reproach they heaped upon the One who loved them and gave them life. Whatever loss I might feel immediately dissipates when I consider the disgrace they heaped upon the Father of us all.

"Go," Asah said, waving his hand in the direction Adam had been heading. "You must do what you must do. Satisfy your curiosity. But don't ever forget who you are and how much YHWH loves you. I would not want to see Him lose you as well."

"I'm sorry," Adam said, not sure whether it was the right thing to say. "I won't do what they did, Asah, of that you can be sure."

Asah watched Adam walk down the path. He wished he could have said more. He wished he could have explained to Adam that everything in the garden was under his dominion, including the tree of knowledge of good and evil. Most of all he wished he could have told Adam that he had the authority to utterly destroy the tree, to hew down every branch and dig up every root. It would have been an arduous task, but not an impossible one. YHWH had told Adam not to eat of the tree, but there was no prohibition against him touching it, and YHWH had never said or implied that its presence in the garden had to be tolerated. Annihilating the tree was the only way Adam could forever silence its whispers and sever its influence. It was Adam's way of escape.

Asah understood it was not his place to say these things. Wisdom could speak these things to Adam, if he was listening. YHWH could speak these things to Adam, if Adam thought to ask him. But Asah could not speak these things. Asah could only wait, watch, and trust in God. And hope that YHWH would not lose what He loved so much.

TWELVE

And do not lead us not into temptation, but deliver us from the evil one.

— Matthew 6:13b NKJV

The four watchers had given their reports and they were all in agreement. The man-creature Adam had spoken and commanded with the power of YHWH. The force of Adam's command on the mute spirit and the Daimónia provided clear evidence that Adam was more than just an intelligent flesh-creature. Some of the watchers had been in a position to see Adam's face when the mute spirit's sentence had been pronounced, and they were sure that there had been God-light emanating from Adam's eyes. Adam was a flesh-creature and a spirit being at the same time. Truly this was a new thing with a distressing array of implications.

After the Council finished questioning the watchers, Satan admonished them to never speak of this again and dismissed them. There was much yet to discuss with the Council, but these deliberations would be kept private. Satan was ever-mindful of the possibility of internal treason, and would afford no opportunity for the rank and file Daimónia to defect and ally with this new spirit being. For the time being, the best way to guard against this was to control their knowledge of Adam's existence and his powers. Satan didn't know if an alliance between disillusioned Daimónia and the man was likely, or even possible. But if it were to occur, the effect upon Satan's dominion could be devastating. While Satan still lusted for the subservience of the man-creature, he knew his initial focus had to be on keeping the man from becoming a serious challenge to his dominion.

After the dismissal of the watchers, the Archon deferentially waited for Satan to speak again. They were always careful not to display too much initiative. Independent displays of leadership tended to arouse Satan's suspicions, and that was never a good thing. After thinking for awhile, Satan finally spoke.

"We still don't know enough about this Adam. That he poses a threat to all of us is clear. None of the angels have the authority to command lesser Daimónia into the Abyss, and yet this creature obviously does. While I am not concerned that his powers might challenge mine," Satan lied glibly, "he could diminish our numbers over time. I still want him turned; I'm sure we could find ways to use his powers to our advantage. But to do this, we must first understand him."

Each of the Archon nodded whenever Satan looked at them. "So tell me your thoughts, counselors. How can a spirit being be clothed in flesh? Is Adam a created spirit just like us, differing only in his fleshly housing, or does the elusive Spirit of YHWH somehow co-inhabit the man's body? What are his abilities and limitations? What are his appetites and desires? And for all of these questions that we cannot answer now, how do we get the answers? Start with the first question."

Shaarur, a horribly disfigured prince of wickedness, was the first to speak. "There really is no precedent for this. We know that the higher animals are soulish — they have varying degrees of intelligence, have feelings and desires, and can communicate. But they lack eternal spirits. When they die, they cease to exist. They are confined to space and time and never enter the spiritual dimensions.

"This Adam," Shaarur said, "appears to have body, soul, and spirit. He can interact with the spiritual realm, and that sets him apart from the animals, but he hasn't shown any ability to move about in the spiritual realm like we can. That, aside from the fact that we lack physical bodies, makes him different from us. It appears that his spirit is bound to his body and that he is, therefore, anchored in the material realm. Yet he possesses incredible power in the spiritual realm."

"One wonders what would happen to his spirit if his body was destroyed." Ghanph said, his face frozen in a perpetual scowl that didn't soften even when something pleased him. "Perhaps his spirit would die along with his body."

"Or perhaps his spirit would be fully released into the spiritual realm and then he would be more dangerous than ever," countered Ptha. Ptha was a prince of lies and had a finely honed ability to formulate alternative viewpoints. He had been an early recruit to Lucifer's ranks and had enticed more angels into the cause than any other spirit except Lucifer himself. Ptha also delighted in posturing as the intellectual superior of the other Archon.

"I wasn't finished." Ghanph said, his voice expressing his unconcealed disdain. "One also wonders how his spirit exercises control over his body. Whenever we attempt to enter the bodies of higher animals, they usually run away in terror. And when we do succeed in penetrating, the best we can do is send them into convulsions."

Satan fostered a certain level of animosity amongst the Archon. He never wanted them to believe they could fully trust one another, but he also didn't want their antagonisms to reach the point where nothing could be accomplished. He wanted them to work together but feel isolated at the same time; to greatly fear him as their master and yet feel he was their only friend.

"Maybe your approach should be more delicate, Ghanph," Ptha said. "This isn't your area of expertise, of course, but consider how a carefully delivered progressive lie works where an outright lie will not. Maybe the key to usefully inhabiting an animal's body is to approach it gently and quietly. Allow it to acclimate to your presence. Don't do anything to alarm it. Try to act in accord with it until you can learn how to assert some control."

"I don't see how this is relevant to the question our Lord has asked." Ratsach, the least subtle of the Archon, had been quiet until now. Brute force was what he was best at. "We don't gain anything by learning how to inhabit animals. The question is how a spirit can dwell in flesh to begin with. Except for this man-creature, animals don't have spirits."

"It's very relevant." Ptha said condescendingly. "If you, being a spirit, learn how to inhabit an animal's body, then you would learn things about how a spirit and body can operate together. That in turn might provide useful insights on how Adam's spirit inhabits his body. You might even be able to learn how to co-inhabit Adam's body while his spirit is still there.

"Of course, I don't mean you personally Ratsach," Ptha concluded. "I'm not suggesting that you try to inhabit any animals. That would require finesse that is beyond you."

This was productive dialogue. Ptha could be brilliant at times. Satan wasn't inclined to think that a demon could inhabit Adam's body while Adam's own spirit was there. After all, there had never been a truly workable habitation of an animal. But Ptha's approach had never been tried, simply because there had never been any reason to.

Satan was pleased; this conversation was raising many possibilities worthy of exploration.

Shaarur spoke up. "I think we shouldn't quickly dismiss this idea of Ptha's. If, in fact, the spirit of God can co-dwell within the man, then theoretically it might be possible for us to do the same."

"The problem is in the approach," Ghanph said, stating the obvious. "Every time a demon gets anywhere near this Adam, he confronts them and commands them into the Abyss."

There was an extended silence while they all considered this.

"But if we learned to inhabit animals," Ratsach offered, "then we could approach him in one of those. He allows the animals to get close to him." Coming from Ratsach, this insight surprised everyone. Even Ptha nodded begrudgingly.

"Useful, Ratsach, but that's still not getting inside him," Ghanph reminded him. "That's still not exercising any direct control over him."

"But if you get close to him, even in an animal, you can speak to him. And if you can speak to him, you can control him if you know what to say and what not to say. If we can learn how to inhabit and speak through animals, I can handle the rest, our Lord permitting," Ptha reasserted his superiority over the Archon while glancing over at Satan with lowered eyes.

Satan spoke up. "Ptha, your approach has merit. Work with Shaarur and develop protocols for inhabiting and speaking through the animals. When you have accomplished that, return to me and we will discuss the plan for contacting Adam. For the present, do not approach him. In fact, I want these field trials conducted away from the area where the man is dwelling. There is no need for some animal telling the man about a botched inhabitation. That would only serve to alert him."

Satan looked at the two Archon to be sure they understood their assignment, and feeling satisfied, continued. "Now, what about the man-creature's strengths and weaknesses? What are his strongest desires?"

"We know he eats, drinks, and sleeps." Shaarur said. "He probably both needs and wants these things. But if you are thinking of enticing him with any of these, YHWH has provided him with an overabundance of feed and water; he suffers no lack."

"He converses with both angels and animals," Ptha said, "so there is at least an inclination to communicate. Perhaps he needs companionship, or perhaps he has an appetite for knowledge."

"He is male, is he not?" Satan asked.

"Clearly," Ratsach replied.

"Is there no female?"

They all shook their heads no.

"So he is not reproducing then. How curious that there is no female. That might have been something we could have used against him. I don't suppose we have any intelligence on his interactions with YHWH?"

They shook their heads no again. This was no surprise. Even Satan would not dare to draw near to YHWH to eavesdrop on his conversations with Adam. He could not realistically expect his minions to do so.

"As you know, my Lord, the light prevents our approach," Ghanph said. "We have only been able to catch brief glimpses from a great distance, and that with great pain. From these, all we have learned is that the man regularly talks with YHWH and also worships."

Satan's countenance changed for just a moment, and then it was past. But the Archon understood. They knew that Satan's lust to be worshiped was all consuming. In the final analysis, it was why all of them were no longer in heaven. The Archon also knew that Satan would gladly risk losing any or all of them if he could have the worship he hungered for.

Satan knew he had lapsed. There was something intoxicating about the thought of being worshiped by this man-creature.

Satan broke the silence. "Perhaps the man can be taught to worship correctly. However, for now the question remains as to whether the spirit of God co-resides within the man. Continue to observe him and to learn about him, but do not approach him or harm him."

If God did dwell inside the man, then Satan already had the beginnings of a plan. While the details of it would have to be carefully thought out, the essence of the plan was simple and elegant. All Satan had to do was to draw the man into some sin against God. Any sin would do, and just one sin would be sufficient. If that could be accomplished, Satan was confident that God would abandon the man of His own accord.

THIRTEEN

... the tree was good for food ... pleasant to the eyes, and a tree
desirable to make one wise ....
                    — Genesis 3:6b NKJV

... no tree in the garden of God was like it in beauty. I made it
beautiful with a multitude of branches, so that all the trees of Eden
envied it, that were in the garden of God.
                    — Ezekiel 31:8b-9 NKJV

Adam knew the tree as soon as he saw it. In many ways it was like any other tree. It had leaves and branches, roots and a trunk. The leaves were dark green and glossy above, but had a red-brown sheen on their undersides. The fruits of the tree were about half a hand across, perfectly spherical with smooth, tight skins that showed a faint dusting of fine white powder in the depressions around the stems. The fruit color was variable, ranging from yellow-green to ruby red to deep purple. Some of the fruits lay fallen close to where Adam had stopped, and these showed a dark venation in the skin, giving the appearance of something that was both plant and animal at the same time.

When Adam first arrived, he didn't approach the tree closely, but squatted a comfortable distance away. Even though he had not followed Asah's suggestion to avoid the tree, he wasn't about to dismiss Asah's other cautions. The last few days had been full of unpleasant experiences caused by Adam acting impulsively rather than deliberately. So Adam sat beyond the reach of the tree's canopy, studying with his eyes and listening with his spirit.

From his vantage point, Adam felt absolutely nothing in his spirit — no anxiety, no disquiet. He felt exactly like he would have if he had sat in contemplation of any other tree. He noticed that the usual grass and herbaceous cover were absent beneath its canopy, and thought this was a bit odd. The lack of ground cover didn't seem to be due to the tree's shade, for the tree was high and the ground beneath it was well dappled with sunlight. Rather, it seemed that the tree exerted some invisible influence that kept the surrounding vegetation at bay. *Perhaps the tree is unwilling to share its water and soil with other plants*, Adam thought.

There was no question that the tree was magnificent. It had almost perfect symmetry and balance in the arrangement of its branches, creating an overall form that was very pleasing to look upon. It was higher than the surrounding trees, though not by a great deal. The tree also conveyed a sense of much greater age than the other trees, though Adam couldn't pinpoint what gave him that impression.

Adam stood up and walked five strides until he stood just inside the clear zone beneath the tree's canopy. The effect of those five steps on his spirit was profound. His inner man immediately went from a relaxed, curious state to one of acute awareness and sensation. The heightened awareness was exhilarating, and Adam found himself paying more attention to what he was feeling than to the tree in front of him. Adam momentarily considered stepping back, but the sensations and amplified awareness were so pleasurable that he didn't do so. Remembering that YHWH's prohibition was only against eating the tree's fruit, Adam decided he was safe in remaining where he was until he had finished his observations. Nevertheless, he resolved not to approach any closer.

From this position, Adam could see that some of the fruits still on the tree had been pocked by birds. Adam looked around but didn't see any dead birds, so he concluded that the tree's fruits were not dangerous for birds to eat. Adam picked up a small stick and poked at one of the fruits on the ground. A milky sap exuded from the puncture and then quickly formed a thin, white skin over the wound. Even detached from the tree, the fruit seemed to have life within itself.

When Adam had seen and studied enough, he turned to leave. Only then did he perceive something that had been lingering outside his thinking, just beyond his conscious awareness. He knew that the tree was alive in the way that all growing plants were alive. But as he turned to go, he sensed that the tree was alive in another way, a way that other plants were not.

The tree has *desire!* In some wordless way, the tree was conveying that it wanted him to stay, to come closer. And upon realizing that, Adam felt an answering desire starting to form within him.

Adam turned and ran until the tree was far behind him.

FOURTEEN

And you shall remember that the Lord your God led you ... to humble you and test you, to know what was in your heart, whether you would keep His commandments or not.
— Deuteronomy 8:2 NKJV

Asah had seen it all, watching Adam from just beyond the interface between the realms. As relieved as he was that Adam's first encounter with the tree was over, he was already concerned for the next one. Asah had not expected Adam to approach the tree so closely, and realized he should have known that Adam's curiosity would drive him beyond what was prudent. However, what really troubled Asah was something he had discovered about the tree, something which he had never anticipated.

Asah had complete freedom of movement, both within the material realm of Earth (or the created universe, for that matter) and through the interface between the spiritual and material dimensions. Asah could enter or leave the material realm as easily as Adam could slip into or out of one of the garden's pools. Just as the interface between the water and air was identifiable but easy to penetrate, the surface between the material and spiritual realm was permeable to angel and demon alike.

But the interface around the tree was different. When Adam had first paused to study the tree, Asah had remained at his side, watchful and alert, just inside the spiritual realm. At any time Asah could have extended himself into the material realm had he willed to do so. When

Adam moved beneath the canopy of the tree, Asah had moved with him, still in the aetherial realm. But the moment Adam stepped beneath the tree's canopy, Asah sensed a change in the interface. While Adam was poking at the tree's fruit, Asah extended his hand and was shocked to find that the interface was hardened and impenetrable.

Asah instantly grasped that if the interface beneath the tree's canopy could not be crossed, then his ability to protect Adam was compromised. Asah gathered himself and flung himself against the interface with all of his angelic strength, but it was of no avail, he only bounced back stunned and shaken. The interface had become an impassable wall. Asah moved around, probing to see if there were any passages, but he could not enter the material dimension anywhere beneath the tree's canopy.

By the time Adam had run away, Asah realized there was something else he could try. Asah entered completely into the material realm well away from the tree's perimeter, adopted a physical body, and walked toward the tree. As he reached the clear zone beneath the tree he again encountered a wall just as solid as the one in the spiritual realm. It wasn't visible or discernible in any way other than the fact that it denied him passage, but it was there.

Asah turned and quickly caught up with Adam. He would watch over and stay close by him, as he always had. He would protect him to the full extent of his abilities, whether from physical harm or spiritual threat. He would do this whether Adam was awake or asleep, no matter where he was. Unless he was under the tree. When Adam was under the tree there was nothing Asah could do to help him. Adam could not be close to the tree and remain under Asah's protection at the same time.

Asah surmised that this was YHWH's doing. The Most High had placed a barrier around the tree to ensure that the choice to obey or not obey was Adam's alone. No angel would be allowed to interfere or intervene. Asah wondered whether the barrier would also exclude the Daimónia. More important, Asah thought, was the question of whether the spirit of YHWH remained with Adam while he was under the tree's canopy. That, and the question of whether Adam would discern it if YHWH's spirit was suddenly no longer present.

FIFTEEN

God is love, and he who abides in love abides in God, and God in him.

— I John 4:16b NKJV

Adam did not see Asah for two days after visiting the tree of knowledge, and had begun to wonder whether he had offended him. He knew that Asah withdrew at times to encourage Adam's reliance upon YHWH, as well as to develop Adam's self-reliance, but this was the longest period yet between visits. So when Adam awakened on his ninth day and Asah was sitting nearby, Adam was very pleased. He had missed Asah. He had also accumulated more questions.

"So! You're back," Adam said. "I'm glad. I've missed talking with you."

"Always at your service," Asah said, giving Adam a broad smile. "Even when you can't see me."

"Asah, I thought I might have offended you by not following your advice the other day. That is, if angels have the same kinds of feelings as I do, which I wouldn't necessarily assume to be the case. But did I? Hurt your feelings, I mean?"

"Be at peace, Adam, you didn't offend me. You constantly surprise me, and at times may disappoint me, but you can't offend me. And if I am disappointed it is for your sake, not for my own. For me to be offended with the one whom YHWH loves would be sin.

"As for feelings, of course angels have feelings. Proper worship of the Most High is not possible without feelings. He desires more from his creatures than a barren mental acceptance that He is God. The Daimónia understand that YHWH is God, but that understanding most assuredly doesn't qualify as worship. In the spiritual realm, feelings are what give color and vibrancy to worship. The more passionate our worship, the more urgent our yearning for Him, the more pungent and pleasing our worship becomes.

"But I wouldn't say I have all the same feelings you do," Asah concluded. "After all, I don't dwell in a body of flesh, and your body apparently has many strange feelings that are unique to creatures of flesh."

"And the demons, do they have feelings?" Adam asked.

"Yes, they do. They were originally created as angels with the ability to worship and to deeply experience the joy and wonder of bringing YHWH pleasure. Having scorned that privilege, they will one day experience His displeasure just as deeply. Thankfully, those are feelings neither you nor I need partake of."

"So the Daimónia were loved by YHWH when they were still angels. But now they are no longer loved. Does that mean that YHWH changed?"

"Not at all. The Daimónia are no longer capable of giving or receiving love. In rejecting God, who is Love, they separated themselves from and have become forever impervious to love. They are the unloving, and as such, have absolutely nothing in common with YHWH. They themselves would not willingly choose to be in His presence. Furthermore, now that they have chosen darkness, where love is absent, they would never survive being exposed to the light of His glory. They would be consumed in an instant and cease to exist."

Adam splashed water on his face, cupped water in his hands and drank, and began walking toward the nearest cultivated terrace, deep in thought. Asah kept pace and kept silent, also in thought. He had been sent to tutor Adam in spiritual matters, but Adam's questions were revealing a depth of insight and inquiry that Asah had not expected so soon.

Before you know it, Asah mused, *angels will be learning the mysteries of YHWH from a man.*

Adam finally broke the silence. "If the Daimónia have nothing in common with YHWH, then why does He suffer their continued existence?"

Another excellent question, Asah thought, one that required a moment's reflection before Asah answered.

"Because YHWH granted them an eternal existence when He created them. It was His gift to all of the angels. It is not YHWH's nature to recall such gifts once they are given."

"Could they not decide to turn away from darkness; to cease their rebellion against YHWH, and thereby regain their former state?"

"Some decisions, once made, can never be reversed," Asah answered. "This is something you must never forget Adam. Free will that cannot make final, irreversible decisions is not truly free will. The Daimónia understood that if they chose to follow Lucifer, they would never be able to return. But they chose anyway."

"And that decision represented their partaking of the tree of knowledge of good and evil?"

Asah was astounded. Adam had gone to the very heart of the matter.

"Well spoken, Adam. One cannot acquire such knowledge without being changed. One can understand evil as an abstract concept, and still remain pure and blameless. But transgression, once tasted, becomes one with the partaker. Even if the partaker were never to sin again, the knowledge and memory of sin would always be there. Consequently, even the simplest transgression leaves an indelible mark on the soul and mind that can never be erased. The actual nature of the transgression is of less importance than the fact that it occurred. Adam, you have been made in the image and likeness of God; holy and without sin. But you must understand that if you commit even the smallest transgression, you will no longer look like Him. You will only look like something that once looked like Him, and has since become ruined."

They had reached the terrace and Adam stood surveying it, deciding on his tasks for the morning. "Well then," Adam said, "we'll both just have to avoid all transgressions, even small ones. I'll warn you if I see you straying too close to the edge. I wouldn't want you to sin and transform into a demon. Then I would have to cast you into the Abyss."

Asah knew Adam's words were meant to be playful. He could have commented on what Asah might have to do to Adam if he ever sinned, but gentleness restrained him. He remembered that it was pride that brought Lucifer down, and pride had many faces. For all of Adam's keen insights, the man still needed Asah's instruction.

Asah's response was gracious but firm, "Adam, that's really not funny. Always remember that your words have power. Therefore, you shouldn't speak lightly of transgression, nor casually regard those things which YHWH abhors. Transgression rarely occurs without one first becoming familiar and comfortable with it in one's thoughts and words."

Adam was instantly smitten and looked at Asah with wide, imploring eyes. "Asah, I am so sorry. You are absolutely right. I spoke foolishly." And then Adam smiled, recognizing the irony of what had just happened. "Well done, Asah, surely you have just now warned me back from the edge!"

Asah bowed slightly with a suppressed smile.

Adam returned his attention to the terrace. The cultivated areas required very little in the way of maintenance. Unlike the lands outside the garden, where plants of all kinds grew mixed together, the food plants of the garden remained within their original planting areas and didn't encroach upon the territories of other plants. That being the case, Adam wondered what work really needed to be done in the garden, for in many respects, the garden tended itself. Furthermore, YHWH had indicated that Adam should work to expand the garden's cultivated areas, but there seemed to be more than enough ground already in production to provide Adam with his daily food.

"Asah, why don't the terrace plantings grow all mixed together like in the uncultivated lands outside the garden?"

'The first answer is that the garden is a place of order; the plants respect each other's space and defer to one another, thereby making your job of tending and harvesting them immeasurably easier."

Adam found that puzzling. "I haven't seen any plants with eyes, how would they know where they are in relation to each other?"

"By their roots. Each plant releases substances into the soil from its roots, giving the soil the flavor of that kind of plant. If the flavor is strong enough, seeds of a different kind of plant will not germinate there, nor will other plants spread into that area. This same phenomenon also occurs in the uncultivated areas, but to a lesser extent; there the plants are more tolerant of each other's flavors."

"And is there a second answer?"

"Of course. As you have noticed, the garden is full of hidden mysteries and messages. Some are simple, some profound. The garden is always silently speaking of the One who planted it and of His ways. This in itself tells you something about YHWH, namely that He wants to be known. So if you have eyes of understanding, the garden can teach you a great deal about the Most High."

"That was the second answer? What does that have to do with plant roots and soil flavors?"

"That was the preface to the second answer," Asah said patiently. "One hidden message of the cultivated areas is this: YHWH's creatures do not seek their own advantage at the expense of other creatures. In this way they reflect His nature."

Adam wondered if eating was a violation of this principle, and then realized that nothing he ate ever robbed the life of the plant — for the fruit or grain was already destined to be released by the plant, and did not cause the plant's death. Even the grazing animals didn't kill the plants they ate, but simply cropped the growth which the plant quickly replaced.

"Now I have a question for you, Adam," Asah said. "Have you noticed that many of the animals are caching and storing food?"

"Well, yes … not that I have given it much thought. Only some of them do it; not all of them."

"You haven't been here long enough to notice, perhaps, but those that aren't storing food have been eating all day long for many, many days to build up fat reserves."

Obviously Asah was leading up to something. Adam knew what fat was in that it was a soft tissue and that it gave a more rounded appearance to some of the animal's bodies, but he didn't know its function or what it should be reserved for.

Asah sensed the gap in Adam's knowledge and proceeded to explain what body fat was. He ended by pointing out how little body fat Adam had.

Adam had come to recognize this as one of Asah's favorite teaching styles — providing partial information and then withholding the rest until Adam asked the right question.

"So are you saying I need to eat more than I do?"

"You can if you wish, but you could never eat enough to get you through the winter."

Adam knew the winter was a period of colder weather that would visit Eden some number of days ahead. That much he had learned from the animals.

"Then you must be saying I need to cache food. But why would I do that when I can just walk to the nearest terrace or grove of fruit trees and gather all I need?

"Because when winter comes most of those trees will be at rest and will no longer have any fruit on them. The grains and pulse will also have long since dropped to the ground. Virtually all of the plants you presently harvest from will have become dormant until the next growing season, which will follow only after many days have passed."

Adam felt a rush of anxiety. He could run out of food! His mind started racing. He could start by gathering the barley and lentils from the terrace he was standing on, but then he realized he needed a place to store the food. And he needed a better way to carry food than just with his hands.

"Adam, may I suggest that you relax, think, and develop a plan? You still have enough time to gather ample food reserves before winter comes, but you do need to get started."

"I need a way to carry the food and a place to store it."

Asah walked to a nearby barberry shrub and extricated an abandoned waxwing nest from within its branches. He tossed it to Adam's feet. "This should work. As for your storage locations, they should be dry and under cover where rain and snow can't reach them."

Adam knew what rain was only from watching it fall on the high peaks; thus far it had always dissipated before reaching the elevation of the garden. As for snow ….

"You mean there will be snow in the garden?" Adam asked. He had always wanted to see snow up close.

"Quite right, lots of it." Asah turned and began to walk away.

"Wait, Asah. I still need a way to carry food. This nest is hardly big enough to be of much use."

"Quite right again. Maybe you should learn from it rather than use it."

Adam started to ask why YHWH had told him to expand the cultivated areas, but he was too late. Asah was gone.

Adam decided to eat before doing anything else. Only when he was completely full did he sit down to think about nests and storage sites. In his wanderings through the garden, Adam had noticed bird nests on many occasions, both in the trees and in the marsh reeds. Some nests were simply loose arrangements of sticks or grass, while others were intricately woven like the one Asah had tossed to him.

And that, of course, was the answer! He would weave carriers out of reeds or sticks. If he used green sticks, like the willows that grew in the sand bars of the garden's central river, they would be more pliable than dead sticks. Some of the carriers could be made large to contain harvested items of greater size — dried apples, pears, figs. These carriers would work without further modification. For foods of smaller size — grains, peas, lentils, almonds, and pistachios — Adam would try lining the carriers with large, broad leaves; perhaps pasting the leaves together with smears of mud. Better yet, perhaps he could just daub mud so that it completely covered the inside of the carriers and then let it dry — an idea borrowed from the crag martins, whose mud-twig nests sometimes fell from the valley's cliff faces.

By midday, Adam had constructed several baskets of different size. Those with a mud coating were left to dry in the sun, and the rest he filled with fruit. Adam knew that dried fruit was both sweeter and smaller in size than fresh fruit, and reasoned that any fresh fruit he gathered would end up drying in storage anyway. Consequently he only put dried fruit in his baskets; the ripe fruit he cut in sections with a sharp fragment of chert and laid the pieces out on sun-baked rocks to dry.

By dusk Adam had gathered or had drying a large volume of food, more than enough to sustain him for several days. While he needed to ask Asah how many days winter would last, it was apparent that the only way he would run out of food was if he failed to put enough aside. The garden already had more fruit on the limb and in the field than he could gather in many tens of days.

Adam devoted the last few hours of the day to exploring the valley walls for storage sites. He found numerous sites where there were large rock protrusions with sheltered undercuts beneath them. Some of these were wet or had indications of periodic water flow or moisture, but Adam found others that appeared to be permanently dry. Adam decided these would suffice until he found something better.

SIXTEEN

Now a river went out of Eden to water the garden, and from there it parted and became four riverheads.
— Genesis 2:10NKJV

Along the bank of the river, on this side and that, will grow all kinds of trees used for food; their leaves will not wither, and their fruit will not fail. They will bear fruit every month ...
— Ezekiel 47:12a NKJV

By the end of the second week, Adam had settled into a daily routine, gathering and storing food in the mornings and making exploratory trips in the afternoons. He had spoken with Asah about the onset and duration of the winter season, and had concluded that by working half of each day he could put aside more than enough provisions to last him until the advent of spring.

Adam usually woke up before dawn, just as the night softened and the high peaks began to blush. It was his favorite time of day. He would clamber up to a high terrace and sit where he had an unobstructed view of the day's emergence, remaining there until the daylight became constant. Even though each sunrise was different, they were all captivating, and Adam could recall the highlights of each.

The early mornings were also special times of communion with YHWH. Just as the sunrises were endlessly variable, so were his times with the Most High. While they often met and talked and laughed face to face, this almost always occurred later in the day, after Adam's work and explorations were done. The morning meetings were different, for in the mornings there was rarely a visible expression of God's presence. As Adam sat and watched the dawning, his own heart would unfold in soft songs and quiet commentary, almost like he was being careful not to awaken the Earth as he spoke to God. And in response, YHWH's spirit would draw near. It was a different kind of intimacy than that of the afternoons, and Adam could never decide which he liked better.

On the morning of his fifteenth day Adam chose a vantage point that offered a superb view of the upper valley. The morning was somewhat colder than usual, and when Adam reached his perch, his attention was immediately caught by the sight of low clouds rising from the far end of the valley. Adam was accustomed to seeing clouds scudding high overhead or cloaking the mountain peaks, but he had never seen them at ground level before. The prospect of touching a cloud was enough to instantly arouse his curiosity.

As he watched, the low clouds occasionally thinned to reveal what appeared to be wet, glistening snow on one of the distant valley walls. Adam felt a tingle of alarm. According to Asah, snow was not due to appear in the garden for many days yet. He strained to see better, but the distance and the clouds prevented a clear view.

Adam decided that he would trek up-valley and explore the area after his morning communion was over. He had learned that after enjoying YHWH's company for a while, there always came a time when the Spirit gently withdrew, which Adam regarded as the signal that it was time for him to begin his day's activities.

When the time came to go, Adam set off with a brisk jog, and by late morning he had already covered half the distance to his destination. The cloud had dissipated as the day warmed, but Adam had marked the spot in reference to the mountains and no longer needed the cloud to guide him. His route paralleled the small central river that ran the length of the garden valley, and as he kept gaining elevation, he eventually rose above the level of the highest planted terrace. As he left the last terrace behind him, the fruit and nut-bearing trees of the lower valley gave way to stately cedars and pines.

The valley pinched together at its upper end, flanked on both sides by sheer rock faces and ramparts of loose rock that had tumbled down from the heights. Everywhere Adam looked he saw water. It oozed from rock faces or trickled from beneath rock piles to converge into small brooks, which in turn wound their way downslope in search of the central stream. This over abundance of flowing water was one of the features that distinguished the garden from the lands Adam had journeyed through in coming to Eden. In those lands, water was confined mostly to larger watercourses that were separated by stretches of well-drained terrain. But it seemed to Adam that all of the garden's encircling mountain walls were dripping, seeping, or gushing water. The streams that gathered this mountain water were also very evenly distributed, ensuring that every part of the garden valley was well watered. It appeared to Adam that the garden simply didn't contain any arid land.

All morning long Adam had been crossing streams and streamlets that ran down to the river. Whenever he came to these he would look for a place to jump across from rock to rock, entering the stream only when there was no alternative. Wading through the rushing, icy water was a slow process due to the force of the water and the unsure footing, and the cold water caused painful cramps in his feet. So when Adam reached a point where the river meandered hard against a near-vertical section of the valley wall, he knew he would have to cross over and that it would be a very unpleasant crossing.

Although the central river here was only a quarter of its size where it exited the garden, it was still much deeper and wider than its tributaries. Adam backtracked, looking for a shallow place to ford, but the best crossing point he could find still had sections of waist-deep water. Even at that depth, the strength of the current would make it hard for him to keep his footing on the slippery, loose cobbles of the river bottom.

Adam could swim well. He had discovered that his body instinctively knew how to move through water just as it knew how to walk and run. But Adam had never been in deep water for more than a few moments, and that had been in an isolated rock pool that had been well warmed by the sun. Adam had no doubt that if he lost his footing, the river's cold swirling water would create painful body sensations that were not limited to his feet.

But Adam was not willing give up his trek to the end of the valley.

He would just have to weather the discomfort. *Unless*, Adam thought, *there is another way. Asah is undoubtedly nearby, watching over me as he always does.*

It was worth a try.

"Asah?" Adam said. "Would you be so kind as to part the waters like you did in the cave when we came to Eden?"

No answer. Not that he really had expected one.

Perhaps a less dramatic request would be allowable.

"How about just carrying me across?"

Adam was sure that Asah was close by and had heard him. He could almost imagine Asah's unspoken response: "I'm here to protect you Adam, not pamper you. This is your garden and your exploration. Enjoy the journey. By the way, don't slip on the rocks, or you might get swept downstream into deeper water where you would have to swim all the way across."

That was an unsettling thought, and Adam wondered whether it was his own. After all, if the Spirit of YHWH could speak through mental impressions inside Adam's mind, maybe the angels could do so as well. Adam wondered if falling completely in the water would appeal to an angelic sense of humor, and whether Asah might actually cause such a mishap.

Adam steeled himself and moved forward, sliding down the short, steep bank into the thigh-deep water.

And whooped in delight! The water was warm!

After splashing about for awhile, Adam braced his feet down-current against a larger submerged rock and squatted down, letting the water pummel his back and sluice over his shoulders. What an incredibly exquisite, delicious feeling!

The river water didn't look any different than it did in the lower valley, but this part of the river was obviously fed by something other than lofty mountain snowfields. Although it would have been quicker to cross all the way over and walk along the far stream bank, Adam took pleasure in sloshing from shallow to shallow and paddling through the deeper pools. He came to a place where one side of the river spilled forcefully over a long section of sloping rock, and discovered he could crawl upstream against the current to the top of the rock and then ride the current back down to his starting point. He did this over and over again, though for every time he succeeded, there were several times when he lost his grip and was swept flailing downstream. It was a great game, and the river was a tireless adversary.

Eventually Adam resumed his journey up-valley. The river channel continued to hug the rock face, and as Adam pushed upstream he passed several thermal springs issuing forth from cracks in the rock wall. These springs ranged from pleasantly warm to very hot — sometimes too hot to touch for more than a moment. In between the hot springs there were still the usual cascades of icy mountain meltwater.

The river eventually eased away from the rock face back toward the center of the narrowing valley. As Adam continued upstream the thermal springs and pools feeding the river became both more abundant and larger in size. Some of the lower pools close to the river were deeper than Adam's height, fed by powerful currents welling up from dark, gaping holes below their surface. Other pools were hardly a hand's-breadth deep. Many of the shallower pools were lined with smooth, slick layers of brownish-red calcite that had precipitated from the mineral-laden waters.

As Adam moved further up-valley, he noticed that the vegetation was again changing. The unbroken cedar and pine forest became thinner and then abruptly ended, yielding to waist-high thickets of mixed raspberry and blackberry. The bushes were full of pendant fruit clusters, and Adam stripped handfuls of berries as he walked, but didn't stop. Something else had captured his attention.

Up ahead was a broad, level shelf situated just above two hot spring boils. The shelf was perhaps forty paces wide by fifteen paces deep, and while it wasn't very large, it supported a lush assemblage of fruit-bearing plants that were completely new to Adam. As Adam climbed up on the shelf, he could see that the soil was deep and rich, moist but not sodden in spite of its proximity to the springs.

As before, Adam recognized and could name the plants even though it was his first sighting. With wonder he walked from plant to plant, touching, studying, and best of all, tasting their fruit. There were small groves of banana, which in turn could be separated into at least three varieties. Pomegranate, citron, persimmon, medlar, jujube, and tamarind were all present. Adam ate his fill and then descended to the river to wash the drying fruit juices from his face and hands.

The planted shelf was obviously YHWH's handiwork. As Adam continued up-valley he passed by scores of similar plantings, all in protected locations and all close to sources of warmth. But YHWH's plantings were not limited to those warmed by hot springs. There were also broad, sunken fissures where hot, steamy air vented from holes and cracks in the earth's surface, and in these enclaves Adam encountered yet more assemblages of fruit trees.

Adam descended into one of these and was immediately struck by the depression's clammy heat. It felt like he had just jumped into a hot spring without the water. Although the individual vents were small in size, they collectively discharged a large volume of heated air. Some of them roared, some hissed, some blew almost silently. All of them exhaled air that was much hotter than the air outside the depression. In fact, it was only the mixture of the cooler valley air with the vented air that made the palpable heat bearable.

It's as if the weight of the mountain is pressing a sigh from the belly of the earth, Adam thought.

Adam examined the plantings and tasted their fruits sparingly; still being full from surfeiting at the first shelf garden.

Maybe accumulating body fat isn't so easy after all. Adam couldn't imagine eating all day like some of the animals.

Adam wondered whether the hot springs and fumaroles were the source of the mysterious cloud he had sighted just after dawn. On chilly mornings, their warm, humid air might form a fog just like Adam's breath did, only on a much larger scale. Perhaps he would spend the night in the upper valley just to see if this hypothesis was correct.

By mid-afternoon Adam could see that he was approaching the unbroken mountain wall that marked the valley's end. There were still garden enclaves tucked away in sheltered locations, and Adam continued to tromp through the ever-present berry thickets. He could now clearly hear the thunder of falling water, the sound of which had been growing louder as he moved up-valley, and he caught occasional glimpses of a majestic waterfall at the valley's head. It had truly been a day of delightful discoveries.

Adam's view of the valley's head had been obstructed both by the slope of the valley floor and the tall escarpment over which waterfall tumbled. Although the waterfall itself was nearly vertical, the terrain on either side was an easy climb. As Adam crested the brim of the escarpment and was afforded his first view of the valley's head, he was awe-struck, just as when he first looked upon the garden of Eden.

Nestled at the foot of the curving mountain wall was an elliptical tarn lake that had been hidden from sight until now. Adam was looking at the headwater of the garden's central river. Scattered around the lake's circumference were several large, turbulent inflows, many with wisps of steamy mist suggesting their thermal nature. But the most magnificent feature of the lake was at its far end, where the lake basin actually met the sloping mountain wall. Here the lower wall sparkled with countless small pools, all stepping down in series before finally emptying into the lake.

The uppermost pools were arrayed in two main series that started on either side of a high stanchion of rock, converging and ultimately merging halfway down the slope to the lake. While just the arrangement of these pools and their flow-ways would have been remarkable enough, it was their color that made them so strikingly beautiful. They were all a brilliant, glistening white — as white as any snow-covered peak.

The center of the tarn was dark blue, indicating water of considerable depth. But the lake also had a wide, shallow perimeter that was adorned with colorful, concentric bands of lotus, water lily, and other aquatic plants. The innermost band, next to the open water, was comprised solely of lotus, their broad circular leaves and crimson flowers standing above the water surface, all bowing in unison to the occasional gust of wind.

The fist-sized, semi-spherical seed pods of the lotus were as abundant as the flowers, and after confirming that the lake's water was neither too hot nor too cold, Adam pushed through the shallower vegetation until he reached the lotus stands. He snapped off several pods and retreated to shallower water to pop the spherical seeds out of the pods and peel away their inedible skins. The flavor of the kernels was sweet and nutty, their flesh crisp and succulent. Adam added lotus kernels to his mental list of foods that could be gathered, dried, and stored.

Shoreward of the lotus stands were floating mats of water lily, undulating in synchrony with the lake's ripples, their soft white blossoms all sporting vibrant yellow centers. Water chestnut was interspersed amongst the water lilies, with edible nuts that grew on short stalks at the base of the plants. Adam had to grope around, his arms extended and his head barely above the water, to retrieve the nuts, but soon realized he could use his toes with equal facility.

Adam set out along the shoreline, heading for the end of the lake. He skirted upslope of the shoreline springs; their voluminous discharges and high temperatures making them impassable on the lakeward side. One of them erupted with such pressure that a frothy mound boiled in the center of the pool that was several hands high.

Adam finally reached the staircase of white pools and began climbing. Each pool was fed by water trickling over the semi-circular rim of the pool above it, and while the white, lustrous rock was smooth, it offered numerous grips. All of the pools were lined with the same white calcite, though their water varied in hue from light to dark blue according to each pool's depth. On several occasions Adam paused to lounge in the soothing waters; the pools were hot, but not uncomfortably so. His view of the valley, and the staircase of pools below him, improved the higher he climbed.

When Adam reached the base of the rock column where the two series of pools diverged, he followed the right prong. He had spotted the opening of a large cave a short climb above the highest pool, and wanted to see if it might serve as an adequate winter den. Adam had noted that some of the animals were also preparing for the coming winter by the construction of dens and burrows. Even though he had never been uncomfortably cold for more than a brief span of time, wisdom whispered that he should follow their example by finding a shelter of his own. The problem, of course, was that he had already cached several stockpiles of food a full-day's walk down-valley. This had to be weighed against the advantages of living in an area with an abundant supply of hot water.

The entrance to the cave was large, affording a panoramic view of the garden valley and allowing copious amounts of light into the two outer chambers, both of which had high ceilings. The cave floor was dry, a mixture of water-worn flat stones, washed sands, and beds of cushiony moss. Water had once flowed out of the mountain through this cave. The walls of the first chamber were covered with moss and lacy ferns. The fronds gently fluttered at several points on the cave wall, and closer examination showed that they were next to small holes through which warm air was venting.

Adam walked back into the cave, through the first chamber into the second, noting the rise in temperature as he walked. The second chamber still had a reasonable amount of light, but it eventually narrowed into a broad tunnel that continued deeper into the mountain. Here the twilight and moss gave way to darkness and bare rock, and Adam could not see to go further.

"*Where is Asah when I need him?*" Adam thought to himself, remembering how Asah had provided light when they passed through the dark tunnel leading from Eden's outer valley.

But it didn't matter. The cave looked like it would be perfect for weathering the winter season. Not only would it provide shelter from any cold winds moving through the valley, but the scattered vents would ensure a steady supply of warm air. Two smaller vents were located just above a flat shelf of rock that looked like it would be suitable for sleeping. Adam hoisted himself up onto the shelf, scooted across, and then turned and laid back.

Perfect! One of the vents was gently blowing on his chest and face.

He would wake up every morning with a warm reminder of the breath.

Adam went back out to the entrance of the cave and sat, enjoying the view. He would spend the night here and return to the lower valley in the morning. He had thought of a way to transport his existing food caches to his new location, and if it proved successful, he could harvest and carry food easily from anywhere in the garden.

Although Adam still bestowed names upon new animals as he encountered them, he was not in the habit of naming places. However, this place was so special he thought it deserved a name of its own. He decided to call it Kikwmillu, the "Place of Warm Water." It would be his cold-weather home. Once he had stockpiled enough food, Kikwmillu would have close to everything he might ever need.

"*And I will be nowhere near the tree of knowledge,*" Adam thought, as the memory of the tree intruded upon his thoughts.

SEVENTEEN

*And they heard the sound of the Lord God walking in the garden
in the cool of the day ...*
— Genesis 3:8a NKJV

Adam made rapid progress in accumulating a winter stockpile
at Kikwmillu. He usually dried his harvest close to where it was gathered,
and then enlisted the help of onagers and bezoar goats to carry it up-valley.
He had rigged pairs of baskets tied together with lengths of twined grape
vine, and these he draped across the backs of the animals. In the beginning, he had connected each pair of baskets with a single twined cord, but
to his horror he found that this caused raw, swollen welts on the backs of
the animals underneath their fur, though the animals never complained.

Adam improved his harness design by weaving a lattice of supple
grape vines that draped over each animal's entire back, and then tied
multiple small baskets onto the lattice. This worked much better, though
Adam learned that the load had to be carefully balanced to avoid spilling
his harvest — something which happened occasionally and which the
animals always found humorous. Adam eventually added loops of twine
around the girth and necks of the animals to further stabilize the loads, but
he still had to constantly check the train of animals and their loads as they
journeyed.

Adam had found that his presence was vital to the success of the
journeys. The animals would walk tirelessly and without pause as long as
he accompanied them, but they couldn't be counted on to make the trip

by themselves. Only once did he attempt to send a group of animals that already knew the way to Kikwmillu on ahead of him. When he followed up with a second group a day later, he found members of the first group scattered all along the intervening valley. Only those group members that were part of the same family or herd stayed together. Upon his questioning, the animals all maintained that they were on their way to Kikwmillu and didn't understand how they had varied from his instructions. Adam realized that onagers and goats simply didn't share his sense of purpose or his awareness of time.

Adam still regularly took time away from his labors to explore new areas of the garden. Yet by the end of his first month, Adam had developed only the most rudimentary understanding of the garden's layout and features. This was due in part to the garden's size, for the garden was in fact much larger than it had at first appeared. From Kikwmillu to the opposite end where the river gorge exited was a distance that required two full days to traverse, and at its widest point, the garden was a half-day's walk across.

Nonetheless, if the garden's size were the only factor, Adam still would have been able to mentally map out its features. He possessed an acute memory for both objects and places, and once he examined something or visited a location, he mentally retained virtually all the details of his observations.

But the garden had an incredible amount of embedded complexity and diversity that far exceeded the mental organization of what and where things were. It abounded in patterns and symbols and mysteries; and these expressed themselves in so many different ways that Adam could not consider all of them at once. Oftentimes he was in the middle of untangling the meaning of some recurring pattern when he would inadvertently discover some brand new aspect of the garden that had nothing to do with his initial contemplation. He then had to choose whether to continue along his original line of mental inquiry or abandon it to follow his latest discovery. Sometimes this happened several times in a single day. It was wonderful and maddening at the same time. Exhilarating, but mentally exhausting. More than anything else, it was this aspect of the garden that defied his attempts to analyze and characterize it.

Adam's appetite for mental inquiry was usually satiated well before he was ready to quit exploring, and when that happened, he would just walk or run or climb and try not to engage in any more analysis. But even these times of unfocused wandering contributed to his understanding of the garden, as both insights and new questions intruded upon his thoughts. As the days passed and Adam grew in knowledge, he came closer to believing that he would never fully comprehend the garden. He couldn't help but recognize that in this regard the garden mirrored the One who planted it.

During his explorations Adam had observed that there were specific places in the garden that YHWH was most likely to frequent in physical form. Adam had discovered three of these, and felt sure there were more to be found. Each of these places differed from the others in terms of their physical appearance, yet they all possessed a certain unmistakable atmosphere. An ambience. An emotional fragrance. Not a fragrance that could be physically discerned, but rather one that was recognized by the stirring sensation it caused in the depths of his being.

Adam didn't know if the spiritual fragrance was left over from recent visits by YHWH, or whether the places exuded the fragrance in anticipation of the Creator's arrival. But when Adam entered one of these places (he called them the Ey'mru — the holy meeting places), his mental exertions ceased and any mental fatigue vanished. He immediately lost interest in whatever endeavor or exploration he had been pursuing. In its place, he felt a sweet but urgent yearning to see YHWH, to talk to Him, to be with Him. This yearning grew in strength and soon became so compelling that Adam couldn't simply sit idle and wait for YHWH to appear.

Sometimes Adam would run through the meeting place in an attempt to search YHWH out; sometimes he would stand and call, sometimes he would sing love songs to coax YHWH into view. Once Adam began pursuing YHWH, it was only a matter of time before He appeared. It was almost as if YHWH was unable to resist being found when Adam was adamant and relentless in his pursuit.

Not that YHWH always revealed Himself right away. On one occasion Adam had quieted himself after entering an Ey'mru and began speaking softly, inviting YHWH to join him. Every so often he paused to listen for the sound of YHWH's approach. When Adam finally heard the sound of YHWH's footsteps, he ran to the spot the noise had come from, only to find no one there. There was a lingering radiance that was visibly fading before Adam's eyes, evidence that YHWH had been there seconds earlier. But the Most High had slipped away. A few moments later Adam again heard YHWH walking and chuckling a short distance away. Adam ran there even more quickly, but only found the radiance a little brighter than the time before.

That made Adam even more determined to catch Him. He continued his futile mad dashes toward the sounds of God. And each time he arrived too late.

Under other circumstances Adam might have found the game frustrating. But the Most High was clearly having such a grand time and his laughter was so infectious that Adam couldn't help but smile. In fact, YHWH was now laughing so much that Adam didn't go to the sound of His footsteps; he just ran toward His laughter.

Adam abruptly changed his strategy, running toward the sound of God but stopping midway to shout "Where are you?" Adam then dropped into a silent, running crouch and circled around to stealthily approach God from the far side. As he finally came to the spot where he had thought God was, he heard YHWH's joyful reply coming from the spot Adam had just left.

So Adam turned and ran hard, away from God, toward the far edge of the meeting place, all the while yelling "You can't catch me!" Adam was still running at full speed when his foot caught a loop of woody vine and he tumbled forward. Just before his body slammed into the ground Adam's fall was arrested by two gentle, strong hands.

"I just did," was God's reply.

Adam immediately threw both his arms and legs around one of YHWH's outstretched arms.

"Gotcha!" Adam replied in turn.

They both laughed until Adam had to beg God to let him catch his breath.

The Ey'mru were such quiet, comfortable places that Adam liked to frequent them even when not visiting with YHWH. They were filled with perfectly formed spots for reclining and relaxing; the boulders, tree trunks, and larger boughs having hollows and contours that were precisely shaped to fit Adam's body, often facing toward some beautiful vista or other pleasing feature of the garden. Once Adam properly situated himself in one of the sitting-places, it cradled his body so perfectly that it created a sensation similar to floating. While Adam could find rest anywhere in the garden, only the Ey'mru contained these precisely crafted sitting-places so well suited for relaxation.

After Adam learned how to recognize the sitting-places, he systematically searched each Ey'mru for new ones. Although the sitting-places were present in all of the Ey'mru, they were often located in places that were difficult to reach. He particularly liked those that were in the highest treetops, though these were the hardest to find, for obvious reasons. Adam climbed countless trees that had no sitting-places to find the few that did. He found it a strange irony that he was willing to exert so much effort to discover places where he could rest.

The Ey'mru, like the rest of the garden, also had their mysteries. The most notable of these was that they contained sitting-places that didn't fit Adam's body. When Adam first reclined in one of these, he initially assumed that he wasn't correctly positioned. But no matter how much he shifted and squirmed, the sitting-place simply didn't fit his body. It not only didn't fit; it was downright uncomfortable. On closer inspection, he could see where its dimensions differed from those of his body.

And that, of course, was the mystery.

Adam knew that everything in the garden was a product of YHWH's design, so the presence of sitting-places for bodies of other dimensions could not be without significance or meaning. As he set his mind to reasoning out this mystery, he could think of only one reason why YHWH would have done this.

I am not the only man!

It was a startling thought; one followed by hours of pondering. Perhaps there had been a man living in the garden before him who was a different size, or perhaps even men, since the "other" rest-places seemed to come in more than one size and configuration. Or maybe YHWH was going to make other men someday in the future. Another possibility was that there were other men now, but Adam just hadn't encountered them yet. Perhaps there were even other gardens!

Every animal Adam knew of was not represented by a sole individual, but by multiple individuals of the same kind. So if Adam was the only man ever created, then that would have distinguished him from the animals in yet one more unusual way.

On the other hand, Adam knew he was created in the image and likeness of YHWH, and there was only one God. So it made sense that Adam was also only one. Adam had been created to commune with YHWH in a way the animals could not, and unless YHWH was somehow dissatisfied with that arrangement (which didn't seem to be the case), there really was no need for another man.

Adam thought about asking YHWH about this, but decided not to, at least for a while. He would take on the mental challenge of discovering the answer by himself. Once he had reasoned it out he would present his conclusion to God to see if he was correct.

But after a week of contemplation, Adam had progressed no further on the topic and was beginning to think he might have to ask YHWH after all. On his twenty-seventh day, his work for the day finished, Adam strolled along the escarpment that formed the dividing line between the calm, scenic lake of Kikwmillu and the plunging waterfall that marked the beginning of the Eden River. The broad stony rim was much wider than the waterfall, and on both sides of the main channel there was an abundance of dry rocks and gently sloping sluice-ways along which tendrils of warm lake water slid toward the rim's edge. The footing was secure in the shallow flow-ways, and Adam found it pleasant to sit where he could see the waterfall and river below while being caressed by the warmth of the running water.

Eventually Adam waded across a flow-way to an isolated portion of the rim he had not examined before and to his surprise, spotted not one, but several sitting-places. He had discovered a new Ey'mru! Adam counted at least eight different rest-places, all arrayed in close proximity to each other, each one with different dimensions, and only one of which fit his body. And some of the sitting places were much smaller than any of the others he knew of.

Adam sensed this new Ey'mru held some important clues on the question of otherness. He thought about how different individuals of the same kind of animal all had slight differences in body morphology from one another. He remembered the pair of onagers that had escorted him as he first entered the garden, and how they differed not only in body size, but in personality. And how the two adults had quarreled over the male's relentless pursuit of the female, and how their young colt had the most placid personality of the three.

Adam's mouth fell open. "Ahhhhh!"

It all fit! The smaller rest-places were for young. YHWH was going to make young! Undoubtedly in the same way he had created Adam. And in time those young would grow into adults, just as young always do.

EIGHTEEN

Now a large herd of swine was feeding there near the mountains.
So all the demons begged Him, saying, "Send us to the swine, that
we may enter them." And at once Jesus gave them permission.
Then the unclean spirits went out and entered the swine (there
were about two thousand); and the herd ran violently down the
steep place into the sea and drowned in the sea.
— Mark 5:11-13 NKJV

Since his awakening, Adam had encountered dead creatures on two occasions. The first time occurred when Adam was slowly walking through one of the garden's quiet places, reflecting on the things he had learned from YHWH during the previous day's communion. By chance he came upon a narrow, sinuous column of shiny, yellowish-brown army ants scurrying beneath and between the thick clumps of sedge and grass. The ants were mostly less than half a fingernail in length, though there were occasional larger ones, and they ran in both directions along an invisible trail they rarely strayed from. Many of the ants carried bits of organic material, which Adam surmised was food, though the food-bearers headed in only one direction.

Adam followed the column until it diverged into multiple spurs. One of the spurs led toward a mound of moss-covered cobbles beneath a dripping rock overhang. Sprawled across the top of one of the cobblestones lay a dead yellow-spotted newt. The ants were in the early stages of dismembering the newt, cooperatively cutting and tugging apart tiny pieces of newt flesh that, upon their liberation, were quickly carried back down the ant trail.

Upon Adam's closer approach, the ants ceased their activity and withdrew in a wide circle around the newt, apparently sensing Adam's presence. Adam stooped and picked up the newt, examined it, and then placed it back within the circle of ants. As if some signal had been given, the ants resumed their work. Adam watched the ants for hours, mentally cataloging their patterns of movement and trying to decipher their mode of communication. When he left, nothing remained of the newt except tiny bones.

The second encounter with a dead animal involved a black grouse. When Adam first saw it, it was being carried in the mouth of a steppe cat. As Adam drew near, the steppe cat gently laid the limp grouse down and sat back on its haunches, looking at Adam. When Adam asked what the cat was doing, it replied that the grouse's time had come and that it had given itself to be meat for the steppe cat's family. Adam's examination of the grouse showed no marks or signs of injury other than a set of small punctures on the grouse's neck. As he was turning the lifeless form over in his hands, the cat asked Adam if he wanted it for his own food. Adam shook his head no and handed it back to the cat, which then bounded off, clearly jubilant that Adam had declined the offer.

From these two experiences, Adam learned that not all creatures ate just fruits, seeds, and herbs. There were animals that also ate the flesh of other creatures. While this was not personally attractive to Adam (he couldn't imagine eating the flesh of something he had spoken with), it was easy to see how this brought balance to the Earth. Apparently the animals did not live forever, but lived for their appointed season and then returned to the soil from which they came. There was a certain economy and efficiency in certain creatures deriving sustenance from the flesh of other creatures before their bodies returned to the earth.

Although Adam had become acquainted with the reality of death, it wasn't until his fifth week that he witnessed a dying. One morning Adam decided to ascend one of the narrow passes in the mountains that ringed the garden. If he could reach the top of the pass, it would afford an excellent view of the garden valley, and also allow a glimpse of what lay on the other side of the mountains. And throughout the trek, Adam would be on the lookout for the tree of life. Adam expected the journey to take the entire day, maybe even two if he descended and explored on the other side of the pass. Mindful that the garden was in his charge, Adam conferred with Asah to be sure the garden would have angelic protection during his absence.

The climb to the pass was challenging and invigorating. There were faint trails up the precipitous rocky slopes, worn by the constant passage of the bezoar goats and mouflon sheep that inhabited the sides of the mountains. Adam negotiated the steep passages with relative ease, and by late morning, arrived at the broad saddle between two towering peaks. From there, Adam could see that the descent on the far side of the pass was more gradual, sloping gently down into another mountain valley.

A strong, steady wind whipped up over the pass from the far valley. The valley floor was mostly obscured by low, misty clouds, some of which were carried up over the pass with the wind. Adam sat on a flat rock, feet dangling over the edge, watching the damp clouds rush at him. One moment he was enveloped in whirling fog, and the next moment the wind whipped the cloud away and he was bathed in sunlight again.

Adam stayed at this perch for a long time, enjoying the hurtling clouds and straining to form a picture of the neighboring valley from the fleeting gaps in the clouds. Every hair of his body was covered with tiny droplets of cloud-dew, so that Adam was cloaked in a white sheen while in the cloud and sparkled when he was in the sun. There was fresh snow on the high peaks on either side of the gap and the wind was cold, but Adam felt only mild discomfort.

As Adam gazed into the valley below, he caught the briefest glimpse of a procession of creatures far below on the approach to the pass. Fixing his eyes on the spot, Adam waited several minutes for the next break in the clouds. When it came, the group was a little closer. Adam eventually concluded that the creatures were Caspian tigers, three of them, padding their way up towards pass between the two valleys. The middle tiger appeared to have a smaller animal draped over its back.

Adam thought about walking down to meet them, but the risk of passing them in the cloud-fog was too great. If Adam remained where he was, they could not pass unseen, because the valley clouds quickly dissipated on Eden's side of the pass. So Adam waited patiently, marking their slow progress and periodically repositioning himself to intercept them where it appeared they would crest the pass.

They saw Adam before they reached the top, and from that point they headed straight toward him. The animal being carried by the middle tiger was a roe deer, which lay balanced on the tiger's upper back with its front legs and head hanging over the tiger's left shoulder and its hind legs lying across the tiger's middle back. The deer's haunches were streaked with blood, and Adam could see that both of its rear legs were broken, one with the splintered bone extending out through ripped flesh. The middle tiger was clearly walking as gently and carefully as possible to avoid jarring his load. As they drew nearer, the deer kept lifting its head to look toward Adam, only to drop it a moment later.

Adam knew all three tigers, having named them weeks before when they had come to the garden. The tiger in the lead was named Ezuz, and was the first to speak when the group came within range.

"It is good that you climbed up to meet us Adam; the descent into the garden would have caused her more pain than the ascent. She has much to tell you."

The second tiger settled low to the ground and rolled carefully to its side while the third tiger steadied the deer's hind quarters with its head. Moving in synchrony, the two tigers gently deposited the deer on a patch of soft ground in a gentle, fluid motion. When they were done, the deer lay with her head resting on her forelegs so that she could easily see all of them. Ezuz delicately licked the dirt and leaves clean of the deer's face.

Adam knelt in front of the deer, slipped one hand gently under her jaw and raised her head. The deer's body was trembling; pain evident in her dark eyes.

"What would you tell me, graceful one?" Even as Adam asked the question, he silently asked YHWH to ease the creature's pain.

The trembling became intermittent and then stopped. Still looking in the deer's eyes, Adam watched as the pain was slowly replaced with relief and gratitude.

"It's the dark ones," the deer whispered. "They are doing wrong things to the animals."

As he remembered his own encounter with the mute spirit, a chill run down the back of Adam's neck and settled between his shoulder blades. This was immediately replaced by a suffuse warmth spreading through his upper body as his anger began to build.

"Tell me everything." Adam gently laid the deer's head back down, kneeling and leaning close to hear what she would say.

"In the past the dark ones rarely approached us." Her voice was weak but clear. "Usually, if they drew near, we sensed them and simply ran away. If they did catch us, they would throw us to the ground, but that was all. Although we had heard stories of the dark ones causing injury or even death, that had never been our experience. After a few moments on the ground, they always grew tired of the game and released us. It had been many seasons since any of us have been caught and thrown."

"But yesterday was different. There were four of us grazing when suddenly the shadows were alive with dark ones. They were everywhere. We all ran in different directions. I didn't see what happened to my brother and sisters after that. I only know what I have been told — that they are all dead, and that they were not proper dyings. I had to come and tell you."

The deer's breathing had become labored from the exertion of speaking, and she lay quiet while she caught her breath. Adam understood and waited, stroking her neck. Eventually he asked a question. "What is a proper dying, and how were these dyings improper?"

Even the tigers wondered that Adam did not know this. "A proper dying," the deer answered, "is a gift. When life has been fully lived and a creature knows its time has come, it lays its life down. Before the dying, it chooses who will receive the gift of its body. Only then should the dying occur."

"And the dyings of the others were improper because they did not first choose who would receive their bodies?"

"Yes," she replied, "but not just that. It is sad that they could not give themselves before their dyings. But the greater wrong was that their blood was spilled before they died."

The deer paused, trembling again, this time from great emotion rather than from pain.

"According to what I was told, all three were horribly injured, worse than me."

Another pause.

"Their injuries were so severe that they shed their blood while their life was still in them. Their life left them through their spilled blood."

The tigers had been listening quietly, respectfully, to the conversation. Upon hearing the fate of the three deer, the three tigers stood almost in unison, clearly disturbed. Two of them began pacing back and forth. Adam was surprised at their reaction and guessed that they had not heard the whole story.

"Do you understand, Adam? You seem not to know about dyings, so I think that perhaps you don't understand." It was Ezuz. In his agitation, he addressed Adam with a frank boldness that bordered on disrespect.

Adam wasn't offended. "Explain it to me, Ezuz."

"Surely you know that life is in the blood," Ezuz answered, already mentally chiding himself for his outburst. "Blood that contains life is sacred, and should never be spilled while a creature's life is yet in it. To do so brings great dishonor upon the one dying. It changes the dying from a giving to a taking. And it wrongs the ground receiving it. Surely you know these things and can explain to us why they are so."

"I have much to learn, Ezuz. Many of YHWH's ways and works have not been revealed to me. You serve me well in sharing your knowledge."

Adam turned back to the deer. He sensed that her strength was waning, and there was more of her story still to be heard.

"Before you go on, tell me graceful one, would you like to be named?"

"Yes," came the whispered reply. "Please."

It was, in fact, the other reason the deer had asked the tigers to bring her to Adam. Adam needed to be told what the Daimónia were doing, but her last wish was to meet Adam and be named before her dying.

"I name you Charise and I will never forget this day of our meeting. I honor your strength and will in making this journey to meet me. Now tell me the rest of what happened."

"We saw them in the shadows and ran. But there were too many. I could feel them slipping inside me. I have been thrown once before, but that was only one. This time they all threw me, and then they started making me do things."

"What kind of things, Charise?"

119

"Ordinary things. Jumping, eating, talking. At first they just tried to force my body to do things, but that didn't work well for them because I could resist them. Not completely, but enough that they didn't really have control. But then instead of forcing my body to do things, they started making me want to do the things myself."

"How did they do that, did they speak to you?"

"Not like we are now. There were never any spoken words you could hear. Just cravings; strong desires I couldn't resist. That's when I started doing things that weren't ordinary. Wrong things. Things I didn't want to do. And as I did these things I could feel their pleasure in my doing them."

Adam's anger grew steadily as he listened to her words, but he contained it. Even as he was listening, he wondered if there was a way for him to find and sentence these demons. One of the tigers was still pacing.

"How were you injured?"

"I did it to myself. They made me climb to the top of a small cliff. Well … made me want to so badly that I did it. Then they made me want to run over the edge. I turned away from the edge to resist them, but the desire was too strong. Eventually, I walked backwards over the edge. Then they left me. I lay there all day until Ezuz found me just before dark."

Her breathing had changed. Its rhythm was uneven and there was faint rattle each time a breath went out. Now that her story had been told she was starting to let go.

The tigers were finally still. Ezuz came closer, watching her intently. "Adam, her time is here. Can she go?"

Adam felt water forming in his eyes, just like when he had laughed so hard on his first day, but this time the feeling was very different. It was nothing at all like laughing, even though his stomach was tight like when he laughed. A drop of eye-water rolled down his cheek to his lip. His first tear. It had a different taste than stream water.

Adam leaned down, kissed her forehead, and whispered a prayer to YHWH. As Adam sat back, Ezuz scooted up close to Charise and lowered his head until his nose was touching hers. They remained that way for many minutes, not talking. Waiting. The other tigers remained still, sitting and watching. The wind had finally died down.

"Ezuz, I give you my body, so that you may have life," she whispered, almost inaudibly. Then there was a gentle spasm and her last breath rattled out.

"You honor me so greatly," Ezuz replied. But she didn't hear him. She was already gone.

Ezuz spent several minutes licking her face and head, even though they were already clean. When he finished grooming her, he extended a single claw, pressed it in, and delicately tugged. He did this on each side of her neck and then stepped back. Charise's blood ran out onto the grass, strongly at first, and then with less and less force.

Adam watched until the flow of blood stopped. When he looked up, he saw that Ezuz was looking at him rather than at her.

"Will you eat her now?" Adam asked.

"We have young ones two valleys away. With your permission we will take her there."

Adam thanked them for bringing her to him and granted them leave. Ezuz clasped her neck in his powerful jaws and loped back down the way they had come, his companions running smoothly at his side.

When the sun set hours later, Adam was still sitting next to where she had died.

NINETEEN

Now the serpent was more cunning than any beast of the field which the Lord God had made.
— Genesis 3:1a NKJV

S haarur had made excellent progress in learning how to exercise control over some of the higher animals. In particular, Shaarur's demons had discovered that they could arouse the natural desires and instincts of animals by stimulating neuroelectric impulses in specific microregions of their brains. Through much trial and error, they learned how to manipulate the intensity and timing of desires to wear down the subject animal's resistance. The optimal approach varied with the species of animal, and to some extent, even amongst individuals. It also differed between males and females of the same species. But given enough time, the demons could cause most of the animals to do things they wouldn't have without their influence.

Shaarur's legion explored the full range of animal desires — hunger, thirst, the urge to mate, the desire for sleep, the desire to scratch, the impulse to migrate or to hibernate, and the urge to take flight. In some cases the maintenance of a steady, low-intensity desire was most effective. In other cases, bursts of high-intensity desire interspersed with dormant periods produced better results. By the end of the first few days of field trials, the Daimónia had become so proficient in their manipulations that the animals were doing many things in unnatural ways and to unnatural extents.

Shaarur understood that controlling animals through their desires was only a first step. Making an animal eat to excess, or run for no reason, or mate out-of-season was not the same as enticing an animal to approach and engage Adam in casual conversation. Furthermore, most of the animals possessing the ability of speech didn't have strong inclinations to use it. They spoke when it was needful, but didn't derive pleasure from it, nor did they feel lack if they refrained from speaking. This made it very difficult for the Daimónia to create enough desire to control an animal's speech.

But Shaarur was patient and methodical. As a second step, he directed his demons to begin introducing spirit-thought commands in conjunction with the stimulation of intense desire. The goal now was to cause the animal to do something only distantly related to the desire, and to withhold satisfaction until the creature complied. This required the Daimónia to identify and learn how to activate other areas of the brain — those associated with the animal's perception of pleasure and fulfillment. The Daimónia discovered that many animals had an innate sense of "rightness," and that the animals would expend great effort to restore and maintain the perception that they and their environment were in order.

Through the manipulation of desire and satisfaction, combined with implanted spirit-thoughts, the Daimónia achieved progressively greater levels of control. They made a fallow deer walk all night to drink from a distant stream, all the while passing by numerous sources of water along the way. The demons enticed male bezoar goats to want to mate with each other, even though there was no way for them to actually do it. They drove many animals to kill themselves in strange ways, though Shaarur put a stop to this simply because the creatures most susceptible to their control were the ones they were destroying.

But as fruitful as these exercises were, Shaarur's demons hit an impasse when it came to making the animals use intelligent speech. The only successful exercise involving significant amounts of speech was with the jirds. In this instance, a team of demons caused two groups of jirds to disdain their own food reserves while intensely desiring the food caches of their neighboring clan. With gently whispered spirit-thoughts and constant inflammation of their desire to cache, the demons were able to guide the jirds in their speech until they eventually agreed to trade with each other. It was a start. But it was also a finish, because none of Shaarur's troop could formulate a plan for transforming the jirds' willingness to discuss food into an approach to Adam.

Shaarur had shared his achievements with Ptha, and while Ptha thought they were commendable, he also thought Shaarur's approach was too direct and would ultimately fail. By Shaarur's own account, the attempts of the Daimónia to exercise control over the animals always elicited resistance. Shaarur's techniques involved wearing down the animal's resistance, but they could not entirely eliminate it. And reduced resistance was not the same as the absence of resistance. For Adam to be successfully approached by an animal, its behavior would have to be completely normal. The creature's words and their delivery would have to arouse no suspicion. This would be impossible to achieve as long as the animal was actively resisting its demonic controller. While Shaarur's field trials had taught the Daimónia much about inhabiting and controlling animals, it really hadn't moved them much closer to their goal — that of being able to approach and speak to Adam without revealing that the Daimónia were involved.

The problem, Ptha thought, was that the higher animals were too intelligent. They knew when demons slipped inside of them and they knew when they were being controlled, even when the control was being accomplished through desire. Furthermore, the sensory perceptions of the higher animals were acute, and they often seemed to see or otherwise sense when the Daimónia drew near. This ability of some animals to sense the presence of demons when they hadn't materialized was something for which Ptha had no explanation.

But using the lower animals posed a different problem. Most of them did not have the gift of speech, or if they did, it was limited and unequal to the task of intelligent conversation. Perhaps, Ptha mused to himself, *one of the serpents might do.* Most of the reptiles in the region of Eden were not eaters of warm flesh, but instead fed upon insects and other cold-flesh creatures after their dying. The serpents, however, were exceptions to both rules. They were capable of intelligent speech and they also frequently fed upon warm-flesh animals.

It took Ptha all night to locate what he hoped to be a suitable serpent, and he spent most of the next day observing it. The length of the creature's body was three times the height of the man, and was comprised of solid cords of muscle rippling beneath a smooth, glossy covering. The body scales were as black as obsidian, with a black-red underlying skin that showed whenever the body flexed. The scales were unkeeled except on the upper portion of the head and feet, giving most of the serpent's body a glassy iridescence that flashed with color in the sunlight.

The keeled scales of the head gave the serpent's face a rougher texture than the rest of the body. Its head also differed in other respects. It was both broader and flatter than the serpent's upper body, and was a sandy-gold color that gradually shadowed into black a short way down its neck. The most visually remarkable thing about the head, however, was the horns. Two forward-curving bony horns protruded from just above its eyes. These were covered by shiny black scales, which except for their smaller size, were identical to those on the rest of the body.

The legs were strongly muscled and smooth-scaled, though smaller in proportion to the body then would be the case for a similarly sized mammal. The feet were black-red beneath, four-toed and clawed, the claws being longer on the hind legs than on the forelimbs. As Ptha would discover through his observations, the serpent could either walk erect or could fold its legs into shallow indentations along each side of its body and slither noiselessly through the brush.

When Ptha first came upon the serpent, it was sunning itself on a flat shelf of rock, raising its body temperature after the chilly evening. It would occasionally raise its head and look around, only to settle back down and soak up more warmth. After an hour or so, it left the rock, presumably in search of a meal. The serpent continued its search for most of the morning, and while it came across a variety of small animals during this time, these scurried away and the serpent did not give chase. Like all the other flesh-eaters, the serpent was looking for the about-to-die for its meal.

When Ptha was ready, he crossed over into the material realm several paces behind the serpent. At the precise moment of his crossing, the serpent coiled tightly, low to the ground, and whipped around to face Ptha. Ptha was surprised at how quickly the creature reacted to his presence.

"Why have you been watching me?"

Ptha was shocked. During his period of observation, he had never approached the serpent within the material realm. He had indeed spent many hours close to the serpent, watching it, following its movements and activities, but always without breaching the interface. Yet the serpent had not only sensed Ptha's presence, but had correctly deduced what Ptha had been doing. And it had also addressed Ptha the moment he crossed the interface.

"I have been nowhere near you," Ptha half-lied. "Why would you think I have been watching you?"

The serpent rose higher until it was standing on its hind legs and looking directly at Ptha, its upper body a series of sinuous curves with its tail coiled behind it. "You speak in part-truths. You have been near me, and you have been watching me since this morning. But you did it from the other side."

There was a short pause and then the serpent concluded. "And you know what I am saying is true."

Ptha was completely nonplused. He had formulated several alternatives for approaching the serpent, intending to adapt them as necessary as their conversation progressed. But in all of his planning and forethought, Ptha had never considered that the serpent would have this level of insight.

"What do you know of the other side?" Ptha asked, trying to regain control of the conversation.

"What do you know of this side?" the serpent countered. "You are not a creature of flesh. You have come here because you have some purpose in mind. So I ask again, why have you been watching me?"

Ptha abandoned every plan he had made. None of them fit what was happening. If Ptha were to control the serpent, it would have to be because the serpent willingly chose to allow that control. Ptha would have to seduce this creature with his words, just as he had seduced so many of the angelic host. He could not risk alienating the serpent by overtly attempting to control it. One thing Ptha was sure of — if it consented, the serpent would be the ideal creature to use in approaching Adam. It was quick of mind and spoke readily, and its awareness of the spiritual realm could prove useful.

But Ptha would not concede the advantage to the serpent so easily. He would not answer the serpent's question until he was ready to. "You are truly a beautiful creature. When I saw you, I couldn't help but pause and admire. Watching you has been most enjoyable. If I were a creature of flesh, I think I should like a body like yours. But I certainly never meant to intrude or cause you any alarm."

"Then why did you just now enter this side? Until a moment ago you were content to watch me from the other side. You could have kept doing that until you had your fill of my beauty. But now you have come to this side. You must have had a reason."

"Well, for one. I can't speak with you from the other side." This wasn't completely true, but it was a plausible explanation. Ptha was recovering his equilibrium. "And I thought that conversing with you might be as enjoyable as watching you."

"Surely there are other creatures like yourself that you can converse with."

"Yes there are. But that doesn't mean they are all worth talking to. Some creatures are more intelligent than others, something I am sure you have observed for yourself."

The serpent wasn't convinced. This creature from the other side clearly wanted more than conversation. But the serpent knew how to wait. He would engage the creature in conversation until he knew exactly what it wanted. Once he knew that, he would be in a better position to name his price.

The serpent settled back down in a comfortable loose coil with his legs folded back into the sides of his body. "So let's talk. I'll start. Why don't you have a body like other creatures?"

"My body is a spirit body, and it suits the realm I live in. But my spirit-body is not well-suited to your realm. That's why I spent so much time admiring you. Your body must bring you much pleasure, but these are things I cannot properly experience, though I wish I could."

"If you cannot experience body pleasures, why would you desire them in the first place?" The serpent's question was an astute one.

"Ahhh ... but there is a way for me to experience them. It's true that I cannot experience them as a disembodied spirit. But if I enter into the body of a creature of flesh, then I can share in its pleasures." Ptha had never actually done this, but he knew from Shaarur's reports that the demons experienced a wide variety of sensations while inside the bodies of the animals.

"So perhaps you would like to enter my body. Is that why you have been watching me?"

Ptha had not expected to reach this topic so early in the conversation. The serpent's skill at controlling the direction of their conversation was impressive. Ptha had planned on broaching this subject only after he had fully won the serpent's confidence. However, now that the opportunity had presented itself, he dare not pass it up.

"Watching you has been a pleasure in its own right; and I never expected anything more. But to share your body for even a brief period — that would be a pleasure I cannot even imagine. I would never presume to ask such a thing, though, at least not without giving you something in return."

Ptha and the serpent both understood what had just happened. The offer had been made. All that remained was to establish what Ptha would give in return for the privilege.

"What you suggest is a strange thing. How can you share my body without pushing me out? Maybe your plan is to take my body from me and leave me bodiless like yourself."

Ptha recognized this as a legitimate concern. He also suspected that the serpent was laying the foundation for asking a high price. The serpent didn't know that Ptha would give him virtually anything he wanted in return for his cooperation.

"If you were to leave your body, your body would be dead and of no interest to me. If I shared your body, it would only be with your permission, and when you chose to end the sharing, you could cast me aside like an old skin."

"You mentioned giving something in return?"

"Certainly. I would become your teacher. I can teach you things it would be impossible for you to learn without me." Ptha had originally thought to offer the serpent material benefits, such as an abundant supply of food. But during the course of their conversation, as Ptha's estimation of the serpent's intellect grew, he realized that knowledge might be the most alluring bait of all.

"What kind of things?"

"Things about the other side, things about this side, things about yourself that you have not yet discovered."

"Give me an example."

"A reasonable request. You may not know that of all of the material creatures, your intellect and insight is virtually unrivaled. Most creatures do not have your depth of understanding, nor can they grasp the subtleties of complex topics the way you can." As Ptha spoke these words, he extended one clawed finger into the spiritual realm, unseen by the serpent. Ever so gently the tip of the finger re-entered the material realm to touch and stimulate a pleasure center in the serpent's brain. Ptha let the finger rest there as they continued their conversation. Shaarur's research did have its applications.

"The only animal that may be your equal in intelligence and dialogue is the man-creature named Adam. He may, in fact, be wiser than you. In either case, I know that you would find conversing with him to be immensely enjoyable." Another gentle release of pleasure. "I also know where to find him, which is something you do not know."

The serpent knew of Adam's existence, of course. All of Earth's creatures knew that Adam was Earth's sovereign, even if they knew nothing else about him. But the serpent had never considered that Adam might be close enough to visit and speak with. This truly was a desirable thing that the spirit-creature offered.

"I should like to meet Adam and speak with him. Take me to him and I will consider granting you your request of body-sharing."

"The journey will not be an easy one. We need to cross two mountain passes and last night the temperatures were quite low. I fear the cold will make the passage difficult for you, if not impossible. May I suggest that we share your body now? I can shelter your body from the effects of the cold, but only if I am inside you. Plus, I would find the journey inside you much more enjoyable than traveling beside you."

The serpent knew this moment would come. If he wanted the knowledge the spirit-creature offered, sooner or later he would have to grant him his request.

"And how will we speak, once you are inside me?"

"As we do now, that will not change at all." Ptha nudged the serpent's pleasure center once again.

The serpent finally acceded. "Very well, Teacher. Let us go together. We can talk as we travel."

Ptha released a massive burst of pleasure as he slipped inside the serpent. He did this for two reasons. He wanted the serpent to always associate his coming with pleasure in order to cultivate an appetite for body-sharing. He also wanted to mask whatever subtle awareness the serpent might have of Ptha's entering in the absence of pleasure. Ptha could foresee a time when he might wish to enter the serpent without permission, so he would train the serpent to always associate Ptha's entrance with a certain set of sensations. That way, Ptha might be able to slip in unrecognized in the absence of such sensations.

The serpent slumped gently to the ground, uncoiling as it did so, and then started turning over and over, writhing in pleasure. As soon as he entered, Ptha was immediately overwhelmed by sensations of intense pleasure and strong feelings of disorientation. The feelings of pleasure were different from anything he had ever experienced, even before the Great Fall, perhaps because they were originating from a body of living flesh. The disorientation, which was emanating from the serpent as it repeatedly rolled over, was also enjoyable, though not nearly as strong.

Ptha knew from his discussions with Shaarur that demons experienced the feelings of their host animals, but he had no idea it was like this. As the pleasure began to subside, Ptha tapped the serpent's pleasure center again, releasing a second pulse of sensation. This one was not as strong as the first, and Ptha realized that the creature's brain could not generate such feelings indefinitely.

Ptha relaxed, allowing himself to fully enjoy the experience. After a few minutes the sensations abated, and the serpent righted itself. A moment later it lifted its head to look for the Teacher.

I am here. You cannot see me when I am sharing your body.

It wasn't plain thought and it wasn't spoken words. The serpent heard the Teacher's voice clearly and knew it was not his own. Yet it sounded exactly like his inner voice.

Shall we be going then? The serpent thought the question.

In a moment, Ptha answered, thinking there was ample time for one more sensation. *Indulge me if you would. I have never eaten anything before. And you need strength for the journey.*

Earlier that morning the serpent had passed through a rocky, dry meadow where three brown hares had bedded down for the day. Because the hares were all alive and healthy, the serpent hadn't given them a second glance. But Ptha urged the serpent to return to the meadow, explaining that one of the hares was on the verge of death.

The serpent was familiar with hares and their ways. It knew that every morning they made shallow depressions in the soil or grass to rest in until becoming active again in the evening. The serpent knew that they remained immobile in these resting places for long periods of time, but never actually seemed to sleep. What the serpent didn't know was that each hare entered into deep sleep for only a minute or two each day. During this time the hare would lay on its side rather than on its belly, its eyes tightly shut.

But Ptha knew about the deep sleep cycles of hares, and from Shaarur's research, he knew how to induce deep sleep. As they reached the meadow they headed straight toward one of the hares, all three of which were remaining perfectly still, aware of the serpent's approach.

Teacher, we cannot eat any of these. They are all still alive.

Ah, my friend, there is so much for me to teach you. Teacher can see when death is imminent. This creature's time is almost here; we are just a few moments early.

They slithered to a halt within striking distance of the hare. *You will see that what I say is true. We will watch this hare together.*

The serpent wasn't convinced, but was willing to wait and see. For effect, Ptha did nothing for several minutes, letting tension build in both serpent and hare. The hare still had not moved a muscle, though the tips of its long ears were visibly trembling even though they were pressed hard against its body.

Finally Ptha reached out an invisible finger and touched the portion of the hare's brain regulating sleep. The hare rolled to its side, extended its legs, and lay still. Even the faint trembling of its ears ceased.

Now you see that Teacher knows many things you do not. Before the serpent could even think about what the Teacher had just said, Ptha triggered the serpent's strike reflex. A second later the hare's head and upper shoulders were firmly lodged in the upper throat of the serpent, the forelegs pinned backwards against its body. The hare awakened instantly. It contorted its body in a futile attempt to break free, its powerful hind limbs flailing, beating the ground and raising clouds of dust.

But it is not dead; it is still alive! The serpent was alarmed, and though it thought it should immediately release the hare, it didn't.

No, it is only the death throes of its body, Ptha lied while speaking the truth. *Did we not watch the first moment of death together? Sometimes death comes this way. The hare's moment of death has already passed, but it takes a few additional minutes for the residual life to drain from the muscles. Teacher knows these things.*

As the hare asphyxiated, its wild movements subsided to weak spasms, allowing the serpent to slowly maneuver the hare's body further down its throat. The hare's tremors continued for a full minute after it had been completely swallowed.

The serpent and the Teacher both found the sensation of eating a not-fully-dead meal very satisfying.

TWENTY

And thine ears shall hear a word behind thee, saying, This is the way, walk ye in it, when ye turn to the right hand, and when ye turn to the left.

— Isaiah 30:21 KJV

Adam remained awake the entire night. The temperature dropped steadily as the night progressed; the wind blowing more strongly than it had during the day. Adam started shivering — another novel body sensation — and went in search of shelter, eventually moving to the leeward side of a thicket of low, misshapen junipers. He was able to crawl beneath the mass of scraggly branches and found they blocked most of the wind. Once he was beneath the low canopy the shivering subsided, and while he was not warm, he was not painfully cold either.

By dawn Adam had made his decision. He would hunt down the Daimónia that were tormenting the animals. YHWH had instructed him to subdue the earth and exercise dominion over all living things, and while that command had practical limitations, there was no reason why Adam's dominion should be confined to the garden of Eden. He would pray to YHWH, ask for help, and begin his search. Adam decided to start two valleys over, where the tigers had their young, guessing that the roe deer had been attacked in that same valley.

Even though he had last spoken with Asah in the garden, Adam thought it likely that Asah was somewhere nearby, watching over him. But Adam knew better than to call for him. Asah no longer responded to

Adam's calls when praying to YHWH was the appropriate course. Adam considered returning to Eden on the off-chance that Asah was still there, but that would have entailed the loss of a full day with the descent to the garden and the re-ascent to the pass, a day during which the demons could wreak more havoc on the animals. In the end Adam simply prayed that YHWH would tell Asah anything he needed to know.

Adam emerged from his juniper shelter at first light. The wind had finally lessened and light flakes of snow were drifting down. Adam could see that there were thicker snow flurries obscuring the tops of the mountain peaks. Under other circumstances Adam would have given the snow closer examination, never having seen snowflakes up close before. But today he was full of resolve and would not be turned aside. As he descended lower into the valley, the snow flakes were replaced by tiny drops of water falling from the sky. It was rain. He regarded the rain with great wonder, and remembering his tears, wondered whether there was any connection. The sky seemed to share his sadness.

By the time Adam reached the valley floor, his sensation of hunger had increased to the point of becoming a distraction. He had carried no food with him. While he could forage from the wild pistachios, almonds, and acorns as he crossed the valley floor, it would have been much easier to have brought something from his storehouse with him.

Next time, Adam thought.

Adam gathered and shelled some acorns and then stopped to drink from the valley brook, looking for shadows in the water before he did so. This was something he always did since his encounter with the mute spirit. For several minutes he stilled himself, listening to his spirit and trying to discern whether he should canvas this valley in search of demons or continue to the next valley as he had originally planned. He decided on the latter course.

The problem with continuing to the next valley was that the next line of mountains were much higher and did not have a low, easily traversed pass like the ridge he had just come over. There were gaps in the line of peaks, but these gaps were all higher than he had ever climbed before. Adam wished he had scouted the best crossing place before he had descended from the first pass; when his elevation gave him a much better vantage point. The view from the valley floor was much poorer than the view from the pass.

Adam selected a crossing point and pushed hard toward it all morning. Winding his way higher, he emerged above the increasingly sparse junipers onto a natural staircase of jumbled rock. He was already higher than the first pass where he had spent the night, and the temperature was dropping as he ascended. By mid-day the cloud cover was still unbroken, but at least the rain had stopped. Adam felt a sense of foreboding — a cold feeling in his stomach that seemed to mimic the damp chill around him.

When Adam reached what he expected to be the top of the pass, he discovered it was only the outer lip of a broad expanse of large boulders that lay between him and a still higher ragged notch that would give passage to the next valley. Adam would have to cover another few thousand feet across a boulder field and then climb several hundred feet higher to reach the notch itself.

Crossing the boulder field required jumping from rock to rock. While he had been ascending the staircase, Adam had been sheltered from the wind, but on the open boulder field he was again fully exposed. In spite of his exertions, he was soon as cold as he had been the night before, and numbness was creeping into his fingers, toes, lips, ears, nose, and genitals. The diminished feeling in his feet made navigation of the rocks difficult and dangerous. Every now and then one of the rocks would dip or shift when he walked upon it, so he had to be vigilant with each step and jump.

The wind was also gusty, abruptly becoming stronger or weaker. Sometimes the strength of the wind changed just as he leapt between boulders, and when this happened, his landing was invariably to one side of where he intended. This also increased the risk of falling. Adam had no illusions about the risks he was taking; what had happened to the roe deer could also happen to him. If he were to break a leg through an ill-timed jump, he might have to give his body to one of the flesh-eaters as well.

Three quarters of the way across the boulder field, his body was shaking so much that he had to time his jumps to fall between the waves of shivering. Adam knew that this was his body's response to the cold, and that it was not something to be taken lightly. He also knew that the sooner he got over the notch and down the other side, the sooner he would reach the comparative warmth of the next valley. That, in addition to his concern for the animals, spurred him to keep moving.

But there was a new problem. He was having more and more trouble getting enough air. When he executed three of four jumps in succession, he found that he had to stop and catch his breath. If he didn't do this, he became too dizzy to jump. Even though the boulder field was more level than the rock staircase, the dizziness and the shivering and the wind were greatly hindering his progress.

His hands and feet hurt and had reduced feeling at the same time. Adam saw that his feet and hands had changed in color, and that there were blotches of blood where he had abraded his legs and feet against the unyielding rocks. When he could walk more or less normally on the rocks, he crossed his arms tight across his chest and tucked his fingers into his armpits. However, he couldn't do this while jumping because it affected his balance. He found that bending over when he stopped to catch his breath helped the dizziness subside.

There were shallow caves and dark cracks between and beneath the boulders, and in spite of his discomfort, Adam watched these as he moved along. This would not be a good time to encounter a demon. Adam could see that the bottoms of the deeper cracks were covered by hard water. After cold nights in Eden, he had sometimes seen hard water as thin, clear sheets over seepage puddles, but this hard water looked solid all the way through.

Adam began praying each time he stopped to catch his breath. His anxiety was based partly on not knowing what his body's limits were, and partly upon the certainty that his body did indeed have limits. With all that had transpired the day before, he had come to regard death in a new way. He felt confident that YHWH would protect him from serious injury and death, but his body whispered doubts of its own. His lips were so cold and tight that it was hard to pray out loud. It reminded him of his seizure by the mute spirit.

By the time Adam reached the end of the boulder field, the snow flakes were back, now smacking into his body rather than drifting down. Although the final ascent to the notch was partially sheltered from the wind, gripping the rocks with his hands was brutally painful. Somehow Adam understood that he had passed the point where he could safely turn around. Traversing the boulder field had taken the first half of the after-noon, and Adam intuitively knew his body could not endure the return trip exposed to the icy wind. He had to climb over the notch and descend to the sheltering forest as quickly as possible. The dizziness was still present, though less of a hindrance now that he was climbing rather than jumping. It was late afternoon by the time he peeked over the top of the notch.

The first part of the descent was steep and treacherous, but only for a short distance. It was quickly met by a rounded shoulder of mountain that declined more or less gradually into the valley below. Adam lowered himself down the steep slope as carefully as he could, using the palms of his hands as hooks rather than trusting his senseless fingers. Upon reaching the shoulder, he descended parallel to but just below the ridge-line, thereby gaining a measure of shelter from the wind. He looked long-ingly at the treeline and the valley below him — they were so far away.

Adam still muttered prayers as he descended, though they could hardly be distinguished from his labored breaths. "YHWH, *please keep me from stumbling or injuring myself. Bring me to the trees; let me find shelter there.*" He no longer planned on immediately pursuing the Daimónia upon reaching the valley floor. Now only one thing mattered — finding a place to rest and regain body warmth. At one point he stopped in a rocky alcove that was nearly free of wind, squatting and hugging his arms around his legs while balancing on wooden feet. His shivering started to subside even though he did not feel any warmer. He decided to rest a while before continuing.

"*Get up!*"

Adam opened his eyes, confused, unsure whether he had heard the words or thought them. But there was no one there; he was still alone. He hadn't realized he was falling asleep, and in a distant part of his mind it registered that falling asleep here was not a good thing to do. With great effort he pushed himself erect against the protest of stiffened muscles and left the alcove to continue down toward the treeline.

"If you go that way you will die." It was Asah, standing in front of him, blocking his way. "Cross over the ridge to your right and go to the mist, but do not enter the water until you can feel your fingers. If you enter the water too soon you will die. If you stay here you will die. Go now and you will live."

"But there is no shelter up here; I must reach the trees."

"If you were indeed able to reach them, it would only be to die there. Do as I say and you shall be saved."

Adam was going to ask Asah if he could make a fire like he had on their journey to Eden, but Asah vanished before he could speak. Almost immediately Adam began wondering whether it had really been Asah. He remembered that Asah had warned him about demons appearing as angels, and that to tell the difference, his spirit needed to be quiet and undistracted. Adam spirit was anything but undistracted, and he knew his thinking had become dull. He realized he had not looked closely at Asah's eyes to see if it was really him. Perhaps it was a demon enticing him to take a path that would lead to his death. Or perhaps he had just dreamed it all while he had been asleep.

But it had seemed like Asah ...

Adam trudged up to the top of the ridge, looking upward towards the clouds. He was in the wind again, but barely felt it. Asah's instructions made no sense; to climb up to where the clouds cloaked the peaks was impossible. But Asah had also mentioned water, so Adam turned his gaze downward to the sloping flanks of the rocky shoulder. There was an assortment of pools and streams, even small waterfalls, all of which coursed downwards to eventually disappear into the forest.

"*YHWH, help me,*" he whispered.

On the third scan he saw it. There was a small spring coming out of the rocks a short distance below where Adam was standing. There was nothing remarkable about it at first glance, but every so often, a thin wisp of cloud would come out of the ground near the base of the spring and then be snatched away by the wind.

Adam stumbled downwards toward the stream. As he came alongside it, he saw there was a small pool just inside a rock opening, and that thick tendrils of fog were wafting up from the pool's surface. The fog would collect inside the rock opening and then intermittently spill out of the tiny cave into the mountain wind.

"Ohhh!" Adam exclaimed. Some of the fog had blown across Adam's body, and there was no mistaking its warmth. It was a fumarole! Not as large as those in the garden, but large enough to enter nonetheless.

Dropping to his hands and knees, Adam crawled into the mist-filled opening and was enveloped by warm, moist air. The rear portion of the small cave had two ragged vertical holes through which hot, steamy air was venting. Water slowly trickled from the bottom of the lower hole and accumulated in the shallow basin of the cave floor.

Adam remained on his hands and knees, unmoving, for several minutes, sucking in deep breaths of the heated air and luxuriating in the sensations of warmth dancing over his body. He noticed that the venting air lacked the acrid sulfur smell of some of the fumaroles he had visited in the garden. This fumarole smelled earthy and damp, but otherwise the air was sweet and clean. The spring pool itself felt hotter than the air, not that Adam would have immersed himself after Asah's warning. Asah's counsel had proved utterly trustworthy once again.

Although the cave was not big enough to stand in, there was room to lie down. Adam made a place to stretch out next to the pool by removing the rocks protruding from the ground. He was asleep within minutes. As circulation returned to his extremities, stabs of pain joined the sensations of warmth, but in his utter exhaustion, he was oblivious to these. He slept through the last few hours of the afternoon and well into the night, awakening only once to relieve himself and drink from the pool. Although it was too dark to see when he stood at the cave opening, he could feel the snow falling heavily. Adam returned to his warm, damp bed and slept until morning.

TWENTY-ONE

What is man, that You should exalt him, that You should set Your heart on him, that you should visit him every morning, and test him every moment?
        — Job 7:17-18 NKJV

The Lord your God in your midst, The Mighty One, will save; He will rejoice over you with gladness, He will quiet you with His love, He will rejoice over you with singing.
        — Zephaniah 3:17 NKJV

And I will give you the keys of the kingdom of heaven, and whatever you bind on earth will be bound in heaven, and whatever you loose on earth will be loosed in heaven.
        —Matthew 16:19 NKJV

Asah stood guard over Adam as he slept. It was something he still did, day after day, night after night. Although Asah showed himself to Adam less frequently now, his vigilance on Adam's behalf remained as constant as it had been from the day of his awakening. There were many lessons Adam needed to learn, and with each passing day, YHWH's tests and the training were becoming more arduous. For some of these, it was important that Asah not be accessible to Adam lest the training process be hindered.

Sometimes Asah understood the purpose of YHWH's testing, but oftentimes he did not. YHWH was clearly preparing Adam to fulfill his destiny as the sovereign of the Earth. Asah also understood that by remaining invisible to Adam, Adam was being taught to rely upon YHWH rather than upon Asah. But most of Adam's training regimen was strange to angelic sensibilities. Although Asah had learned many things since his own moment of awakening, he had always understood what it meant to be an angel. There had been no angelic equivalent to the process of self-discovery and growth that Adam was being led through. Asah could hardly imagine how constraining it must feel to be confined to a body of flesh that one could not put off at will.

Asah was particularly puzzled by the events of the last eighteen hours. It would have been safer for Adam to delay his journey over the second pass until the wind had subsided and the early snowstorm was over. Adam's body was marvelously constructed, but for all of its resilience and strength, it was still just flesh and, therefore, fundamentally fragile. Adam had been only minutes away from cold-induced heart failure when Asah received YHWH's command to intercept him and direct him toward the hot spring. Asah could have instantly transported Adam to a place of warmth. He could have shielded him from the wind, or turned himself into a radiant flame that required no fuel and could not be extinguished. He could have supernaturally strengthened Adam's heart muscles so they remained vigorous for hours.

But YHWH did not permit Asah to do any of these. Instead, YHWH allowed Adam to stumble toward the brink of death, only to rescue him at the very last moment. And perhaps even that rescue had not been a sure thing, for if Adam had not strictly obeyed Asah's instructions, he would surely have died. The hot pool on the floor of the cave had been a deadly test — if Adam had entered it prematurely, the constricted blood vessels of his extremities would have dilated, allowing their colder blood to once again move through his circulatory system. This would have delivered a punishing blow to Adam's already chilled heart. Had he chosen to disobey and soak in the warmth of the pool, Adam would have been dead within minutes. Only by breathing in the hot, moist air of the cave was Adam able to slowly and safely restore warmth to his body's core, where the warmth was critically needed.

YHWH was obviously not anxious about Adam's near-approaches to death (not that Asah had ever seen YHWH anxious about anything). Apparently there were lessons for Adam to learn in these experiences that could be gained in no other way. Not having a mortal body, Asah just accepted that there were elements of the training process he might never fully understand.

In the last hour before dawn, YHWH visited Adam for a time, speaking words over Adam while he slept. As an expression of respect, Asah withdrew slightly, still watching but not listening. In one sense, Asah's presence was totally unnecessary — the All-Seeing One certainly didn't need an angel to stand guard on His behalf. But Asah had his orders, and orders from YHWH were never to be trifled with. They were to be obeyed without question or variance, and once given, they stood until modified or rescinded. For Asah to do anything other than to stand guard as commanded would have been to exalt his own reasoning above that of God's. That would have been a grave error, and Asah knew better.

Not that angels couldn't make mistakes. They could and they did. Because they were created beings, it automatically followed that they could fail. Not being all-knowing or all-powerful like YHWH, their service was always constrained by their limitations. Sometimes they had to report to YHWH that in spite of their best efforts, they had been unable to accomplish the task He had set before them. But an honest failing never evoked YHWH's displeasure — admonition perhaps, but not displeasure. YHWH was tolerant, gracious, and patient in His correction and instruction. But above all, He loved each of them individually — and this the angels treasured most of all. Only when a spirit embraced iniquity, as Lucifer and his cohort had, did the love of God yield to wrath. Lucifer's mind had been twisted to think that he could know better than God. No angel in his right mind should ever have contemplated such blasphemous foolishness.

So Asah followed YHWH's orders without question, and was pleased to do so. YHWH continued to hover over Adam, alternately singing over him and whispering, just as if Adam had been awake and could understand what was being spoken. Well ... for that matter, maybe he could. It hadn't occurred to Asah before, but Adam might actually comprehend words spoken over him while he was sleeping. If not, why would YHWH speak to him? Here was another mystery. Asah had been granted special understanding and insight about Adam's fleshy body when YHWH had assigned him to be Adam's guardian. But the capacities and workings of Adam's mind and spirit — these were hidden from Asah, and could only be learned by observation. One thing had become plain to Asah — Adam's inner thoughts were nothing like those of an angel.

Just before sunrise YHWH withdrew from Adam, spoke with Asah, and departed. Adam awoke almost immediately, though he lay still with his eyes open for many minutes. He's thinking, Asah surmised. His eyes were clear and alert, and Asah could see that his body had been fully restored by YHWH's visit. One would not have known, just by looking at him, that he had been so close to death the day before. Asah also saw something new in Adam's spirit. There were tiny points of light lodged deep within the folds of Adam's spirit-man, evidently deposited during YHWH's visit with Adam. Asah studied them for a long time, and while their outer form was apparent to his spiritual eyes, their nature was hidden from him.

Adam crawled out of the cave to stand and look at the surrounding mountains, awash in the early morning light. Asah felt a twinge of excitement and anticipation. From what YHWH had told him, Asah knew his was going to be a momentous day. An ambitious offensive had been planned, one in which Adam would play the central role. In his previous encounter with the mute spirit, Adam had unknowingly been used as bait in a carefully planned ambush. But this encounter would be different. This time Adam would be the hunter rather than the hunted. And this time Adam clearly understood what he was about — he fully intended to cast every demon in the valley into the Abyss. This would be the first time that man and angel truly partnered in the war against the Daimónia.

The angels knew about the demonic activities in the valley below, of course. YHWH's ears were attuned to His creation, even to the smallest of creatures. He knew each one, and to Him none were insignificant. He would not have granted them breath if they were without value to Him. Every creature that had breath, in its own way, gave praise to God. Nonetheless, from the moment the demonic experiments had begun, the angels had been instructed to keep their distance and not interfere.

Asah stayed abreast with Adam as he left the hot spring and began descending into the valley. An hour later, as he approached the sparse, upper fringe of the treeline, Adam again stopped to ask and listen for YHWH's direction.

He learns quickly, Asah thought. *How much better it is to ask for YHWH's directions than to stumble about aimlessly.*

Asah had been fully briefed on the current activities of the Daimónia. They were still engaged in their experiments with controlling the animals, but they seemed to be losing focus and many of their activities had devolved into pleasure-seeking and lounging. Apparently, the demons were able to experience pleasurable sensations when they inhabited the animals, and these sensations could be enhanced by demonic stimulation of neural pleasure centers within the animals' brains. Consequently, the demons had become increasingly reluctant to leave the bodies of their hosts even when they were not actively experimenting.

Asah thought the whole situation was odd. First, an angel would never invade the body of a living creature. Angels could put on bodies of flesh if it was needful, but these bodies were not already living creatures, but simply flesh garments that the angels fashioned for a season. Such flesh garments dissipated as soon as the angels were finished with them. They had no inherent life of their own.

Even stranger was the pleasure-seeking behavior of the Daimónia. Why a former angel would stoop to pleasuring itself in the material realm was hard to understand. The angels of heaven would never have indulged in such self-gratification. Asah and the angels obtained pleasure, great pleasure, simply by executing the commands of YHWH. Doing YHWH's will sustained them and gave them strength. But since such pleasure and fulfillment was forever denied to the Daimónia, perhaps the demons were attempting to fill their gnawing emptiness in this new way. That made a certain kind of sense, pathetic as it was.

Asah had also been surprised to learn how much the Daimónia had let their guard down. As pleasurable as flesh habitation might be, it was foolish for the demons to have become lax about their security. None of the demonic sentries that had stood watch at the beginning of the habitation experiments were still at their posts; they had all joined in. Because the angels had kept their distance and offered no challenge, the demonic cadre had incorrectly assumed that the matter was of no interest to YHWH. If all went as planned, they would pay dearly for that assumption.

In the third quarter of the day, Adam reached the second valley in which the demonic activity had been concentrated. He paused again to listen and then turned to the southeast, weaving his way down-valley. As he traveled, he passed by the bodies of animals with increasing frequency, though none of the deaths appeared to be fresh. Nor did he encounter any living animals.

As Adam approached the portion of the valley where the demons had congregated, the angels began to covertly slip into position in a wide open perimeter around the demons. As Adam drew nearer, other angels behind Adam kept pace, slowly closing the circle, while the other angels remained in position. With each passing moment, the gaps in the angelic ring were filled in by new arrivals, some of which faced outwards. Within minutes the line would become an impregnable barrier to all but the most powerful demons.

It was almost time. Asah drew up beside Adam, close enough to protect him, though Asah really didn't think it would be necessary.

TWENTY-TWO

For if God did not spare the angels who sinned, but cast them down to hell and delivered them into chains of darkness, to be reserved for judgment ...
— II Peter 2:4 NKJV

Therefore hell hath enlarged herself, and opened her mouth without measure ...
— Isaiah 5:14a KJV

... and the ground hath opened her mouth and swallowed them, and all that they have, and they have gone down alive to Sheol ...
— Numbers 16:30b YLT

Shaarur had been amusing himself with an old male boar when he saw the first angels take position. He immediately disengaged from the animal and calmly watched as the angelic perimeter filled in and coalesced into a solid line. As one of Satan's mighty Archon, he could have easily broken through their ranks at any number of locations, but Shaarur had no inclination to do so. He was a veteran of many battles, and was undaunted by the prospect of yet another. Besides, most of his legion of lesser demons would neither prevail nor escape without his leadership. As he gauged the strength of his opposition, Shaarur mentally ran through various tactical options. He concluded that he and the stronger demons should be able to breach the perimeter and hold the gap open long enough for the remaining throng to pour through and escape.

Shaarur didn't need to sound an alarm or call the legion to gather. They were swarming in of their own accord, having seen the angels and not wishing to face them individually. A few straggled back still within their animals, but quickly exited upon his command. Flesh and blood would have no part in this battle, or so Shaarur thought. He was in the middle of explaining his battle plan and assigning positions when the man-creature and his angel walked into plain view.

Every demonic eye fastened upon the pair. Shaarur knew that the man-creature's arrival would require modifications to his battle plan, but he still was not greatly alarmed. The man was formidable and dangerous, with a proven ability to vanquish lesser Daimónia, but that didn't mean he was a match for one of the Archon. The lesser Daimónia lacked this self-assurance and scurried to positions where Shaarur was between them and the man-creature. Most of them had heard the report of Adam's encounter with the mute spirit, the account of which had circulated widely through the realm of darkness in spite of the Archon's efforts to quash it.

One of the demons broke away from Shaarur's shadow and streaked toward a small gap in the angelic perimeter, followed quickly by another fleeing in a different direction.

"*Stand fast!*" Shaarur roared.

A third demon that had broken away turned around and rejoined the group, not so much in obedience to Shaarur's command, but because it witnessed the fate of the first two. Each one had ended up impaled upon two or more angelic swords, and both were writhing and screaming in pain. The demons tried to grasp the swords with clawed hands and feet to push themselves off, but the light-metal of the blades sliced and seared through their spiritual flesh. They were fully stuck.

The extra blades were removed from the demons, and each remaining single sword was passed, with attached demon, around the perimeter to a large angel sporting heavy dark-metal chains draped diagonally across its torso. The chains had self-adjusting manacles designed to shackle demonic limbs, but because the demons had so mutilated themselves in their attempts to extricate themselves from the swords, the manacles wouldn't hold. While humming a hymn of praise, the chain-bearer improvised by passing the chain through the gaping body wounds of the two demons and attached the manacle back to the chain. The chain links expanded in size to fill the wound cavities and soon held the demons firmly.

Unlike light-metal, which could sear through all but the most heavily armored demonic flesh, dark-metal did not cut. It could be used to bludgeon and batter, being wholly unbreakable and unyielding. But it could be severed only by light-metal (which no demon could handle), the touch of which caused dark-metal to instantly dissipate. Consequently, the most frequent use of dark-metal was to bind captive demonic spirits. Dark-metal chains were also well-suited for this application because upon prolonged contact with demonic flesh, dark-metal had the peculiar quality of swelling and binding to the flesh in such a way that it eventually became inseparable from it.

When he was done, the angel hoisted the heavy chain with dangling demons and gave it a few test swings, deciding that it could be used as a weapon in its own right. As the acclamation of the nearest angels died down, the chain-bearer held the chain still, looked toward Shaarur and his throng, and beckoned with his free hand for more demons to attempt to break through.

Throughout this time the man had continued to walk straight toward Shaarur and his demons. Although the man-creature obviously could not see them, he seemed to know they were there. Shaarur was simultaneously trying to formulate a new plan and restore cohesion to his legion, all of whom had been held spellbound by the spectacle of their comrades being threaded with chains. Shaarur understood what they did not — that the spectacle was itself a weapon, one designed to foster fear and confusion, and thereby weaken their strength.

It was working, too. Some of the Daimónia had become so agitated that they were not paying attention to Shaarur's new instructions, but were wrapping themselves in layers of darkness; a futile defensive measure in view of the strength of the angels they were facing.

This wouldn't do at all. Shaarur had to restore single-mindedness in his troops. The laws of unity and agreement applied universally within the spiritual realm. What made the angelic force arrayed against them so dangerous was not the power of individual angels (as formidable as some of them were), but that the angels were of one mind in what they believed and intended to accomplish. Furthermore, they were in one accord not only among themselves, but with the mind and will of YHWH. This always gave the angels an unfair advantage, for while concentrated darkness could weaken angels and cause them to fail in their mission, YHWH was impervious to such tactics. YHWH never wavered. There had been only one time when Satan and the Archon had assailed YHWH with a barrage of their combined doubt and unbelief. That attack had failed miserably and was never attempted again. The fact that YHWH had not counterattacked in any way, but had simply laughed at them, had added greatly to their humiliation.

So ... as long as the angels were joined in faith to the Almighty they could not be overcome. However, if Shaarur could marshal all of the Daimónia to act together and speak with one voice, they might still open a way of escape. Losing some, no doubt; but Shaarur and the stronger should still make it.

"Speak and be like-minded with me legionnaires! We have the strength to break through." Shaarur quickly indicated to them where the focal point of their attack should be, instructing three other small groups to focus their energies at other points along the angelic ring as diversions. For good measure, Shaarur also directed a group to target the man, speaking in unison that he should go back the way he had come. Shaarur noted that the perimeter of angels was not closing, which was an odd strategy, for closing their ranks would have made breaching the ring more difficult. This was most encouraging; victory or defeat often hinged upon such small errors.

Shaarur began the chant, *"You shall not stand; others around you shall stand, but you shall be overcome. You are the weak link in this chain."* As the legion took up the chant and fell into agreement, tendrils of murky darkness snaked outward from the throng toward the targeted areas of the angelic circle. Simultaneously, the ring of angels began to glow with increased radiance in response. Those angels which had not yet unsheathed their light-metal swords did so.

The chants gained in strength. Shaarur glanced at the man-creature and saw that he was standing still with his head bowed and his eyes closed. Perhaps he was tired. Shaarur directed the contingent assigned to the man to add words of fatigue to their litany.

The tendril of darkness associated with the primary chant had become a torrent, enveloping, and isolating the targeted angels in palpable, rolling blackness. These angels had become pillars of bright fire, and continued to stand ready with firmly planted shields and raised incandescent swords, though they could not be seen from outside the torrent, nor could they see each other within it.

"You shall not stand … you shall be overcome … you are the weak link."

Each time the chant was finished the dark river pulsed, disgorging another great bolus of impenetrable darkness. If only one or two of the angels faltered it would be enough. Every angel standing within the streaming river understood that they *could* falter, and therein lay the strength of Shaarur's tactic. They knew that it had happened before, and that inevitably it would happen again. More importantly, they knew that if they wavered for a moment it *would* happen to them. The chant and its black river only had to be strong enough to convince a few of them that *it was* happening to them for the breach to occur. When that happened, the sword of the faltering angel would dim and become heavy, and that angel would cease to be a threat. Upon Shaarur's command, the legion would then dive into the river and make their escape.

Unlike the angels, Shaarur could see clearly through the dark torrent, and watched for signs of weakening even while he continued to lead the chant. No faltering yet. And the remaining angels still had not altered their positions. A glance toward the man found him still standing, apparently asleep.

"They are making this too easy," Shaarur said to himself, wondering what he was missing.

There! The sword of one of the smaller angels dimmed perceptibly. Shaarur redirected the thickest, darkest part of the chant toward this angel while maintaining its isolation from the angels on either side.

"Be ready," Shaarur called out, *"It's almost time."*

When they made their break Shaarur would position himself in the center of the river. This would minimize his chances of meeting an angel wielding an undimmed sword. It would also allow him to speak words of defeat as he passed the angel which had doubted, hopefully weakening him for battles yet to come. Shaarur would mentally mark this angel to ensure he recognized him in any future encounters.

The river had become a black jet, pummeling the small angel.

"... *OTHERS AROUND YOU SHALL STAND, BUT YOU SHALL BE OVERCOME ...*"

The angelic ring had discerned what was happening and the angels on either side were pressing their way sideways through the torrent and toward the small angel. The man remained in his torpid state.

As a look of horrible dismay flashed upon the face of the small angel, the light emanating from his sword blinked out.

"*Go, go, go!*" Shaarur screamed as he leaped into the stream.

"Stop! By YHWH, not one of you shall escape judgment this day!" The man had awakened, and while his words had been spoken quietly and calmly, they were heard by every demon there.

Within seconds the rushing torrent ebbed to a mere trickle and the chant broke apart into confused babble. The residual darkness began to dissipate immediately, and some of Shaarur's legion once again began to wrap themselves in protective cocoons of darkness.

The angel which had faltered had already been reached by three others, two of whom were supporting him from either side while a third was speaking to him over his shoulder while steadying him from behind. In a disgusting display of tenderness, the third angel reached over the small angel's shoulder and placed his palm beneath his chin, gently raising his head so that he was once again gazing at Shaarur and the legion. In spite of his weakened and shaken state, the three angels were keeping their stricken comrade in the battle.

Shaarur was enraged. He knew their power had been broken by the man's words, and that it would now be impossible to rally the confused throng. They had been so close to escape! But the man's words had been perfectly timed. While the angels had not yet closed in battle, it was surely only moments away. Most if not all of his legion would be lost.

But Shaarur's rage did not weaken his mental prowess, and he quickly shifted his strategy and focus. He was one of the Archon. He would not be taken easily. He also could do what was not expected. While the combined strength of the angelic ring was more than Shaarur wished to confront, there was only one angel standing by the man, and he did not look to be Shaarur's equal.

It was a good plan, considering it was the only one that came to mind. Shaarur would strike the man down with a vicious passing blow and hurl himself through the ranks, all in one unbroken movement, seizing the moment of confusion caused by the man's death.

Shaarur was moving even before the plan was fully formed. He materialized his corpus and hardened one claw into a massive lance as he streaked toward the man. The moment he started to move, the angel above the man's shoulder landed on the ground in front of him, also taking material form, his sword blazing and leveled at the oncoming lance.

While the man could not see Shaarur's form clearly, the oncoming lance was plainly visible. The man spoke a second time, "I bind every spirit of darkness here in the name of YHWH."

As these words were spoken, stabs of spirit-light exploded forth from the man's mouth. Shaarur saw his clawed lance-hand drop to the ground in front of him, sliced from his spiritual body by one of the light pulses. While he could still move his head freely, he had come to a complete standstill and his limbs were not functioning properly. Shaarur examined himself in shock. He had been dismembered! His clawed feet and other arm were at rest near him, fizzling as they sublimated into dark wisps of ethereal vapor. The same thing was happening to his materialized lance-hand.

Shaarur could see the man and angel from his immobile position. The angel dematerialized and stepped back to his original position behind and above the man, sheathing his sword and shaking his head with a wide smile. The man was watching the lance boil away with wide eyes. Beyond them, Shaarur could see that the rest of his legion had been similarly stricken.

The angelic ring finally dispersed and began moving amongst the legion, not in battle, but in a leisurely manner. The angels traveled back and forth between the chain-bearers and the inert demons, affixing and securing the dark-metal chains and then stacking the captives in orderly piles.

Shaarur watched in morbid fascination as his severed limbs finished dissipating. Such a thing had never happened to one of the Archon. Nor had any of the Archon ever been taken captive before. It was inconceivable that this was happening to him; that he would be the first of the Mighty Ones to go down.

At this thought his rage crumbled completely into numbing fear. The Abyss! Might they cast him into the Abyss? He strained in panic, willing his body to move, but he was still held fast by some invisible force unleashed by the man's words. He knew that he would need all of his faculties and strength if he were to have any chance of escape, yet as hard as he tried, he could barely marshal his thoughts.

With time Shaarur could have regenerated new limbs, but he knew his fate would be settled long before that. Perhaps he could speed the growth of just one limb, one which could be used if his bonds loosened for even an instant. He had just begun to apply himself to this task when a loop of dark-metal chain dropped over his head and around his torso. The chain immediately contracted and cinched what remained of his arms to his torso. Another loop arced out around the stubs of his legs, pinning them together.

He felt himself being lifted, gently swinging face down in his wrapped chains, and then carried to where the other demons had been stacked three-to-four high in a large circle. All of them were facing inward so that they had a clear view of the circle's interior.

The circle was not quiet. Many of the legion were whimpering; some begging and bargaining; a few uttering threats or curses.

Shaarur was placed in an unoccupied spot in the circle, also facing inward. When he could hold his peace no longer he spoke to the angel which had carried him, trying to make his voice authoritative and commanding, as befitting one of his stature.

"*What is going to happen here?*" Shaarur's voice sounded less imposing than he would have liked. It had been a long time since he had been so afraid.

No answer. The angel didn't even look down, but responded only by placing his foot firmly over Shaarur's mouth, effectively silencing him.

Shaarur could see that the man and his angel were talking. The man finally nodded his head and spoke.

"You afflicted and tormented the innocent and helpless. Therefore, you shall be afflicted and tormented. I sentence you to the Abyss and the judgment YHWH has prepared for you."

The man's words were met with an outburst of forlorn wails and cries from the legion. These quickly died down as the throng watched to see what would happen next.

Nothing happened. Shaarur felt a glimmer of hope. Perhaps there were limits to the man's abilities. Maybe he had overstepped his authority and inadvertently gone beyond what the Most High would permit. If that was so, maybe nothing would come of his words.

Shaarur saw movement in the very center of the circle around which the bound legion had been arrayed. It was peculiar, because the movement was occurring in both the material realm and the spiritual realm at once. Normally the realm of spirits and the material realm of earth were completely distinct. Ever so close, yet completely separate.

In the material realm, the first movement had been a shallow slumping of the sandy soil in the middle of the circle. The diameter and depth of the depression slowly increased, not smoothly, but erratically, as if the settling ground became stable only to be jarred loose again from below.

In the spiritual realm, the first detectable movement had been the appearance of a small wrinkle of blackness. Shaarur was accustomed to darkness, but this wrinkle appeared to be beyond dark, beyond the absence of ambient spiritual light. It was unlike anything Shaarur had ever seen in the spirit realm.

As Shaarur watched, the wrinkle elongated at both ends, becoming a dark sinuous crack in the fabric of the spirit realm, the ends rapidly extending beyond Shaarur's range of vision. The edges of the crack then began to thicken and differentiate into what appeared to be two black, bulbous lips. Shaarur knew this couldn't be right. There was no life form, spiritual or material, that corresponded to what he was seeing. Yet the resemblance of what he saw to a monstrous pair of compressed lips was undeniable.

Shaarur's attention darted back to the material realm. The pit had continued to deepen and expand outward until its perimeter approached the circle of bound demons. The pit then stopped widening but the bottom kept dropping. Sand, rocks, and boulders slid and crashed down the steepening slopes. Trees and shrubs caught in the sloping, earthen current tumbled and turned, branches and tangled roots surfacing out of the flowing earth only to submerge again a moment later. All of this was accompanied by an eerie groan as massive amounts of earth fell away.

The Daimónia were all wailing now, even those who had been cursing a few moments earlier. The angel removed his foot from Shaarur's face, slipped it through the free loop of chain that had been used as a handle to hoist Shaarur, and then placed his foot on the back of Shaarur's neck. Shaarur had resolved not to give the angel the satisfaction of hearing him cry out, yet he couldn't stop himself from shaking uncontrollably.

He was thinking what the legion of demons was thinking. It was the Abyss! And it was preparing to receive them.

In the spirit realm, the black lips were still sealed together, but they were stretching and straining, evidently trying to pull apart. The spiritual entrance to the Abyss had become a trembling, grotesque smile that wanted very much to open.

"*I was wrong. I was wrong to sin against YHWH. I was wrong to listen to Satan's lies. I am Shaarur of the Archon, one of the mighty ones, but I bow before YHWH's greatness and majesty. Only YHWH is God.*" Shaarur didn't realize he was speaking until he heard his own words dribbling out. He stopped himself, but soon the words resumed. He was unable to halt his horrible confession.

The angel gave no indication that it heard him.

The lips finally parted from each other with an incongruously gentle sigh, and Shaarur immediately detected the smell of rancid combustion. In the physical realm, the bottom of the pit abruptly broke apart as the remaining sand and debris quickly plummeted out of sight. Strangely, the sides of the pit remained in place, held by some invisible force, though rivulets of mud and water continued to slough down the inside edges of the pit as groundwater drained from the adjacent soils. The gaping hole had no visible bottom.

In the spiritual realm, the lips of the Abyss remained wide open, quivering and expectant. Everywhere the bound demons toppled into the pit from where they had been piled, screaming in terror. Shaarur felt himself also falling, only to stop suddenly as his chain jerked taut.

The angel's foot, still in the loop of his dark-metal chain, had kept him from falling. The pull of the Abyss was incredibly strong. Even if his legs and arms had been whole and free, he would not have been strong enough to pull himself back up the chain. In contrast, the angels were at ease, unaffected by the force that was tugging against him. Shaarur wondered if his dark-metal chains had a limit beyond which they would break.

Hanging upside down over the chasm, Shaarur gazed into the depths of the Abyss. It was terrible beyond anything he could have imagined. Although his legion of demons had already fallen a great distance, some peculiar quality of the pit kept them clearly visible. In like manner, their faint screams were still audible.

They had not yet reached the bottom. In fact, Shaarur could see no bottom to the Abyss. What he could see were consecutive layers of dancing flames, one after another, in an endless procession. Shaarur wasn't sure if the demons had the same enhanced visual perception that he was experiencing. If they did, then the realization that they might forever be falling through these layers of flames must already be driving them mad.

As Shaarur watched, the tumbling mass of spirits approached the first layer of flames. As they did so, the flames began changing in nature and form, as if anticipating the approach of the falling demons. The flames wrapped themselves together in tight coils of white-hot incandescence, the coils building in height until they extended well above where the layer of flames had formerly been. Soon there were clusters of waving, burning tentacles everywhere, each cluster positioned to intercept one of the condemned Daimónia. They looked like immense, headless worms.

The first of the falling legion had almost reached the flames. To his shock, Shaarur recognized his name in the distant screams, "*Shaarur, save us! You have not yet fallen; you can help us. Shaarur come to our rescue!*"

So they could see him, just as he *could* see them.

As those falling came within reach, the fireworms reached out and stabbed through them, not once, but over and over again. Immediately the volume of the demonic screams increased, only to lessen and then become silent as the voracious fireworms selectively lanced and slashed through the remaining larger pieces of demon flesh. Each time a fireworm sliced through a piece of demon body it released a line of acrid black smoke, a cloud of which was now wafting lazily upward toward the still-open lips of the Abyss.

As the rain of demon flesh fell through the far side of the first layer of flames, the smoldering bits and pieces of their shredded bodies began to join back together. As they reformed, the silence gave way to a rising chorus of dreadful moans. But by the time the demon bodies had fully reformed and rejoined, the screams had begun again in earnest.

The second layer of flames was only a minute away, and the fire-worms were making ready.

"Demon, pay attention! There is someone here to free you of your chains." The angel whose foot was holding Shaarur's chain had spoken.

Shaarur struggled to look up at the angel looking down at him. There was hope! His words of repentance had been heard after all and had won him some small concession, perhaps even liberty and reinstatement as one of the elect angels.

Shaarur redoubled his efforts at repentance; this was no time to spare words. *"I know I have sinned. I deserve the righteous judgment of YHWH, but I have seen my error and will forever turn from it. I will help the Almighty defeat Satan."*

"Silence!" the angel commanded. *"There is one here who would have a word with you."*

A small angel peered over the edge of the pit at Shaarur. *"Do you remember me?"* the angel asked.

Shaarur did. It was the angel who had faltered during the legion's attempted escape.

Shaarur nodded. He was starting to apologize when the small angel spoke.

"And now shall my head be lifted up above mine enemies round about me ..."

Before Shaarur could respond, the small angel skillfully sliced through all of Shaarur's dark-metal chains in one stroke, freeing him of his bonds.

Freeing him to fall.

As Shaarur hurtled past the black lips of the Abyss, they settled gently back together, satiated for the moment.

Shaarur could no longer hear the cries of the falling Daimónia. His own howl filled his ears.

TWENTY-THREE

Every kingdom divided against itself is brought to desolation, and
a house divided against a house falls. If Satan also is divided
against himself, how will his kingdom stand?
— Luke 11:17b-18a NKJV

P tha flew through the aether of the spirit realm with as much haste as he could muster. Normally he would have traveled slowly and with deliberation, choosing his route carefully and taking full advantage of the spiritual shadows that shrouded the planet. But not this time. Satan had summoned Ptha and the other Archon for an emergency Council meeting, and that being the case, Ptha's concern for his personal safety was best served by not keeping the Lord of darkness waiting. Satan could be remarkably patient when it came to laying an ambush or implementing a strategy, but he was never patient when kept waiting by underlings, even underlings of high rank. So Ptha flew in a direct path and in plain view, keeping a sharp lookout for the sudden appearance of angels on intercepting paths.

Earlier that morning Ptha and the serpent had just crossed over the high ridgeline and begun their descent toward the garden of Eden when a flyer found them. The flyer had the presence of mind to appear within Ptha's spiritual field of view without approaching or speaking, using a standard claw signal to signify that it had an urgent message. Ptha slipped out of the serpent briefly, received the message, and returned without the serpent noticing he had been gone.

Ptha then told the serpent he would need to be absent for a while, explaining that he could locate Adam more quickly if they separated, and that they would be reunited soon. As he spoke, Ptha gently prodded the serpent's brain regions associated with sadness and anxiety, wanting the serpent to feel sadness at Ptha's leaving. Ptha had learned much about the serpent's neural structure during the last two days. He had prodded and probed, delicately exciting neural impulses as he watched for reactions in the serpent's physical body or mental state, all while he carried on conversations or engaged in other activities that occupied the serpent's attention. This gentle experimentation had allowed Ptha to expand on Shaarur's early discoveries about animal instinct and desire, and pleasure and pain, to encompass the full range of primary and secondary emotions.

Ptha directed the serpent's gaze to a tall tree in the distance that was easily distinguishable from the garden's others trees, and told the serpent to wait for him there. Ptha would rendezvous with the serpent as soon as he had located Adam, either bringing Adam with him, or returning to escort the serpent to Adam's location.

As he began his journey to the Council meeting, Ptha tried to make sense of what he had just learned. After delivering the summons, the flyer had succinctly filled Ptha in on why he had been summoned, but there were still many details the flyer hadn't provided.

This much Ptha knew: two days earlier a partially incapacitated demon had fluttered into one of the Daimónia's mobile encampments and reported on the fate of Shaarur and his legion. The demon had seen it all, having been intentionally set free by the angels so the tale would be told. The encampment immediately sent out two flyers to find and alert Ptha, while the rest of the group headed straight for the nearest Archon with a known location, carrying the traumatized witness at a speed it could no longer achieve by itself. Because the two flyers had been unable to find Ptha, Satan had dispatched a host of additional flyers on the following day. It was one of these that had finally located Ptha.

Satan's direct communiqué to Ptha had been brief: *Report in immediately, in person, without delay. Your Master awaits your arrival to commence an emergency Council meeting.*

Under other circumstances, Ptha would have been thrilled to learn that the other Archon were being made to wait for him. But this summons left him apprehensive, even though Ptha was not temperamentally inclined to being fearful. As he thought about it, Ptha realized that with his progress with the serpent and with the loss of Shaarur and his legion, Ptha was now the only one who had any reasonable chance of making contact with Adam without ending up in the Abyss. Of course, there was an equally reasonable chance that he would end up in the Abyss anyway.

No wonder I feel anxious, he thought.

Ptha was sure that Satan had been shaken by the loss of Shaarur. He was probably feeling some fear of his own. Satan might be able to hide it from the other Archon, but they hadn't devoted themselves to studying Satan the way that Ptha had, something that Ptha had practiced solely for the sake of self-preservation. Ptha had learned that when Satan became fearful he also became unpredictable. If Satan's judgment was to become sufficiently clouded by fear, Ptha could see himself being sent on some poorly conceived mission that would only lead to his demise.

Ptha would need to have all of his skills of persuasion and influence at the ready. And it would be wise for him to have his own plan formulated by the time he arrived to better allow him to influence the outcome.

And that's when the thought struck him.

The man Adam has incredible power. Perhaps so much power that he could prevail against Satan ....

... What if I could orchestrate an encounter between Satan and Adam, an encounter that ended with Satan being cast into the Abyss?

Such a dangerous thought! But such a delicious, energizing, exciting thought. Satan dethroned! And his dominion seized by one more worthy than he.

Ptha had long been convinced that Satan would never be able to prevail against the Almighty. At first, Ptha had really believed Satan might emerge the victor. But over time, as the Daimónia failed to achieve a single, meaningful victory, Ptha had become more realistic, and the realism had been replaced by fatalism. Having cast his lot in with the insurrection, Ptha had no alternative but to continue the battle.

But now there just might be another way.

If Ptha could single-handedly engineer Satan's demise, and then accede to power, he might be able to negotiate a truce with heaven. This was not something Satan had ever been willing to consider, nor would it likely have been well received in heaven. But Ptha did not aspire to replace God, only His fallen archangel. And that might be just enough of a difference to end the war. Ptha would commit to never troubling or threatening heaven, if heaven in return allowed the Daimónia to continue to exist in exile. That seemed fair to Ptha. And if Ptha offered the Daimónia an escape from the Abyss that awaited them all, surely they would accept and even acclaim him.

It was betrayal, of course. But Ptha had betrayed before, and this time it was a much easier choice.

All of this merited very careful thought, though now was not the time, of course. Ptha needed to finish his mental preparations for the Council meeting. He still needed to develop contingency responses if Satan decided to embark on a plan with unacceptable risks.

As he corralled his thoughts, Ptha decided to never think on matters of betrayal when he was in Satan's presence, lest some trivial slip of expression or word rouse Satan's suspicion. To accomplish this, Ptha would have to become two-minded. When he was with Satan or the Archon, he would be the wise, devoted counselor. But when he was with the serpent, he would be the soon-to-be recognized sovereign of the Daimónia.

TWENTY-FOUR

... the rulers take counsel together, against the Lord and His Anointed ...
— Psalms 2:2b NKJV

The battle of Shaarur had been an utter disaster. As the surviving demon gave its detailed account to the Council, Ptha felt deep dismay. Satan's face was a mask that revealed nothing, but Ptha could see that the other Council members were as demoralized as he. When all of its facets were considered, the battle of Shaarur was arguably the greatest defeat the Daimónia had suffered since the Great Fall. The rank-and-file Daimónia would need time to mentally recover from the loss. And the Archon would need time to fully comprehend its implications and to formulate an appropriate response.

They had lost a total of one hundred forty two mid-rank demons (the minimum grade that Shaarur had allowed to participate in the field trials), eighteen commanding demons, two under-Archon, and Shaarur himself. While Ptha had periodically received Shaarur's verbal summaries on the legion's habitation experiments, (which Ptha had adapted to his habitation of the serpent), the findings had not been compiled, analyzed, or reduced to written protocols. Consequently, they had lost much of the detailed knowledge that Shaarur's legion had accumulated.

They had also lost the element of surprise. Adam now knew of their activities, even if he didn't know the strategic objective behind them. They could engage in new field trials in a location more remote from the garden (and probably should do so for the sake of general knowledge), but Ptha didn't believe that would help them in their approach to Adam. Ptha was still convinced that they would never be able to adequately control animals that were forcibly inhabited. Secondly, even if they perfected the habitation of some susceptible species, and even if those animals and their handlers were able to successfully journey to the garden, Adam would now be on the alert. Upon meeting a new animal, it would only be prudent for Adam to command any demon in the vicinity to disclose itself, and they all knew what would happen after that.

Ptha had to admire the psychology behind the angels' tactics. The release of one demon was a small price to pay for the distress this whole event was causing amongst the Daimónia. To be effective against the angels, the Daimónia needed to be able to operate in one accord, and to do that they needed to maintain a certain level of corporate confidence. Ptha knew that the stories about Shaarur and his troops must already be spreading from legion to legion. By now some of the stories no doubt had embellishments that made them even more demoralizing, if that were possible. To the extent that the morale and resolve of the Daimónia had been shaken, their strength had been reduced.

The demon finished telling its story, answered several questions from the Council, and was dismissed. Satan then asked Ptha to brief them on his activities with the serpent. Ptha recounted how he had first met the serpent and described the creature's formidable intelligence and keen spiritual intuition. He told how he had negotiated entry into the serpent, how they had subsequently journeyed together to the edge of the garden, and how they would rendezvous in a few days.

The first question came from Ratsach. "The early reports from Shaarur said that inhabiting animals was pleasurable. Did you find that to be so?"

Ptha hesitated before answering. He felt reluctant to disclose how pleasurable it really was, but there was no valid reason for him to withhold such information. And then, having hesitated, he wondered whether his hesitation had been noted and whether it might somehow be misconstrued. Ptha stopped himself just as he was about to look at Satan, regained his mental control, and focused on answering Ratsach.

"Yes, it is indeed pleasurable. I was just thinking about how to explain it and realized I don't really understand it myself." Ptha was mentally chiding himself as he spoke. He had done nothing more than entertain disloyal thoughts earlier that day and he was already reacting in ways that could arouse suspicion. He *had* to appear to be completely truthful, and the best way to do that was to *be* as completely truthful as possible.

"After entering the serpent," Ptha continued, "I experienced the sensations and emotions of the serpent, as well as my own, though I could always tell the difference. That perhaps was to be expected. What was surprising was that I perceived the serpent's feelings as more heightened and more intense than my own. To experience such intensity of emotion is unquestionably pleasurable."

Ptha remembered that prior to the rebellion, his existence had been rich with vibrant, joyful emotion, but he said nothing of this poorly timed reflection.

"Based on Shaarur's reports and my own field experience," Ptha continued, "habitation appears to be pleasurable regardless of whether it is forced or consensual. The degree of pleasure appears to be correlated with the intensity of the host's emotions rather than the specific type of emotion. So inhabiting an utterly terrified animal would be more enjoyable than inhabiting one that is content, even though the animal would obviously prefer the latter."

"This raises a concern," Irkmattu said. "Such powerful pleasure is something that most Daimónia are unaccustomed to, given our present war footing. Could such pleasure affect the habitant's judgment?"

Satan had appointed Irkmattu to serve as Shaarur's replacement on the Council of Archon. Prior to this meeting Ptha had known of Irkmattu only by name, but he had the reputation of being a shrewd battle planner. Considering the increased frequency of battles and skirmishes lately, his elevation to the Council was a wise move.

Much of Irkmattu's spirit-body had eroded away during the Great Fall, so his size was not imposing. His face and corpus had a gaunt, stretched appearance, not unlike the animals Shaarur's legion had deprived of food to weaken their resistance. In contrast, Irkmattu's hands and feet were still their original size, making them disproportionately large for his diminished body, and he had long, curving talons on the end of each digit. However, the darkness behind his black eyes was unusually steady. This feature in particular spoke of Irkmattu's menace in spite of his small size. Any angel seasoned in battle would have quickly recognized that Irkmattu was a very powerful, very dangerous spirit.

"It's a fair question," Ptha replied, "and yes, it could influence the judgment and performance of the habitant. The degree of influence would depend upon the mental discipline of the habitant. In fact, I have wondered whether Shaarur and his legion were so distracted with their new-found pleasures that they failed to maintain proper readiness."

Ghanph scowled, making no effort to conceal his contempt for Ptha or his dislike of Ptha's slight on Shaarur's abilities. It was also likely Ptha's single-handed success with the serpent, when all of the other efforts of the Daimónia had come to naught, did not set well with Ghanph.

Ptha knew Ghanph regarded him as condescending, and in truth, Ptha was — with Archon not his equal. But Ptha's statement about Shaarur was worth thinking about. It would be wise for all of them to learn from Shaarur's mistakes. Nevertheless, Ptha didn't want to be at odds with Ghanph right now.

"Of course," Ptha said, "we never would have learned any of this without Shaarur's excellent work. His efforts and his subsequent sacrifice gave us essential knowledge about what not to do."

Ghanph's countenance didn't soften.

"It seems clear," Irkmattu said, looking first at Ghanph and then at the others, "that habitation does indirectly put the habitant at risk. If we were not at war, we could pleasure ourselves with the animals, there certainly are enough of them and we would never use them all up. But given the situation, I wonder what is to be gained by more experimentation along these lines. Perhaps we need to conceive an entirely new strategy."

"And perhaps it is time to just kill the man-creature," Ghanph said. "If he can't be turned as our sovereign hoped, then perhaps it is time to rid ourselves of him before more damage is done. I would be willing to take such an assignment. With one stroke I could scatter his body over the entire valley."

Ptha was tempted to remind Ghanph of the outcome of Shaarur's attempt to do just that, but redirected the conversation instead. "I do have a plan," Ptha said, looking at Satan.

Satan nodded his consent for Ptha to continue, his eyes revealing nothing.

Ptha's plan had been hastily developed during his flight to the Council meeting. It was simple and sensible, and he objectively believed it stood a reasonable chance of success. Equally important, at least to Ptha, it also minimized his risk of meeting Shaarur's fate.

"As you recall," Ptha said, "the primary objective of the field trials was to learn how to converse with Adam through the animals without being detected. Shaarur's approach was essentially one of force. His troops entered animals without invitation and then used a variety of techniques to press their will upon the animals. We know that they met with some success in prodding the animals to do certain things, but Shaarur never succeeded in achieving controlled conversation. Or at least he never reported that he had succeeded."

"Shaarur's approach failed because it was flawed," Ptha continued. "Any animal with enough intelligence to carry on a meaningful dialogue with Adam knows when it has been forcibly entered. And the universal response of animals to a demonic intrusion is always resistance. Although this resistance is expressed in different ways, all of them involve some alteration of the animals' natural behavioral patterns. Needless to say, now that Adam knows of our experiments, it would be foolish for any of us to approach him in an animal that is acting oddly."

"But if an animal has both granted consent and become accustomed to our habitation, its behavior should be normal. We know from my work with the serpent that this is achievable. All that remains, then, is to engage Adam in conversation. Once that has been successfully accomplished, it is just a matter of time before we first sway him, and then turn him with our words."

"Are you really ready at this time to approach Adam with your serpent?" Irkmattu asked. "If you do so prematurely, before you are sufficiently practiced, you and the serpent could both be lost. And having failed, such an approach would not work a second time."

"I have thought of that. And it probably is too soon for me to personally speak with Adam through the serpent. But it isn't too soon for the serpent to approach Adam without me. My plan is to use a carefully constructed ruse to get the serpent to speak with Adam without me, having guided it beforehand on what to say and what not to say. The serpent's relationship with me would never be revealed, of course.

"In time," Ptha said, "Adam will become completely accustomed to speaking with the serpent, and perhaps will even look forward to doing so. When the time is finally right, I will enter the serpent and begin to actively participate in the conversations."

"Perhaps this will work. What will you say to turn Adam to our side?" Ghanph asked.

"That wouldn't be for me to decide. That moment will require the ultimate skill and wisdom of our master." Ptha lowered his head respectfully while glancing toward Satan. "Once I have fully prepared the serpent for our sovereign's entry, my work will be done."

Still sullen and in thought, Ghanph nodded his head in support of the plan. Ptha could guess what he was thinking: *If you succeed, Ptha, that will be good for all of us. If you fail, then you will be in the Abyss instead of attending Council meetings, and that will be good, too.*

Satan smiled. "It is a good plan, Ptha."

Indeed it is, Ptha thought.

TWENTY-FIVE

*But ask now the beasts, and they shall teach thee; and the fowls of
the air, and they shall tell thee.*
— Job 12:7 KJV

The serpent was there, waiting at the tree where Ptha had said
they should meet. It was lying along one of the lower horizontal branches,
its upper limbs folded beneath its body, its hind limbs clasped together
around the branch, and the rest of its length wrapped around it in loose,
draping coils.

It had been three days since they had parted, and Ptha had been
worried that the serpent might tire of waiting and move on. He was still
worried about encountering Adam before the elements of his plan were
fully in place. For all he knew, Adam might already be back in the garden.
A chance meeting at this point could ruin everything.

Ptha crossed the interface, materializing in plain view in front of
the serpent.

"You do like to watch me before crossing over, don't you?"

Ptha had forgotten how perceptive the serpent was. The lapse
goaded him to dismiss all competing thoughts and to focus on the task
before him.

"One of the small pleasures I allow myself," Ptha said. "It was a
tedious journey and I apologize for being away so long. I have missed your
company and our conversations. May I join you?"

"Of course, Teacher. I have been waiting."

Ptha noticed there was no hesitation in the serpent's response. *A good sign,* he thought, *the creature trusts me and desires my entry.*

As Ptha entered the serpent he compressed and contorted his corpus until it fit entirely within the serpent's linear body. Although complete containment wasn't necessary for Ptha to communicate with the serpent or to stimulate its nervous system, Ptha's plan would eventually require him to inhabit the serpent in the presence of the man, and probably his angel. While the man's ability to see the Daimónia might be underdeveloped, the angel's vision would be sharp. Ptha was gambling that with time and practice he could become so well acclimated to the serpent's ways, and his corporeal form so well camouflaged within the serpent's body, that he would be invisible to all but the closest angelic scrutiny. Furthermore, the serpent's initial conversations with Adam would occur without Ptha being present. By the time Ptha started accompanying the serpent, the angel would have become used to the serpent and Adam conversing, and that familiarity would hopefully lull the angel into looking for demons everywhere other than inside the serpent.

Ptha secreted most of his spiritual body into the serpent's open body cavities — the anterior portion of the single functional lung and the posterior air sac; vacant portions of the esophagus, stomach, and intestines; and the peritoneal cavity. Ptha had learned from experience that this was more comfortable than residing within the fluid or solid portions of the body — just as it was less taxing for materialized Daimónia to dwell in or travel through air than through solid materials.

When properly situated, Ptha could easily reach out and touch any portion of the serpent's nervous system, from its brain to the furthest nerve endings of its tail. As was his habit upon entering the serpent, Ptha stimulated a burst of neuronal impulses within the serpent's pleasure center.

I have missed this, Ptha thought to himself, selectively shielding the thoughts he didn't want the serpent to hear — something else he had learned how to do during his initial habitations. Ptha relaxed, savoring the sensations. The serpent's head slipped off the branch and lolled to one side while Ptha steadied the rest of the body to keep it from sliding off the branch.

So what would you like to know about Adam? Ptha asked after the snake had regained its faculties.

Ptha was ready to begin constructing his deception. He had learned from Satan long ago that a complex web of lies was always more believable if the one being deceived came to the erroneous conclusions through its own mental process. Ptha had not met a creature yet that didn't believe its own thoughts more readily than the words of another. The more intelligent the creature, the more this seemed to be the case. The mark of a truly great deceiver was that he guided the deceived into articulating their own lies.

And Ptha had always been a great deceiver. *It's my gift*, he thought to himself with dark sarcasm.

Are we ready to meet him?

No, Ptha answered. *He is still away on a journey, but he will be returning soon. We will wait for him here rather than try to find him elsewhere. This garden valley is his home.*

What is he like? Is he a spirit like you?

Not at all. He is a creature of flesh like you, though not a flesh-eater. He is quick of mind, well-spoken, a capable sovereign. And as I told you before, he is exceedingly wise.

Is he wiser than you?

The serpent had intentionally thought the question in a neutral tone, masking the wry, teasing humor underlying the question. This presented Ptha with a double opportunity. The serpent didn't know that whenever Ptha was in residence, all of its thoughts were open to Ptha. And Ptha didn't want the serpent to know that. So whenever he could, Ptha would intentionally miss some nuance, or feign a lack of understanding of the serpent's thought-question, thereby bolstering the illusion that Ptha knew only what the serpent chose to communicate. Ptha had done this so effectively to date that the serpent had already concluded that its private thoughts were hidden from Ptha.

The second opportunity came from the subject of the question, for it opened a pathway to precisely the area upon which Ptha would build his system of lies. Ptha had not yet worked out the details of how he would achieve this; the process of building false belief systems always had to be flexible and opportunistic. One worked with the subject's thoughts, questions, feelings, and desires as they presented themselves. When a useful idea or perspective arose, Ptha could select it, reinforce it, and then carefully weave it into the overall belief system being constructed.

I am not a creature of flesh, so my wisdom and understanding of all things material is limited. It is something I cannot help, Ptha answered, in all seriousness and with a touch of embarrassment, pretending he was unaware that the serpent had been teasing him. *But it is something I am working hard to overcome.*

But your first question suggests a second, Ptha continued, *and one that is worthy of our exploration. And that question is whether Adam is wiser than you, my student.*

The serpent was surprised. *Surely he must be. YHWH has placed Adam as sovereign over all the creatures of Earth; how could he not be wiser than those of his dominion?*

A very reasonable assumption. I'm sure there are many areas where his wisdom surpasses yours; but what you don't realize is that you in turn understand things he doesn't. YHWH has given to every creature its own kind of wisdom, to each as they have need.

Perhaps that's true, the serpent replied. *But what could I possibly know that would interest him? Shall I teach him how to slither and eat warm flesh? Or show him which rocks warm most quickly in the morning sun? Or instruct him on the fastest way to shed old skin? Even if he had interest in such things, it wouldn't take me long to tell all I know.*

You underestimate yourself, my student. You have more wisdom than you know. Not only that, but it is YHWH's intention that you increase in wisdom.

Ptha paused to allow that to sink in.

Why would YHWH want me to increase in wisdom? The turn in the conversation had the serpent completely baffled.

An excellent question; and a very wise one, I might add. One that deserves a proper answer. I can see that the time has come for me to confess that our first meeting did not happen by chance. Nor did I become your teacher simply because I desired to dwell with you. These things occurred because I had an assignment, a mission given to me by YHWH Himself.

Even as Ptha was verbalizing one lie, his mind was evaluating and choosing between alternative storylines several lies ahead. It reminded him of the countless deceits he had fashioned during the great rebellion, when every angel that was turned represented an important victory. Ptha had known then what few Daimónia knew to this day, namely that Satan's strategy was to amass the largest number of angels possible by whatever means necessary, and that any falsehood that worked was acceptable. It was immaterial whether they joined the ranks willingly and knowingly or whether they were tricked into crossing over. Satan had correctly deduced that once a spirit had been enticed to turn against YHWH, it could never turn back.

My assignment was not an easy one, Ptha continued, *nor did I have an abundance of time, for reasons you will understand shortly. Simply stated, my instructions were to search out the wisest creature in this region of Earth and to make it wiser still. There would only be time to choose and teach one student. That is why I observed you for so long before first speaking with you, and that's why I have spent so much time with you since. Although it is my nature to be forthright, I couldn't speak of this when we first met because I had to be sure I had chosen wisely. I know now that I have, and can now speak of these things with you.*

Ptha was pleased to see that faint traces of pride were already forming in response to his words. Ptha still marveled at how easily a creature's self-concept could be manipulated. Even though the serpent had not yet heard the rest of Ptha's deception, it had mentally accepted that Ptha was speaking truthfully, and that it had indeed been chosen above all the other creatures of the Earth.

But you still haven't told me why YHWH would wish me to increase in wisdom.

I'm coming to that, Ptha replied. *You may or may not know that Adam was only very recently placed on Earth. For every other creature of flesh, YHWH created female for male, and male for female. But for Adam there is no female. Consequently, Adam needs a suitable companion to converse with, one that can both understand and challenge his brilliant intellect. One that can learn from him the deep things of his mind, and one that can open his eyes to things he has not yet thought of. You, my student, are that one.*

The serpent's pride swelled. It was amazed that it had been chosen for this task, and was eager to hear more. Even as it was listening to Ptha's words, another part of the serpent's mind had filled with imaginary scenes in which it was patiently explaining hidden mysteries to the amazed and grateful sovereign of the Earth. Ptha paused for a few moments, allowing the serpent's imaginations to run their course; resuming only when the serpent's imaginations became repetitive.

So here is what we shall do, Ptha said. *I shall spend the next several days teaching you all that I can, preparing you for your first meeting with Adam. I warn you now that this time of preparation will be rigorous. Exhausting, in fact. And if we are to prepare properly, I must demand your complete trust and unquestioning obedience. Some things I will explain in detail, so that you can understand the why as well as the what. Others I will not have the time to fully explain and you must just accept what I tell you.*

I am honored by your choice Teacher, and will do all that you say. But I must ask — why wouldn't YHWH just have you converse with Adam, or another spirit like you?

It was a shrewd question, one that Ptha had anticipated and also hoped for. Ptha examined the serpent's thinking but detected no underlying suspicion.

Well, as it turns out, Adam does have a close spiritual companion; a spirit who accompanies him, converses with him, teaches him. His name is Asah. He doesn't look like me, but we came from the same father long ago. Sometimes he appears in material form, just as when I first met you; other times he is invisible. But there is a problem ...

Ptha paused, seemingly reluctant to continue.

What is the problem Teacher?

Asah was in fact sent to Adam to do just what you spoke of — to be his companion, to teach him and learn from him. And Asah was certainly qualified in terms of his intellect. There is no question that Asah is a brilliant spirit, much more so than I. Ptha knew the double meaning of his last statement wouldn't be perceived by the serpent, who knew nothing of the differences between spirits of darkness and angels of light. But Ptha loved to deceive while telling the truth, and considered it good sport to liberally sprinkle true statements amongst his lies.

But Asah's behavior has been increasingly strange of late, and has become a matter of concern to all of the spirits. More importantly, it has become of concern to YHWH. You see, Asah has always been a creative storyteller; it is one of his most enjoyable attributes. But it appears that his imagination has somehow gone awry, and that he now regards preposterous imaginations to be real. *As I am sure you realize, this is a very serious development. Particularly with him having been assigned to be Adam's intimate companion and guide.*

How can such a thing happen? The serpent was genuinely alarmed.

We don't know, Ptha replied. *Such a thing is without precedent. But whatever the reason, Adam needs to be weaned away from Asah's influence, and safeguarded from even the possibility of being harmed. That is where you come in. You are to become Adam's new friend and companion.*

Asah would harm Adam?

We hope not. But he could — if he ever chose to do so. You see, sometimes when Asah is not visible to us he is inside Adam, speaking with him just as I do you. It is possible that Asah could damage Adam's mind while he was a habitant inside Adam's body. That is one reason why you were chosen to be Adam's new companion. Being a creature of flesh, you could never pose such a danger to Adam. Not that YHWH thinks your imagination will ever run away with you, Ptha said, simulating laughter.

Also, Asah has become protective of his relationship with Adam. Think of how male rams protect and keep their ewes away from other rams during the rutting season and you'll grasp the concept I am speaking of. Asah has shown some antagonism when other spirits have come to visit with Adam. But we believe Asah is unlikely to object to Adam becoming friends with another creature of flesh.

So the habitation of flesh-creatures by spirits is a common practice then?

Ptha hadn't expected this question, but could use it nonetheless. Ptha wanted the serpent to feel both exclusive in its relationship with Ptha and a sense of rivalry toward Asah. By the time the serpent had finished thinking the question, Ptha was already stimulating the neurons that caused feelings of jealousy and competition. It was a mild stimulation — Ptha only wanted the serpent to feel a glimmer of the emotion — at least for now.

Simultaneously Ptha provided the basis for the feeling he had just initiated. Using all of his skill to mimic the sound and rhythm of the serpent's self-talk, Ptha whispered: *My relationship with Teacher is special. As sovereign of the Earth, Adam is also worthy of such a relationship, but it should be with a creature equal to the task. And while Teacher's words have been kind, Asah obviously is no longer worthy of being Adam's teacher.*

Ptha paused for a moment to see if the serpent owned the thought he had just planted. Satisfied, he then answered the serpent's question using the thought-voice the serpent was accustomed to. *It is actually quite rare. There are very few creatures with sufficient intellectual prowess to be of interest to the average spirit. And to my knowledge, our collaboration is the first time a spirit and creature of flesh have ever partnered to accomplish a mission on YHWH's behalf.* As he said this, Ptha loosed a diffuse feeling of well-being.

But returning to the topic at hand, you can now see why there is some urgency to this matter. I will go over the details of what you should and shouldn't do when speaking with Adam, but for now, you should remember two things. First, you must never mention in front of Asah that you and I have ever spoken, much less shared your body. To do so would stir up Asah's jealousy. Secondly, to be safe, I wouldn't even mention our relationship privately to Adam, lest he casually speak of it to Asah later, or worse, it happen at a time when Asah is indwelling Adam.

I will do as you say Teacher, the serpent answered. *Adam will only know me as the serpent that enjoys his company and delights in speaking with him. But what shall become of Asah?*

When the right time comes he shall be separated from Adam, but only when it can be done safely. Hopefully it will not be something you will have to witness.

Very well. I am ready to begin my preparation.

And I am ready to prepare you, my student. But you will need strength. Perhaps we should first find something to eat.

TWENTY-SIX

Mischiefs doth thy tongue devise, like a sharp razor, working deceit.

— Psalms 52:2 YLT

The time of preparation had been every bit as rigorous as Ptha had promised. The first four days had been filled with hour after hour of instruction. After the first night Ptha paused the training during the cold hours just before dawn, when the serpent's mental acuity invariably dipped along with the temperatures. But except for this nightly period of rest, the training continued non-stop.

Ptha had developed a detailed plan for teaching and preparing the serpent, and he followed this plan carefully, moving to the next stage of instruction only when he was comfortable that the serpent had mastered the current lesson. In some cases Ptha was simply trying to convey knowledge, and this was relatively easy because of the serpent's sharp intellect. But Ptha's training program encompassed more than just transferring knowledge. He was also trying to cultivate certain automatic responses from the serpent. In particular, he needed the serpent to be able to lie without hesitation and to deceive without discomfort. Even though the serpent had mentally accepted the need to be duplicitous (based on Asah's supposed instability), the creature was not yet emotionally comfortable with being deceitful. Ptha had anticipated this and was focusing much of his training regimen toward eliminating that discomfort.

Repetition is the key, Ptha thought. *The first lie is always the most troubling. But the more lies one speaks, the more natural it becomes.*

Ptha remembered his own "first lies" and his subsequent progression. At the time, it had surprised him how quickly he became accustomed to being untruthful. He attributed that in large part to his working so tirelessly to recruit other angels into the rebellion — meaning he was either speaking lies or conceiving lies every time he spoke with another angel. From his initial turning, it had been only a short period of time before Ptha was fully immersed in deceit.

Ptha had quickly reached the point where it was not only second-nature to deceive, but where he derived pleasure from it.

Lying is a most pleasant art, Ptha thought as he looked at the sleeping serpent. *I will teach you that pleasure. The day will come, my student, when you will lie without being aware of it. And if you do think about it, you will be proud of how well you do it.*

Dawn was an hour away and Ptha was still refining the day's study plan. During the preceding days, some of their conversations occurred while Ptha was in-dwelling the serpent; others while Ptha was in a materialized, visible form. But today the regimen would be different. From now on Ptha would no longer be visible to the serpent during their conversations, nor would he share the serpent's body while training was underway.

There were two reasons for this. Ptha had a growing concern that they might be observed speaking together, either by Adam or Asah. Although he remained vigilant while training was underway, there was still the chance that they might be observed from a distance. Secondly, because the serpent's initial conversations with Adam would all occur without Ptha being resident in the serpent's body, Ptha thought it prudent to complete the training in that mode. Ptha had no way of knowing for sure, but he suspected that his indwelling might subtly affect the serpent's thought processes even when Ptha wasn't doing or saying anything.

Ptha wasn't going to take any chances. He would do anything and everything he could think of to reduce the risk of the serpent erring and the mission being detected. Ptha knew that YHWH was not subject to odds or probabilities if He chose to be directly involved. But YHWH often seemed to allow events in the created realms to unfold without His direct intervention, a phenomenon most Daimónia believed was linked to God's irrevocable gift of free will. The proponents of this perspective argued that there would be no point in granting free will if YHWH then disallowed the implementation of freely made decisions just because they were contrary to His will. For obvious reasons, this topic was of great interest and relevance to the Archon as they considered alternative strategies for furthering the rebellion.

Ptha shared the opinion that the original grant of free will to the Daimónia was still in full effect, and that the Daimónia retained the external power "to do" along with the internal ability "to choose." The fact that Satan's rebellion had been permitted in the first place suggested how unalterable the original bequest of free will was. Yes, there had been the Great Fall, but that was a response, not an annulment of their initial decision to rebel. YHWH did nothing to stop Lucifer from seducing a third of the angelic host. Presumably He would have allowed all of the angels to defect had they chosen to do so.

The unchangeableness of God once a matter had been established was perhaps the one thing that offered their rebellion a slim chance of succeeding. Satan and all of the Archon knew that the Daimónia were incapable of mustering enough power to pose a direct threat to YHWH (though they never acknowledged this in front of the rank-and-file demons). The All-Powerful One really was all-powerful.

So Satan's current strategy was to somehow maneuver YHWH into a position where He could avoid defeat only by violating some aspect of His unchangeable nature. If that were ever to happen, it would *theoretically* leave God in conflict with Himself. YHWH would be forced to choose — either stay true to His unchangeable nature and voluntarily allow His own defeat, or violate His nature and become something other than what He has always been. Although either scenario would be a win for the Daimónia, nobody really wanted the latter scenario to occur. There was no telling what a dethroned but still all-powerful No-Longer-God might do.

What a bizarre irony, Ptha thought, *that we all desperately hope YHWH will remain true to His nature and behave like God even after defeat.*

Of course Ptha's fledgling plan of simultaneously betraying Satan and engineering a truce with heaven also carried immense risk. But Ptha simply didn't believe that Satan would ever be able to stalemate YHWH.

And failing such a stalemate, the current trend suggested that it was only a matter of time before they all were cast into the Abyss.

Ptha shuddered and pulled his thoughts back to the matters at hand. The sun had risen, the serpent was awake, and there was work to do today. For the moment at least, God's lack of direct intervention in the war between the Daimónia and the Anhailas meant that happenstance would continue to affect demon and angel alike. Consequently, Ptha had to assume that carefully laid and skillfully executed plans could affect the ultimate outcome.

The serpent was clearly ready to start and kept looking around even though Ptha had told him he would not be visible to him today.

"I am ready when you are," the serpent finally said quietly.

"You should always allow me to speak first." Ptha's reply was clear and easy to hear, but came from no place in particular. "My vision in both realms is much better than yours, and it is better that I first make sure there is no danger of our being overheard."

"Of course, Teacher."

"And do not call me Teacher any longer. If you were to be overheard, that might result in some awkward questions."

"I understand. Perhaps from now on I should speak as if I am musing to myself. Of course, you would know that it is really for your benefit, and could answer if and when you wish."

"Let's not make things more complicated than they need to be. When I am with you and it is safe, we can speak as we do now. But your idea may have its place. If you should absolutely require some guidance from me while you are with Adam, that might be a good way to communicate."

"Now I have some good news for you," Ptha continued. "Today we will complete your training, and once we are finished you will be ready to introduce yourself to Adam."

An iridescent sheen flashed across the serpent's normally glossy black surface, indicating excitement.

"But we still have one more training exercise. This morning you will pretend you are meeting and conversing with Adam. I will play the role of Adam. Take a few moments to prepare yourself and then begin when you are ready. If it helps to have an object to speak to, you can pretend this tree is Adam." Ptha struck a lower limb of the tree while remaining invisible. One of the tree's fruits fell and split partially open, revealing a firm, dark red interior that was quickly obscured an opaque, milky juice oozing out from the bruised flesh.

TWENTY-SEVEN

Every one that is proud in heart is an abomination to the LORD:
though hand join in hand, he shall not be unpunished.
— Proverbs 16:5 KJV

They were nearing the completion of the exercise. The serpent had handled the imaginary conversation with "Adam" well, even better than Ptha had hoped for. The creature didn't break character once, and its words seemed to Ptha to be genuine, natural, and at ease. The serpent had intuitively grasped the principle that the most effective deception was one that used falsehood sparingly, thereby minimizing the number of lies one had to keep track of.

Although it really wasn't necessary, Ptha kept the dialogue going. *I am being overly careful*, he thought. *I have covered every imaginable contingency and am starting to repeat myself. It is time to put the student to the test.*

Even though Ptha had maintained his normal vigilance throughout the exercise, his absorption with the question of whether he had done everything possible to prepare the serpent had commanded too much of his mental attention. It was for this reason that he didn't see the distant angel until it began moving toward them.

The serpent continued to talk but Ptha was no longer listening. He felt a surge of panic and quickly scanned the surrounding countryside. There were two other angels, both of which remained stationary for a few moments longer and then also began moving. All three were heading toward the serpent and the tree, approaching from different directions in

a deliberate and cautious fashion. Ptha surmised that their careful movement was not out of fear, but because they didn't want to call attention to
themselves as they drew nearer.

"Adam, are you there?" The serpent had sensed the break in Ptha's
attention, but was still maintaining the charade.

Ptha forcibly calmed himself. He wasn't afraid of a confrontation
with the angels, but he was terrified that they might have been found out
and that the plan would be compromised. Being ever cautious, he had kept
his body positioned inside the trunk of the tree, and he knew it was
unlikely that they had actually seen him from their distant vantage points.
Nor was it likely that they had overheard the quiet conversation between
Ptha and his student.

*No, their attention was captured by a serpent speaking to itself, or
perhaps to this tree,* Ptha reasoned. *They were watching discreetly and from a
distance to see who the other participant in the conversation might be, and seeing
none, finally decided to take a closer look.*

"Have I tired you with my many words, Adam? If you would like to
sleep, perhaps we could chat again later," the serpent quipped wryly, still in
character.

Ptha estimated that he had only a brief span of time left to speak
before the visitors arrived.

"Yes, I am rather tired," Ptha said. "And you, my student, have
exceeded my expectations. You truly are ready and have no further need
of speaking with old, tired trees. It is time for you to embark upon your
mission."

"I am ready, and am most pleased that you are pleased. Will you
take me to him?" the serpent asked.

"No, that would be unwise," Ptha said quietly, his eyes fixed upon
the nearest of the approaching angels. "But I will tell you where to find
him, and you can handle it from there. Go to the upper end of the valley,
where the hot springs flow down the mountainside of white rock. That is
where he dwells when he is not wandering or gathering food. If you start
now, you should reach the first hot springs along the way by early evening
— which I think you will find most enjoyable by the way — and should
arrive at his dwelling area before the end of the following day. Spend as
much time with him as he will allow, and we will meet again here, after

dark, in eight days. If for any reason I am delayed, remain in this area and I will find you."

"Is there time for us to find something to eat?" the serpent invited.

"No, you need to be on your way. But I promise we will when you return. And now I must be off to attend to other pressing matters. We will meet again soon."

The serpent lingered for a moment. "Very well, then. I will not fail you."

Hearing no answer, the serpent turned and began its journey up-valley.

TWENTY-EIGHT

And the angel who was speaking with me said to me, "I will show you what these are ... these are those whom the LORD has sent to patrol the earth." So they answered the angel of the LORD who was standing among the myrtle trees and said, "We have patrolled the earth, and behold, all the earth is peaceful and quiet."
— Zechariah 1:9b, 10b-11 NASB

They were part of the angelic rearguard. Their mission was to detect any incursions of the Daimónia into the garden and thereby prevent surprise attacks upon Adam. Although Adam and Asah had both been at Kikwmillu for the last four days, it was only a matter of time until Adam resumed his explorations of the garden. It would be very demon-like for some malevolent imp to slip into the garden under the cover of darkness and hide, perhaps for days, until Adam happened to pass by. As keen as the senses of the angels were, it was very difficult to intercept a demon entering under the cover of darkness. And during daylight hours it was equally difficult to find a demon that was well hidden and immobile. The angels might be able to discern that demons were present in the general vicinity, but pinpointing their precise location was another matter.

Rearguard units usually consisted of three or four angelic warriors. Their unit had been together since the beginning of the rebellion, having been one of the first to learn the tactics of war under Michael's brilliant and creative tutelage. They had now fought together, trained together, talked together, and worshipped together for so many centuries that it was a rare occurrence to see any of them by themselves. Although each member of the unit retained his individual personality, when the need arose they could function as if they had only one mind instead of three.

When patrolling the garden valley they often used a dispersed formation where only one of them moved at a time — the others watching for any response their moving comrade elicited. Each of them possessed a nearly infallible sense of location. Even when they all moved at once, they instinctively knew just where to look to find and communicate with each other. Although they were masters at fading into the landscape, they had long ago lost the ability to hide from each other.

Charuzt stopped moving forward when he spotted the serpent. It was apparent that a conversation was underway, but it wasn't clear whom the serpent was speaking to. Charuzt watched for a moment and then looked back at Emunah and Lahatmakaz, both of whom had stopped scanning the landscape and were watching Charuzt intently.

No words or hand signals were necessary; the subtle expression on Charuzt's face told them all they needed to know. Emunah, the unit's leader, was the first to reposition, swinging in a wide arc to Charuzt's right side and stopping where he had a clear view of the serpent, Charuzt, and the terrain behind Charuzt. When he was situated, Lahatmakaz duplicated the movement on the other side.

For a while they just watched, waiting for the other party of the conversation to show himself. It didn't appear that the serpent was talking to himself because his speech had the characteristic rhythm of dialogue. Yet the other party remained invisible.

Emunah eventually signaled for them to move close enough to hear what the serpent was speaking. But shortly after they started to reposition, the serpent ceased talking, dropped to the ground, and glided away in the direction of the upper valley. Lahatmakaz inquired via hand-signal whether he should break away to follow the serpent, but Emunah decided they should continue their convergence toward the tree. Nobody had seen the other participant of the conversation leave, if there was one.

They halted upon Emunah's signal, their positions forming an equilateral triangle with the tree in the center. They were close enough to the tree that nothing could be hidden from their collective view, yet far enough away that the tree didn't obscure their view of the areas behind and above their comrades.

They all had expected to find some small creature that the serpent had been conversing with, and when they didn't, it further aroused their curiosity and caution. While it seemed unlikely that a demon would be conversing with a serpent, they all knew that the Daimónia had shown an unprecedented interest in the animals of late. Even though that interest had been of a cruel and self-gratifying nature, none of the ranking Anhailas assumed that it was wholly without purpose. The fact that this new interaction between the Daimónia and the animals had occurred only in the region around Eden and nowhere else on the planet was a strong indication of some demonic intent behind the interaction.

Emunah signaled Charutz to "examine" the tree, which meant that Charutz would penetrate the interior of the solid trunk and incapacitate or flush out any demon that might be hiding there. If the trunk was unoccupied, Charutz would next examine the soil column beneath the tree. Emunah and Lahatmakaz would remain in their positions, at the ready to intercept any spirit attempting to make a quick exit. If the soil beneath the tree was also vacant of any inhabitant, then it would be just one more unsolved mystery.

In a flash Charuzt drew his sword, increased his brilliance, and streaked toward the tree. An instant later, just before he reached the tree, Charuzt was thrown backwards with terrific force. To his two comrades it looked like he had been dealt some massive blow from an invisible adversary, and they rushed to stand on either side of their stunned comrade, swords drawn and at the ready.

But nothing happened. No enemy materialized and there was no further attack.

"What happened?" Emunah asked, still facing outwards from Charuzt, who had regained his feet but was still shaken.

"I don't know. I hit something or something hit me, I'm not sure which. But it felt more like a wall than a blow."

Lahatmakaz, who was closest to the tree, walked forward with his light-sword extended while the others watched. While still several paces from the tree, his sword silently deflected to one side. Tapping with his sword to identify the location of the invisible wall, Lahatmakaz slowly extended one hand to touch the wall, unsure whether the wall would react differently to the touch of an angel than it did to that of a light-sword, and not wanting to repeat Charuzt's experience.

Lahatmakaz kept his hand against the wall as he slowly walked along it. The wall was smooth and hard, and had a slight curvature with the tree in its center.

"It is the tree Asah told us about," Lahatmakaz called back with astonishment. "We cannot approach any closer because of ..." Lahatmakaz stopped in mid-sentence as he finally looked up toward the other two and was summarily silenced both by the rebuke in Emunah's eyes as well as his hand signal to be silent. Emunah had already deduced where they were and what this tree was, but had retained the presence of mind to not say anything.

Lahatmakaz realized his mistake instantly, but was too seasoned and well-trained to dwell upon the ramifications of his error. His eyes spoke a brief apology to his comrades and then he waited for Emunah's decision on how to proceed.

Emunah realized they could accomplish nothing further and finally signaled for them to resume their patrol. They would speak more of this later when they were no longer near the tree. If a demon were hiding in the tree, which Emunah now thought was fairly likely, there was no way for them to make it show itself. Any further activity on their part would only make it clearer than it already was that they were incapable of doing *anything* inside the barrier. And attempting to out-wait the demon would be equally futile and also demonstrate their limitations — not to mention how much time they would waste if it turned out the tree was vacant after all. The best thing to do was to move on and hope this entire spectacle had not been observed by the enemy.

TWENTY-NINE

Revealed to thee were the gates of death? And the gates of death-shade dost thou see?
— Job 38:17 YLT

For all that is in the world, the lust of the flesh and the lust of the eyes and the boastful pride of life, is not from the Father ...
— I John 2:16a NASB

Several hours after the angels had left, after it had become fully dark, Ptha emerged from the trunk of the tree. He was still astounded at his good fortune, and chuckled every time he recalled the sequence of events. He had been tempted to taunt the trio when he first realized they were unable to approach the tree, but since that would only confirm that their mishap had been witnessed, he restrained himself.

Ptha examined the area where the angel had circled the tree, but could discern nothing out of the ordinary. He could neither see nor feel the barrier that had excluded the angels. Standing at the same point where the angel had halted, Ptha mentally projected a circle around the tree of equal radius, carefully noting where the circle occurred in relation to features on the ground. If he couldn't feel or otherwise sense the barrier, then he would memorize where he believed it to be before he left.

Ptha considered traveling up-valley and catching up with the serpent, wishing he could observe its first encounter with Adam from a distance. But there was little to be gained by that course of action — the serpent would either succeed or not, and Ptha's presence would do nothing to increase the chance of success. In fact, his presence could complicate matters if Asah or some other angel sensed he was in the vicinity.

Ptha decided to finish his examination and then report his new findings to the Council. He was relieved that the mission had not been compromised, but he also felt a strange excitement about the discovery of the tree. It took some time and reflection for him to put a name on the emotion.

I do believe I am feeling hope, Ptha thought to himself. *How unusual. Maybe it will even last for a while.* It was so hard not to be pessimistic.

Without question there would be return trips to study the tree. They would need to verify whether the tree's exclusionary properties were permanent in nature rather than temporary or episodic. It would also be useful to know if Adam was subject to the barrier, or if that was not the case, whether his normal spiritual powers were reduced or absent within the "zone." And once the properties of the tree and the zone were fully defined, they then had to develop a working theory as to why such a phenomenon should be present in the garden of Eden.

That's the real mystery, Ptha thought. *Why would God allow the garden to contain an area from which angels are excluded and to which demons have free access? And what are the odds of my being safely inside the tree precisely when an enemy patrol is passing by?*

If Ptha had been one of the rank-and-file Daimónia he would have attributed his good fortune to the powerful hand of Lucifer. But as one of the Archon, he knew that Lucifer had no such power.

But that won't stop him from taking credit for it, Ptha thought. He knew that his encounter with the angels would be transformed into an epic account that would be widely circulated among the legionnaires. He was so certain of this eventuality that Ptha decided to be the one to suggest it at the next Council meeting. There would be embellishments, of course, and the very existence of this strange place would be attributed to Satan. But that was all as it should be.

This couldn't have come at a better time, so soon after the loss of Shaarur and his legion. The hordes need to believe that they can win battles as well as lose them. And when they hear how their sovereign craftily implanted an unassailable fortress of darkness in the very midst of YHWH's special garden, they will scream with delight.

If the tree never serves any useful purpose other than lifting the morale of the Daimónia, that will be enough. But Ptha was confident that the tree and its properties *would* be put to good use; the Council would see to that.

Having completed his examination in the material realm, Ptha slipped back into the aether. He returned to the area where the exclusion zone ended, this time on the spirit side of the interface. But just like before, he found no evidence of any invisible barrier. He shifted his position to the area above the tree to see if a change in perspective made any difference. It didn't. And then, being thorough, he moved to the area below the tree.

He sensed a change as soon as he moved under the tree. After losing his light-craft during the fall, Ptha had developed a honed sensitivity to nuances in the strength and spectral composition of the aetherial realm's ambient light. There was a shadow beneath the tree, one that seemed to extend from beneath the canopy of roots downward. Even though it was only slightly darker than elsewhere beneath the soil surface, it was clearly discernible. And the shadow was not only discernible to the eye; Ptha could feel it as well. Each time he crossed back over its edge, it triggered a faint sensation at some deep level.

Ptha flew in a trajectory that would have been downwards into the earth if he had been on the material side of the interface. The shadow continued, undiminished and unchanged in its dimensions. Interestingly, it extended in the same direction that Ptha would travel in returning to Satan's domain.

Perhaps it's not a shadow at all in the sense of being caused by the tree. Perhaps it is a corridor of darkness that extends all the way to the dark realms. Ptha knew his imagination was running ahead of sound reasoning, but the orientation of the passageway certainly suggested the possibility. He wondered if the Anhailas were excluded from the shadow passage in the same way they were from the area around the tree.

Ptha decided to follow the shadow route as far as it led, but remembering something, returned upward to the tree to check one last thing. Upon reaching the ground surface, he re-entered the material realm and examined the shallow soil around its roots. He had noticed earlier the absence of ground vegetation beneath the tree's canopy, but hadn't attached any significance to the observation.

His hunch proved correct. The only living plant roots beneath the tree's canopy were those of the tree itself. Just as strange was the lack of the normal soil fauna. Insects, worms, and other invertebrates — all were absent. At the edge of the barrier Ptha discovered that the roots of the surrounding plants were all truncated in a neat circle surrounding the tree. Looking more closely, he saw that the root ends were black and dead, almost as if they had been burnt, or perhaps poisoned. He occasionally observed the body of some small burrowing insect, but these were found only just inside the circle

Everything that enters the circle dies, Ptha realized. *This tree kills every living thing, plant or animal, which tries to occupy the soil beneath its canopy!*

I have discovered the Tree of Death! Ptha said to himself in utter amazement.

THIRTY

He who dwells in the secret place of the Most High shall abide under the shadow of the Almighty.
                    — Psalms 91:1 NKJV

The serpent arrived at Kikwmillu falls before dawn, much earlier than Teacher had predicted. The serpent had detected the warming trend of the river while still far downstream of the overflowing hot pools, and since the lower river provided long reaches of easy passage, the serpent swam the first portion of its journey, leaving the channel only where necessary to circumvent the more powerful cascades.

Upon reaching the first hot pools, the serpent didn't stop as Teacher suggested, but continued up-valley. Lingering in one of the pools would have been pleasant, but the warmth of the river water had already buoyed the serpent's metabolism to such an energized state that it chose to press on in spite of the evening chill. Only upon reaching the waterfall, where overland travel was the only way to proceed, did the serpent stop to wait for daylight.

The serpent spent the last few hours before dawn lolling in the steaming shallows of the waterfall pool, exposing just enough of its body to the night air to maintain its body temperature within a comfortable range. Normally it didn't move around much until the morning warmed up, but it was so anxious to meet Adam that it left the pool shortly after first light. The first portion of the ascent next to the waterfall went quickly, but well before reaching the top the serpent's upward progress began to slow. The cold ground, cold air, and lack of direct sunlight all sapped its residual body warmth, resulting in the inevitable loss of strength as its core temperature dropped. The serpent eventually stopped, and resigning itself to the reality of the situation, curled itself into a tight ball on a rock platform that would catch the morning sun once it crested the steep valley walls.

If Teacher were with me he would have kept me warm, the serpent thought through deepening stupor, *just like when we crossed the mountains together into Adam's valley.*

It was mid-morning when the serpent finally reached the top of the escarpment. It immediately submerged into the warm water of one of the shallow sluiceways, scanning the shoreline of the tarn lake for any sign of Adam as its body temperature crept back up. Although the serpent's perception of its immediate surroundings was sharp and clear, its ability to see at great distance was poor. In contrast, its sense of smell was acute and discerning. Every time its tongue flicked out, it gathered dozens of scents from the air, all of which it unconsciously sorted and classified by category and strength. When it chose to, it could just as easily taste the spoor carried in the water or left on the soil surface. The serpent didn't know what Adam's scent smelled like, but it was able to recognize warm-blooded, mammalian scents, and it knew the individual scents of all of the region's more common creatures.

The serpent began gliding back and forth across the lower end of the tarn lake, just above the outflow to the falls, alternately tasting the water and the air, looking for any new scent. The water bore the taste of several different types of waterfowl and wading birds — ruddy shelducks, red-crested pochards, teal, and even black stork. There were detectable undertones of pika and dwarf hamster, the faint essence of their droppings having washed into the lake from hundreds of colonies in the high mountain boulder fields. And in the air there was the ubiquitous scent of bezoar goats and mouflon sheep, which was always heaviest in the morning. In addition to all of the organic scents, there were the pervasive flavors of iron, sulfur, and various other chemicals from the mineral-rich hot springs.

Although the serpent encountered several new scents, none of them seemed right for a large mammal. It concluded that these were probably from alpine creatures that didn't live in the lower valley habitats the serpent was more familiar with. Finding nothing of interest in the water, the serpent left the lake and moved perpendicular away from the lake shoreline, carefully checking the ground for scent-trails, hoping to cross some pathway Adam had used.

This approach worked. Almost immediately the serpent encountered a strange, new mammalian spoor that ran parallel to the lake. The scent-trail was strong, with both fresh and aged layers, and of sufficient width to indicate that the trail had been traveled over numerous times. Unfortunately, this same characteristic made it impossible to determine the most-recent direction the trail-maker had traveled.

The serpent followed the trail for several minutes in both directions to develop a sense of where the trail went to and from. The trail was obviously circumscribing the lake, the upslope route heading toward the white, terraced pools at the upper end of the valley and the other heading back toward the waterfall. The serpent decided to follow the up-valley trail first, reasoning that its length in that direction would soon be limited by the looming rock walls.

Of course, Adam might be able to climb rock walls as well as any ibex, the serpent thought, *in which case the trail might go right up the mountainside.* Although the serpent could climb steep slopes of broken or eroded rock, it knew its limitations and would never attempt a vertical or steeply sloping ascent where the rock had been worn smooth by water and wind.

The up-valley trail weakened and then disappeared at the point where the stepped hot pools spilled into the lake. The serpent considered crossing to the far side of the pool staircase to see if the trail reappeared, but finally decided it was more sensible to turn around and retrace the known pathway rather than spend time searching for the resumption of a trail that might not exist.

As the serpent followed the trail around the lake back toward the waterfall, it periodically sampled the air to see if the Adam-scent could be picked up on the breeze. Its forked tongue gave it the ability to differentiate the direction from which an airborne scent was originating as long as there was at least a slight breeze. But Adam's scent was only detectable on the ground.

As the trail approached the rocky platform of the waterfall, the ground-scent briefly disappeared as the serpent crossed each flow-way, only to resume again on the other side. When the trail reached the edge of the platform it turned right, skirting the edge until finally disappearing at a wide, flow-way that spilled over the precipice in several locations. The serpent checked the far side of the flow-way, but the trail didn't emerge there. Unless Adam made a practice of leaping over the edge of the water-fall, this point represented a destination of some sort.

The flow-way had the same almost-hot temperature as the tarn lake, and while the shallow channel was wide, the force of the water flowing through it was not overly strong. Upon looking over the edge, the serpent saw that unlike most of the rest of the waterfall, the water here did not plunge straight down from the lip, but tumbled and sprayed over a series of three ledges before finally falling free. The serpent surveyed the ledges as best it could from above, but saw no sign of Adam.

The serpent's disappointment began to transform into apprehension. In spite of the scent-trail having been strong and recent, both ends had failed to lead it to Adam. The serpent had never considered that Adam might prove difficult to locate, or worse yet, that it might have to return to Teacher having failed at its assigned task.

The serpent thought through the alternatives. It could backtrack and check the edges of the trail to see if it had bypassed some intersection with a side trail. It could search for completely new trails and follow them to their endpoints, just as it had this one. And it could ask some of the more intelligent animals where they had last seen Adam. But if those approaches didn't work, the serpent would have no recourse except to select one of the better-used trails and wait for Adam to appear.

If the serpent's voice was strong, it might have called out as it searched. But its voice, while clear, would never carry over any significant distance. Listening to the ever-present roar of the waterfall in the background, it realized that its loudest vocalization would be inaudible a short distance away.

And that's when it heard it.

Someone was singing!

The serpent didn't know if the singing had been there all along, almost drowned out by the waterfall, or if it had just started. But now that it was listening, every now and then the faintest snatch of song could be clearly heard. And the song wasn't just melody; it had words as well.

It must be Adam!

It was very difficult to tell where the song was coming from. The serpent's most sensitive method of perceiving sound came through absorbing ground-borne vibrations into its body; the sound waves being transmitted through the air-space of its single lung to the bones of its internal middle ears. But the thunder of the waterfall filled the ground so full of vibrations that nothing could be heard that way. Instead, the serpent had to lift its head high into the air to try to detect where the airborne sound waves were coming from.

At first it seemed as if the song was rising up from below the water-fall, but the serpent couldn't imagine that Adam could sing *that* loudly. The serpent moved and listened; moved and listened, again and again. After several minutes the serpent felt fairly sure that the song was emanating from somewhere on one of the ledges below, but looking from above it could see nothing but swirling water and glistening rock.

I'll have to take a closer look.

The serpent wasn't happy about this prospect. It understood that flowing water could be incredibly strong, and its relatively large body provided a large surface area for the water to push against. Although the flow-way above the ledges was shallow and broad, the water became progressively more concentrated with each drop, which meant that the strength of the currents also became correspondingly stronger.

The serpent reasoned that Adam might have similar concerns about being swept away, and examined each ledge for the safest route Adam might have taken to descend. There was one strip of slightly higher rock that extended all the way down to the third ledge; the rock being wet with spray but not underwater. This route appeared passable. Even if it was not the one Adam had taken, it would at least permit the upper ledges to be viewed from below.

The serpent carefully slid down, bracing its body against every out-swelling of rock and using all four limbs as well. Once on the first ledge, it paused both to listen and to look for Adam in both directions. It repeated the process until it was on the third platform, still catching no glimpse of the one singing.

The singing was louder on the third ledge, but still seemed to be coming from below. The serpent inched its way toward the final edge, keeping its body centrally located on the now greatly narrowed emergent strip of rock. The feeling of fear had become palpable. If it lost its grip here, there would be nothing to save it from a quick and terrible death. It inserted its clawed toes and fingers into the deepest cracks it could find, and only once it had anchored itself did it stretch its neck and head out over the edge.

Adam was directly below the serpent, nestled comfortably and at ease in a concavity of the rock, alternately speaking and then singing at full volume, showing no awareness that he was being watched from above. The serpent could hear the words now, and it was clear that he was communing with YHWH, though the serpent couldn't see anyone else around.

In spite of its fear, the serpent had enough appreciation of beauty to recognize how unusual Adam's perch was. While the water coursed by on either side of them, the area immediately in front provided a clear, open view of the valley below. But even more amazing was the band of brilliant, vibrant colors that hung in the mist and spray of the waterfall just below them. The serpent had seen tiny versions of colors like these on the sheen of its black skin just after shedding, but the bands of vibrant color below them were immense in comparison, both wider and longer than the serpent's entire body.

The serpent returned its gaze to Adam, studying the body cradled in the rock. Adam was soaked, the warm spray dripping off his facial hair and nose, running down his body and gathering in a pool at the base of Adam's seat. Being a mammal, the serpent had imagined Adam would be fully covered with hair, but while Adam's hair was thick in many places, his skin was also plainly visible over much of his body. It gave him a most unusual appearance.

Throughout the serpent's examination Adam continued to sing and speak with his eyes closed. The serpent had assumed that Adam was not aware that he had an observer, and was debating whether to interrupt him when Adam stopped singing, looked up, and spoke directly to the serpent.

"Welcome!" Adam said in a shout just loud enough to be heard over the waterfall. "I have wanted to see a horned serpent, and you are my first. Thank you for waiting while I gave the Most High my full attention. Come; let us find a quieter place to talk."

THIRTY-ONE

… deceit it hath spoken in its mouth, peace with its neighbour it
speaketh, and in its heart it layeth its ambush.
— *Jeremiah 9:8b YLT*

Adam led the serpent away from the waterfall, following the trail until turning aside onto a long finger of rock that extended out into the lake. At the end of the extension Adam slipped into the waist-deep water and began digging up water chestnut tubers with his feet. After snapping off the attached rhizomes, Adam rubbed the tubers between his fingers to scrub off the grit, dipped them for a final rinse, and then popped each tuber into his mouth whole, chewing and talking at the same time.

Adam's questions were endless, and the serpent answered each one thoroughly and thoughtfully. Adam was delighted to learn about the everyday life of horned serpents, commenting on how rare it was to find a reptile that was a worthy conversationalist. And in truth, Adam's conversations with Asah had been less frequent of late and Adam was glad for some intelligent dialogue.

"The ways and natures of reptiles are so different from the ways of mammals; I never would have expected a serpent to be so capable of wit and careful thought," Adam said as he climbed up onto the rock and slicked the water off his body in long, smooth strokes.

"The pleasure and privilege is mine," the serpent replied. "To be able to meet and converse with the sovereign of the earth is an honor and a joy … though I should add that I have met some mammals that are every bit as dull of mind as the average tortoise."

"I didn't realize tortoises could speak." Adam replied. He had occasionally come across spur-thighed tortoises plodding across the dry, rocky hillsides of the neighboring valleys, but they had never engaged in conversation, nor for that matter, paid any attention to him whatsoever.

"My point exactly."

Adam chuckled. He noticed that while the serpent didn't laugh, it *did* bob its head to one side whenever it said something with an element of humor. He realized that part of what made this creature so fascinating was that he couldn't intuitively read its emotions; none of the normal mammalian cues of facial expression or posture applied.

"Well, I am pleased that you sought me out, and hope that you will stay a while. I welcome your companionship."

The serpent's body scales flashed with a slight blush of color, which Adam took to be another indicator of emotion, though he didn't know which one.

"I have nowhere I have to go," the serpent said. "I hadn't planned on overwintering in this valley, but now I have good reason to, having met you. Besides, the mountain passes have already become cold and it is probably too late for me to safely cross back over to my home valley. So … I would be most pleased to stay here, perhaps until next spring's mating season. I need only to wander off every week or so in search of suitable food; otherwise, I am at your disposal."

"Good; it is settled then. Whenever we are both unoccupied and have the inclination to talk, we can meet here."

"Agreed. A delightful proposition. But Adam, why you would choose me for a companion? Surely you have many others to choose from."

"Not so many as you might think. Most animals, mammal or reptile, aren't given to prolonged conversation."

"Of course, but have you no one to talk to; have you no female?" The serpent remembered what Teacher had said about Adam having no female, and had wondered at the time why this should be so.

Adam didn't answer. He looked down at himself; not that it was necessary — he knew that he was male. It's just that he had never wondered about his maleness before. And the fact that he hadn't, when he spent so much time thinking about everything worth thinking about, was in itself unusual.

The serpent's question was so obvious, and it opened the door to so many others. *Why would YHWH make me male if there was to be no female? He could have made me like Asah — neither male nor female. But He didn't. I am male, and surely YHWH had purpose in making me so.*

The thought caused a strange stirring in Adam's body and soul. His mind was consumed with the possibility that there was ... or someday would be ... a female for him. In a flash of insight, he realized that his earlier conclusion that YHWH would someday create children was incorrect. There was still much about the making of young that he didn't understand, but he *had* been observant. With every animal he knew of, the making of young required a female as well as a male!

When Adam finally looked up, he saw that the serpent had settled into a low coil and was watching him intently. He noticed its color had become greatly dulled.

"Did I say something wrong?" the serpent asked, breaking the silence.

"No. Not at all. It's just that I have no female."

THIRTY-TWO

... behold, a throne set in heaven, and One sat on the throne ... before the throne there was a sea of glass, like crystal ...
— Revelation 4:2a, 6a NKJV

And I saw something like a sea of glass mingled with fire ...
— Revelation 15:2a NKJV

... and there was under His feet as it were a paved work of sapphire stone, and it was like the very heavens in its clarity.
— Exodus 24:10b NKJV

For you have said in your heart: "I will ascend into heaven, I will exalt my throne above the stars of God; I will also sit on the mount of the congregation on the farthest sides of the north; I will ascend above the heights of the clouds, I will be like the Most High."
— Isaiah 14:13-14 NJKV

... therefore I cast you as a profane thing out of the mountain of God; and I destroyed you, O covering cherub, from the midst of the fiery stones.
— Ezekiel 28:16b NKJV

Once an assignment was given, angels usually remained on location until their mission was accomplished, or until they received orders recalling them to heaven or redirecting them to some other task. Asah had not been to heaven since Adam's awakening, having either been constantly with Adam or attending to matters related to the security of the garden.

But there *was* a procedure for requesting an audience with YHWH prior to a mission being accomplished, and for only the second time since his own awakening, Asah had sent one of the angels under his command to request that he be allowed to return to heaven. The leave had been granted and Asah was headed heavenward, having left Adam in the charge of several capable Anhailas.

Asah had never forgotten Adam's first encounter with the tree of knowledge of good and evil, or how the interface had been hardened around the tree so that Asah could not approach it. It had been a point of concern at the time, but with the recent report from Emunah's patrol, Asah's concern had blossomed into alarm.

Asah didn't believe for a second that the suspicious activities observed by the patrol were without meaning. The Daimónia knew about the tree — of that he was sure. And even though he had no direct evidence, he was fairly sure that the environs of the tree were accessible to them. If that were not the case, the tree would have held no interest for them.

They will find a way to use this to their advantage, Asah thought. They could entice Adam to enter the exclusion zone and try to kill or maim him. Of course, the results of such an attempt would not be a foregone conclusion. Adam would presumably retain all his authority and power as sovereign of the earth. Just because angels were without power beneath the tree didn't mean Adam was powerless, and that possibility would not escape the Daimónia. The battle of Shaarur had taught them that Adam had the ability to bring destruction by his word even before angels were involved.

Asah knew that whatever plan they chose, it would be carefully thought out; one that offered the Daimónia the greatest potential for a long-term strategic advantage. Killing Adam would accomplish little if YHWH simply spoke a word of healing and breathed new life into Adam. The Daimónia would consider this eventuality as well, and probably reckon that killing Adam would yield little net gain.

But if the Daimónia could entice Adam to sin ….

Even Asah didn't know the full implications of that.

It's what I would do if I were in their place. They know too well there was neither tolerance nor remedy for their sin. If Adam were to join them in their disobedience, they would expect YHWH to do to Adam what they could not do. The thought of inciting YHWH to destroy a creature He loved so greatly would hold irresistible appeal to Satan.

And if YHWH didn't destroy Adam, Satan would reason that Adam would at least be banished from the presence of God, and that Adam's current authority and spiritual power would be rescinded. If YHWH also recalled Adam's angelic protection, then the Daimónia could subsequently maim or torment Adam at will.

The more Asah thought about it, the more convinced he became that Satan's end game had to be to lead Adam into sin. Perhaps they hadn't arrived at that conclusion yet, but they would in time. And once they did, it wouldn't be long before they began setting their traps. Asah's job would be to recognize and disarm those traps, and to teach Adam to do the same.

Asah reasoned that for the Daimónia to succeed, they would have to have direct interaction with Adam at some point. In the entire demon horde, Lucifer was the only one in which sin originated without outside assistance — every other fallen angel was led into sin by persuasion, by deceit, or by implanting the desire for something forbidden.

Of course, Adam's first line of defense would be to do exactly what YHWH had commanded Adam to do: guard the garden. And Asah and his troop would continue to assist Adam in doing that. If the Daimónia were denied entry to the garden, then they would be denied access to Adam. Secondly, Adam had shown he was quite capable of dealing with any demons that did slip in. His responses to demonic encounters to date had been strong and decisive, and he had shown no inclination to engage in unnecessary dialogue. Nevertheless, Asah decided he should reinforce his earlier warnings about conversing with demons.

In spite of his concern about leaving Adam and the garden, Asah was glad to finally be returning to heaven. In the material realm the clouds that shrouded planet earth were bright and white, illuminated by radiant sunshine from the outside. But in the aetherial realm, the environs of the earth were clouded by shadows and opaque mists, all of which were darkened from the earth outward. As Asah moved heavenward and the shadows lessened, he could feel himself being refreshed and strengthened.

I have been down there so long that I have grown accustomed to the shadows, Asah reflected. May YHWH hasten the day when the earth is once again clothed in His undiminished glory.

Asah's first request in his audience with YHWH would be to augment the forces assigned to guarding Adam and the garden, and to have additional forces on call at Asah's request. Asah didn't want to be overwhelmed by sheer numbers if the Daimónia elected to launch some massive infiltration. Asah felt reasonably sure this request would be granted.

Asah couldn't make up his mind about the second request. He would have liked to ask YHWH for the ability to penetrate the barrier around the tree; for the tree to be as accessible to him and the Anhailas as any place else in the garden.

But Asah knew that request would not be granted, at least not in such a direct form. YHWH had placed the barrier there for a reason, and consequently, any request Asah might make would have to give proper regard to that reason. Asah would never ask YHWH to change His mind or reconsider His actions; that simply wasn't the way one approached the Almighty. But Asah could make requests that improved his ability to protect Adam without suggesting the barrier be removed.

To do that, Asah needed a better understanding of the barrier and why YHWH had placed it there. That and any wisdom YHWH might grant on how Asah could best protect Adam with the barrier being in place.

Asah had fully entered the outer reaches of heaven. The shadows of earth were far behind him now, completely dispelled by the light emanating from the presence of God. He still hadn't reached the substantial portion of heaven, where heaven's terrain rose majestically out of the fathomless expanse of the deep, but it would be coming into sight soon.

Asah loved re-entry. The light was sustenance to him, as it was to every angel. He could feel the reserves of his strength being replenished. While he hadn't thought of himself as being fatigued when he had left earth, the effect of the nurturing light clearly showed that he had been.

But the strengthening effect of the light upon his angelic body was only part of it. There was also an effect upon his inner essence, the core being within his spirit body. The weight of the assigned responsibility of watching over Adam was lightening — not lessening, for the responsibility was no less there — but the effort required for him to constantly bear it was perceptibly diminishing.

Asah detected the first stirring of the wellspring of joy within him. It usually happened just before making heavenfall, just before heaven's terrain came into view. It was a delightful sensation, even at this subdued level. From here forward, as long as he was heading in the direction of the presence of God, it would increase in intensity. The stirring would become a trickle, the trickle a stream, the stream an irrepressible fountain. By the time the throne of God actually came into view, Asah would be beside himself with joy.

It was, in fact, God welcoming him back from a distance. YHWH was letting him know that his approach had been noticed, and that the Most High was joyfully anticipating their face-to-face meeting.

It always amazed Asah how God could be so totally immersed in communion and companionship with each of heaven's countless inhabitants at the same time. Asah could track multiple conversations that were within his range of hearing, and he could speak to other angels while remaining fully alert to any word or urging YHWH might give him. But no created being came any where close to exhibiting God's capacity for simultaneous fellowship.

That's what limitlessness is all about, Asah thought. *I am limited; He is not. He is present in every place He chooses to be. And for those places he chooses not to project His presence, He remains fully aware of them. Nothing is hidden from His view. The deepest depths of the Abyss are as plain to Him as my feet are to me.*

Heaven's landscape had just come into view, though it would be several minutes before there was sufficient resolution to make out anything or anyone. Even at this distance the intensity of the light would have been enough blind the eye of any creature of flesh. It was also enough to repulse any Daimónia that might seek to re-enter heaven.

No need to post angelic guards on the outskirts of heaven, Asah mused. *No demon would ever approach this closely; the pain would be too great. And if they could somehow endure the pain, the light would consume them long before they touched down on solid ground.*

One curious thing about the form of heaven was that when it initially came into view, it appeared to be a flat wall perpendicular to Asah's flight path. But as he drew nearer, the orientation of the surface slowly shifted to that of an easy, gentle incline, all without Asah changing his direction of flight. By the time the forests and rivers and lakes of heaven took on clear shape, Asah was no longer flying toward heaven, but up heaven. Notwithstanding the substantial topography of the terrain (for there were tall mountains and deep valleys as far as the eye could see), the landscape as a whole still had a perceptible slope. Upslope was the direction one took to approach the throne of YHWH; downslope was the direction away from it. The Anhailas even had two different words for up and two for down, depending on whether the reference point was the ground surface or the throne of the Most High.

Needless to say, there was nothing higher than the throne of the Most High.

Another minor mystery, at least to Asah, was how unpopulated heaven was. As innumerable as the angelic host seemed, there *was* a finite number of angels, for they had all been individually created and awakened. But here on heaven's outer slopes, Asah had yet to sight one of his brethren. It always seemed incongruous to Asah for God to have created heaven so large and then leave it so empty of inhabitants.

The perception of heaven being underpopulated would change as Asah flew higher. The closer he drew to the throne of God, the more crowded it would become. And the more noisy. This was to be expected, for as one approached Him, one's excitement and joy reached the point where it was delightfully unbearable and progressively less containable. Every angel had their own way of expressing their delight, some shouted, some sang, some laughed, and some did all three. There were also those that suddenly erupted from their line of flight into elaborate aerial displays of loops, spins, spirals, turns, summersaults, and other unnamed maneuvers. This last group of angels always took longer to reach their destinations, and when three or four broke into a coordinated group maneuver, it delayed everyone around them as they stopped to applaud and shout their approval.

Asah passed his first out-bound comrade, an angel traveling downslope on some errand. Asah flashed a greeting and received one in return, neither of them stopping to exchange pleasantries.

Asah had finally decided to keep his inquiry about the barrier short and direct. Rather than trying to puzzle out what the right questions were, he would simply ask YHWH to impart whatever understanding Asah needed to effectively protect Adam when he was within the tree's exclusion zone. This approach also had merit because it was to the point (which was always appropriate during an individual audience with Him) and because it relied upon God to convey what Asah needed to know.

The mount of the congregation was now in view, and Asah angled his flight path upward (in both senses) to begin the long ascent toward the throne. At the proscribed distance from the throne, he would alight on the ground and make the last leg of his approach on foot. Even though Asah knew his arrival would be greeted with warmth and love, there were protocols for how one presented oneself to YHWH. One observed the protocols to show due honor and reverence, even at a distance. One also observed the protocols to preserve one's life.

The origin of the protocols was a mystery. None of the Anhailas could remember ever having been instructed on what was or wasn't appropriate and allowable in approaching YHWH, or while in audience with Him. They all just had a sense of what was right. Some angels believed it had been instilled in them at their awakening. But the majority opinion was that the protocols had in fact never been defined, but had arisen solely out of the innate desire of all Anhailas to show how deeply they honored and loved the One they served. Soon after their awakening, the ways in which that could be done had all been discovered and in short order had been universally adopted. Once adopted they became custom, and at that point any divergence from what had become accepted as customary carried the risk of being regarded as dishonor.

It wasn't that angels had poor memories. They all remembered the awe and wonder of their individual awakenings, and their times of discovery afterwards. But because they lived only to please Him, it never occurred to any of them to identify the limits of what they could and couldn't do and still live. The topic itself would have been unseemly to think about, had it even occurred to them.

But it had occurred to Lucifer, and he obviously gave it much thought. In the end, he convinced himself that he could actually fly above the throne and adorn himself with the glory of God.

Asah still couldn't fathom how Lucifer, with all of his wisdom, could ever have concluded that such a thing was possible. As accustomed as Asah was to the presence of YHWH, the glory of God was never something he could feel *familiar* with. The area above the throne, where the presence of God intersected the created heavenly realm, was a terrifying place, a place where even the substance of heaven melted away. No created being could go there and live.

Asah's arrival had been anticipated by comrades and friends as well, and as they caught sight of him, they began to fall into flight beside Asah one-by-one, peppering him with questions and asking him to recount the stories of the events on earth. They all already knew, of course, but that was no substitute for a first-hand account, and they wanted to hear it told from his lips. Asah found himself repeating his accounts over and over again — especially the one about the battle of Shaarur, which always resulted in shouts of praise.

They were careful not to slow him down, being mindful of the reason he had come. Those that had been the first to greet him had listened for a while and then moved forward, both to yield their place to the new arrivals and to form a vanguard to announce and facilitate Asah's passage.

Although the mount of congregation towered over the rest of heaven's landscape, it did not end in a single pinnacle, like so many lesser mountains did. Instead, the top was a massive plateau, in the center of which was a modest rise above which the throne of God was situated.

Asah and his cortege touched down just before cresting the rim of the plateau and advanced on foot. The plateau was not formed of the same rock as the sides of the mountain, but was instead composed of clear, iridescent crystal. While at first glance the plateau's top might have appeared to be a single crystalline stone, a closer look revealed that it was in fact many stones perfectly joined together, all smooth and level, the seams between them being almost impossible to detect.

It would have given one the impression of walking upon a sea of limpid glass except for one thing: the sea was alive with light. The ambient light that was present above the crystalline floor was several times more radiant than any sunlight one might encounter on earth, even on the brightest of days. But the crystalline sea was not simply reflecting back this ambient light, the crystals contained a fire of their own.

The patterns were complex and varied, having only a superficial resemblance to the patterns associated with a combustive fire. There were bursts of light, rippling waves of light, boils of light, shafts of light — all constantly in motion, all constantly shifting from one hue to another.

The crystalline fire was not only captivating to watch, but it was also invigorating and refreshing. Asah felt like he could fight a thousand battles in the shadows of earth, and had he not had a specific task to attend to, he would have been content to linger and allow the light to wash over him.

But his ascent upon the mount of YHWH did have a purpose, and Asah didn't slow his approach until he drew near to the throne. Before reaching it, the entourage that had been clearing a forward path for him dropped back one by one, repositioning themselves behind him. Heaven's protocol allowed them to approach with Asah as companions and friends — for there was nothing said before YHWH that was not open for all to hear — but they demonstrated proper honor and deference to the one being granted the audience by not approaching more closely than he did.

Throughout their ascent and walk across the crystalline sea, Asah and his companions had been full of shouts and rejoicing. But as they neared the throne, they all fell became silent. The praise of heaven behind and around them did not lessen, and it was no quieter because of their ceasing, but Asah had begun his approach, and the holiness of God demanded that anyone approaching closely come listening rather than speaking.

Asah dropped to one knee, his right hand on his sword and his head bowed. The group with him followed suit as one. They would remain in this position, in unbroken reverence and stillness, until Asah was called forward. Whether it was minutes or hours or days (not that there were days in heaven), they would not depart until Asah's audience was concluded. Nor would any member of the group rise until Asah was given leave to rise — they had joined themselves in unity to Asah and were, therefore, bound by the same conventions that governed his conduct.

Not that the wait would be tedious. Asah would have been more than happy to never leave, to stay there bowed before the Almighty for the rest of his existence. He was, after all, in the presence of God.

But the wait wasn't long.

The voice of YHWH spoke.

"Asah … come."

THIRTY-THREE

... for where there is no law there is no transgression.
— Romans 4:15b NKJV

P tha felt like celebrating, except there really wasn't anything
he could *do* to properly celebrate. Celebration, the noisy cousin of joy and
happiness, was something that could only be fully experienced in the
context of a community of individuals that shared one mind and one
heart. Like so many things that had once been a constant part of his existence in heaven, the ability to truly celebrate was forever gone — left
behind during the Great Fall. But just because Ptha could no longer be
consumed with joy or lost in rapturous celebration didn't mean he had
forgotten the feelings — or that he didn't hunger for them.

*There are so many vacancies inside all of us. Satan grasped for what
was beyond his reach and now cannot reclaim even the small things that have
been lost.*

The best that Ptha could muster was a partial recession of the
anxiety that every demon constantly felt, and a glimmer of hope that their
discoveries about the tree would yield a truly useful advantage to the
Daimónia. Indeed, his report to the Council had been met with a raucous
welcome — a celebration of sorts, perhaps — except that it lacked genuine
good will among the participants. Following that, research teams had been
sent to explore the dimensions and characteristics of the tree and its
shadow, and some of the results of those investigations were already
coming in.

But the most stunning discovery hadn't come from the research teams, but from what Ptha had learned from the serpent. Ptha had met and spoken with the serpent twice since its first encounter with Adam. On their first meeting, Ptha had instructed Reh'mes (the name Adam had given to the serpent) to show interest and make general inquiries regarding the trees of the garden, hoping to elicit some useful information about the tree without being too obvious about it.

It had paid off. In their second meeting, just now concluded, Ptha had learned from Reh'mes that the mystery of the tree went well beyond its unusual biological properties and its ability to exclude the Anhailas.

The tree was forbidden!

Ptha still couldn't believe it. Adam had been forbidden by YHWH to eat the fruit of the tree, supposedly because it would give to Adam some knowledge of good and evil which Adam didn't currently possess.

No matter. The reason for the prohibition is of minor significance. What is important is that a prohibition exists. For where there is a prohibition, sin becomes a possibility.

No doubt the prohibition was why the trio of angels seemed to already know something about the tree when they had passed it on patrol.

If ever we have had cause to celebrate, this is it!

Now they had a goal. Ptha was returning to bring this latest report to Satan, who would undoubtedly call another Council meeting right away.

But now there is no need for us to hurry. We have identified a sin into which Adam can be enticed. We can take as long and be as careful as necessary in developing and implementing a plan.

The development of such plans was precisely the arena in which Satan excelled.

And I will still be watching, Ptha thought to himself, *watching to see if I should develop and implement a plan of my own.*

Perhaps this new knowledge about the prohibition would give them such a powerful advantage there would be no reason for Ptha to depose Satan. Perhaps they might be able to win after all.

But still, Ptha had thought long and hard about what his life would be like with Satan cast down.

In truth, he had grown very fond of the idea and wasn't ready to abandon it.

THIRTY-FOUR

Delight in the Lord, and he will give thee the requests of thy heart.
— Psalm 37:4 DRB

Until now you have asked for nothing in My name; ask and you will receive, so that your joy may be made full.
— John 16:24 NASB

… how much more shall your Father which is in heaven give good things to them that ask him?
— Matthew 7:11b KJV

Sunset was well past, and with moonrise not due until after midnight, it would soon become too dark to move about by sight. As was his custom, Adam descended to the highest terraced pool for one last drink before bedding down for the evening. The nights were growing much colder, and Adam had begun to sleep frequently in the cavern perched above the Kikwmillu pools. It wasn't that he was unable to sleep in less protected locations — he could if he needed to — but his near-death exposure to cold on his first venture out of the valley of Eden had left him with an affinity for warmth.

The plants of the garden were also responding to the lower temperatures and shorter days. Most of the fruit trees had stopped bearing, and all of the succulent vegetables and some of the greens had succumbed to the nightly frosts. Adam found himself making frequent trips to the warm gardens down-valley from Kikwmillu just to have the taste of fresh, undried produce. But even these heated groves were producing less, as one type of fruit tree after another went into dormancy.

Adam clambered back up over the lip of the cavern, settling a short distance back where he could see the spread of heaven's stars and yet still feel the cavern's warm breath at his back. The time between nightfall and when he went to sleep was always a time of reflection.

Earlier that day Reh'mes had left to feed and to search out a suitable overwintering den somewhere in the lower valley. Adam had offered to share his cavern, but Reh'mes thought it unsuitable — desiring a moister, more enclosed location with less airspace; a place where his body would be more fully surrounded by earth. Reh'mes had promised to return as soon as winter was past and the days warmed up enough for him to travel again.

Adam had enjoyed his regular visits with Reh'mes, sometimes meeting at Kikwmillu, sometimes meeting at other locations in the garden. Their discussions were stimulating enough on an intellectual level, but Adam hadn't been able to develop any true feelings of companionship with the serpent — they were just too different. Reh'mes had a dry sense of humor and a keen desire to learn, but otherwise the serpent gave no indication of possessing the emotions and passions so common to mammals. And of late their conversations had languished as they ran out of things to talk about.

Adam might not have been so aware of his aloneness if it hadn't been for Reh'mes. In part this was due to Reh'mes asking why Adam had no female. But it was also due to the kind of creature Reh'mes was. When Adam was with YHWH, the closeness of their communion banished all thoughts and feelings of isolation. But when Adam was with Reh'mes, he felt acutely the lack of a companion that was like him in both body and soul.

The problem with Reh'mes is that there is no comfort in touching him ... or in being touched by him. Any touches that happen are only incidental; they are never an expression of emotion. As a conversationalist, he has no equal among the creatures. But I would never lay my head against his coils and chat as the mountain clouds slipped from color to color at the end of the day.

Adam was very physical in demonstrating his affection to the animals. Sometimes he played rough; sometimes he gently stroked them.

As they had need they would come to him and he would groom them, removing snags and loosening tangles. Other times he would vigorously rub them down — knowing how much they loved that. They played together and they rested together. More than once he had napped with his head resting against a warm haunch. And when the animals brought their young to him, he never failed to lay his hands on them as he pronounced a natal blessing and gave them their names.

They welcome my touch, and I enjoy touching them. There is a physical closeness we share that goes beyond words. Perhaps it was because they all had warm blood and their bodies were fundamentally the same in spite of outward differences.

Most of the mammals talked, of course — when there was something they needed or when something disturbed their sense of rightness. But trying to engage them in discussions about the abstract issues of life was fruitless. Adam knew — he had tried with many of them. They simply weren't concerned about the why or how of anything beyond their daily needs. They experienced their lives, but had no interest in reflecting upon them.

How wonderful it would be to have a creature of warm flesh that had a mind as interesting as Reh'mes.

Adam sighed; his thoughts once again running down the familiar trail. All of YHWH's creatures had mates except him. It seemed to be a universal, fundamental aspect of life. For every male there was a female, sometimes more than one. And from male and female there always came young.

Adam chuckled at his own naïveté, remembering how he had once concluded that YHWH would make children in the same way He made Adam.

I am the first Man, and had to be formed of the earth, just as every first animal was also formed of the earth. But YHWH has ordained another way for the making of young. Adam shook his head, still amazed that he hadn't seen that from the beginning.

It hadn't been that long ago that Adam had been completely content with being the only person in the garden. Even when he had realized that the garden would one day be a home to others, it had not greatly affected him. In fact, believing he had solved the mystery, he had lost interest and stopped thinking about it.

No longer. The prospect of the first other person being a *she* was nothing short of fascinating. She captivated his thoughts and energized his imagination. Adam couldn't recall his thinking ever having been so dominated by something other than YHWH. He tried to imagine what she would be like, but always ended up with an unsatisfactory mental image that seemed to be much more Adam than female.

Maybe it's not possible for me to correctly imagine a female, Adam thought, not for the first time. He might not know what a female really was, but he had a strong inner sense of what she wasn't.

The only thing Adam was sure about was that her body would be different. That was obviously the main thing differentiating female from male. Beyond that, it was safe to say that she would be like him and yet not like him in other ways, too. It was the "not-like-him" part that both teased and eluded his imagination.

If she were here now, I could talk to her. We could sit close to each other, watch the stars, and keep each other warm. Adam suddenly realized that the sleeping bench in the cavern was large enough for two. *Ahhh! We could stay warm through the winter by our shared body warmth, as well as the cavern's warm vents!*

Assuming, of course, that YHWH formed her and brought her to him before the winter. The thought that she might not come before spring, or perhaps arrive even later, triggered a pang of yearning in his mid-section. This acute awareness of his aloneness was a new emotion; one he was now experiencing on a regular basis.

Adam knew that during the coming winter the loneliness would only increase. He knew that most of the mammals would retreat to their dens and burrows for long periods of sleep, just like the serpent. Some would sleep through the entire winter while others would sleep only during the coldest spells. But he knew he couldn't expect those that **were** awake to climb up the terraced pools to visit him in his cavern. Unless they needed him for something, it would never occur to them to do so. Animals just didn't think that way.

"If she is not here, that leaves only Asah to talk to," Adam muttered.

If Adam had to choose between Asah and Reh'mes as a regular companion, he probably would have chosen Asah. Not because Asah was more interesting to talk to than the serpent; they were comparable to each other in that respect. But speaking with Asah usually had an uplifting effect upon Adam, no matter what the subject matter. Conversely, speaking with Reh'mes had no emotional effect whatsoever.

"But I would still rather talk to her than to Asah," Adam muttered again.

"Which is why I am here," Asah's quiet voice came from behind Adam. He was sitting on the edge of the sleeping bench, barely radiant enough to be seen but not so radiant that Adam had noticed any reflected glow coming from behind him.

Asah still had a way of startling Adam with his unexpected arrivals, but Adam very much wanted to speak with him and set his irritation aside.

"Well good, I have wanted to speak with you." As Adam walked over to the bench to sit down, Asah increased his brightness to light the way. Adam didn't really need the light; he knew the inside of the cavern by heart, yet it *was* nice to have light instead of the cavern's usual inky blackness.

"I didn't want to intrude; you seemed to be deep in thought; but there are some things we need to discuss ... and you *did* mention me."

Adam felt a little embarrassed, remembering what he had said. "Asah, I didn't mean to suggest that I don't enjoy speaking with you. I do, very much — when you are around to speak to. But you are an angel and I am a man ...."

"And you would rather be speaking with her. That is completely as it should be. Your desire to be with her does not offend me."

Adam's eyes grew wide. Asah's words had just confirmed that she *was*, or at least that she some day *would be*. It was the first time her existence had been confirmed outside of Adam's thoughts. Adam's eyes filled with tears, a mixture of the now intensified yearning for her with the joy of knowing that she was more than his imagination run wild.

"Then she is alive." It was both a statement and a question.

"I asked the same question," Asah replied. "His answer was that she lived, but not where she can be seen."

"That doesn't make any sense."

"I agree," Asah said.

"Then can I go to be with her?"

"I asked that too. He said she is already with you."

Adam looked around the cavern. "That really doesn't make any sense."

"I really agree."

Adam was at a loss. The hope that had just buoyed him up was already slipping away. "Asah, do you understand? I *really* want to be with her. Is there nothing that I can do?"

"There is something you can do and it's not difficult, but it is something you have never done before."

"And what is that?" The hope was back.

Asah smiled. "I can't tell you, you'll have to discover that yourself."

Adam tightened his lips. From his many conversations with Asah, Adam had come to understand how much angels loved the mystery of hidden things. "Asah, it would be fine with me if this one time you just gave me the answer now," his mood evident in his tone.

Asah lifted an eyebrow.

"I mean, everything doesn't always have to be a riddle. A straight, clear answer would be as refreshing as it would be unusual."

Asah overlooked Adam's sarcasm. "Adam, I am not toying with you. I know how important this is to you and I will answer you as clearly as I can. But I cannot reveal to you what has not been revealed to me, nor can I exceed the bounds that YHWH has placed upon me. I can only share what He has given me liberty to share."

"Then please do so."

"Do you remember when all the animals came to you to be named?"

Adam remembered. He had been naming animals since the day of his awakening, but there had been one day that was different from all of the rest. On that day, the procession of animals had been unending, as pair after pair, family after family came by.

"I remember."

"Do you know why they came to you that day?"

"To be named of course."

"Yes, they came to be named, but that was the lesser reason for their coming. They also came to teach you something."

"Teach me? I don't see how that could have been their purpose. Other than asking to receive their names, they all had very little to say."

"But they did ask, did they not?"

Adam thought back, recalling how as each pair or family of animals approached him he had always asked what he could do for them, and they had always asked in return for their names.

"Did you name any of them without their first asking to be named?"

"Not that I recall … in fact, no. I always waited for them to speak their request."

"Why did you do that? Surely after the first several animals you deduced why they were all coming to you that day. You could have dispensed with the dialogue and just given them their names. Why prolong the process by listening to their requests when you already know what they want?"

"I don't know. I didn't give it a thought at the time. It just seemed the right way to do things."

Asah smiled.

"You are like your Father, son of YHWH," and then Asah was gone and the cavern returned to darkness.

THIRTY-FIVE

*… No tree in the garden of God was like it in beauty. I made it
beautiful with a multitude of branches, so that all the trees of Eden
envied it, that were in the garden of God.*
— Ezekiel 31:8b-9 NKJV

*But each one is tempted when he is drawn away by his own desires
and enticed. Then, when desire has conceived, it gives birth to sin;
and sin, when it is full-grown, brings forth death.*
— James 1:14-15 NKJV

Adam slept fitfully through the first half of the night; his mind
filled with a parade of half-dreamed, half-imagined scenarios of meeting
her. As soon as he had grasped the meaning of Asah's lesson, he had
resolved to seek YHWH out and present his request. He had never before
been apprehensive about meeting with God, but this time the outcome
was so important that the more Adam thought about it the more anxious
he became. Eventually he gave up trying to sleep, though he remained on
the sleeping ledge because the cave's entrance was too cold.

It wasn't that he thought YHWH wouldn't grant his request. He
was sure that He would, and that He would do so joyfully. All of his
reasoning and everything he knew of YHWH's ways gave him this confidence. But there was the question of *when*. Adam had to accept the possibility that YHWH might delay for one reason or another, or for no reason
at all. But the clamor in Adam's heart had grown to the point that he could

no longer put his thoughts of her aside. In that sense what YHWH told Asah was right, she was already with him.

The thought of facing the winter alone, without her, pressed down upon him in a palpable way. What if he had not gathered enough food stores to last them both through winter? What if YHWH delayed bringing her to him simply because Adam had not prepared adequately when the garden contained a surfeit of food? Adam mentally recalled all of his food caches and tried to calculate whether there would be enough for two of them. It seemed like there would be, but he knew his assessment was based on many assumptions. Some of these assumptions were fairly safe — it seemed likely she would eat the same things as he and that she would not differ greatly in size from him. But still, he didn't really *know* how much she would eat, nor did he know how long winter would last or how long it would take the garden to start producing once winter was over.

Adam decided that if the food stores were insufficient, he would simply eat less to accommodate the shortfall. He also would resume his food gathering tomorrow from those dried and scattered crops that would allow it. One way or another he would make sure she was fed. He would also make sure YHWH understood he was willing to go without if only He would allow her to be with him now.

And then he had another thought.

What if she brings forth young during the winter? How many of them might there be? As Adam lay there the sensation of pressure suddenly increased. It felt like some giant creature had its foot planted on his stomach and had just now lifted the other supporting foot off the ground. Being ever the observer, Adam had noted that amongst the animals the lactating females consumed greater amounts of food. His female would surely not differ in this respect. And once their young were weaned they also would need to be fed from the stores.

That could be a very sensible reason for YHWH to delay. Adam chided himself for not preparing more adequately. There was no way the food stores would be adequate if they had to feed the two of them *and* a litter of young.

Adam leaned out over the edge of the sleeping ledge to where he could see the cave's entrance. The subdued light of the half moon had just begun to be overtaken by the new day. Adam rose up and as he approached the cave's entrance saw that while the air was clear at the cave's elevation, the valley floor of Kikwmillu was shrouded in a thick fog that obscured everything.

Adam tended to his morning routine and then plopped down in the nearest hot pool in frustration. He had already chosen the Ey'mru he would visit to seek YHWH's presence, and it was not one of the nearby ones. The mist was so thick it would undoubtedly slow his progress and might eventually halt it all together. He knew Kikwmillu so well he could find his way to the waterfall in the poorest of light. But this particular holy place was not one he had frequented often, and he eventually would need to be able to see at a distance to navigate his way.

No matter. I will start anyway, Adam decided, rising from the pool and stepping his way from one pool rim to another as he headed downslope.

By the time Adam scrambled down around the waterfall, the mists were beginning to lift, and as he proceeded along (and sometimes in) the river, the day not only cleared completely but turned warm and humid. He jogged where the terrain allowed it, reaching the uppermost planted terrace by mid-morning. The plum trees had already dropped all of their leaves; the pear and almond trees were still in the process of doing so. There was no fruit to be found anywhere, only a scattering of nuts strewn among the wet leaves.

In his haste to be on his way Adam had once again neglected to carry any of his stored food with him; in fact he had not even bothered to feed himself beforehand. He *was* hungry, but refused to stop to eat. He settled for snatching dried grapes and figs as he made his descents over the terrace walls, barely slowing his pace as he did so.

At the ledge between the third and fourth terrace Adam faced a decision. The quickest route to the selected Ey'mru would pass right by the tree of knowledge of good and evil. There was an alternate, more circuitous route — but taking that would add considerably to his travel time, and the sense of urgency driving him forward was strong.

There were other holy places where he might meet with YHWH of course, but he had long ago learned to heed his inner sense of when and where they were to meet. Sometimes Adam didn't have an inner leading to go to any specific Ey'mru, and YHWH responded to his worship wherever Adam happened to offer it. But every time a leading *had* been present and Adam had ignored it by going to some place closer, he had spent his time at that Ey'mru alone. And this time the leading was as strong as it had ever been, as strong as the second morning after his awakening when he had run to offer worship to YHWH.

Adam made his decision and set off again. The chance of arriving too late wasn't one he was willing to take. The quickest route passed by the tree, and that's exactly what he would do — he would *pass by it*. He wouldn't tarry, he wouldn't study it like he had before, and he most certainly wouldn't step beneath its canopy. He would give it wide berth. In fact, at first sight of it, he would leave the trail and circle around it at a distance.

But Adam had forgotten how closely this particular trail came to the tree, not having been back to the site since his first visit. He hadn't even thought he was close to it when the trail, having snaked through a dense stand of cedars, suddenly emptied him into the familiar clearing.

The tree was directly in front of him, and not very far away.

Adam stopped in his tracks, at first in surprise at finding himself so close to the very thing he wished to avoid, and then at the appearance of the tree.

It was unchanged! Except for the evergreen conifers, all of the trees of the garden had either lost their leaves or were well into their color change. And none of the broad-leaved trees had any ripe fruit. But this tree was as verdant and vigorous as it had been in the middle of summer. And its outer branches not only drooped under the weight of abundant fruit, but Adam could see that some of the fruits were still green and in the process of ripening.

How can this be? Adam still hadn't moved a step from where he had stopped. *What kind of tree is this? Nothing in the garden is still in fruit; everything is out of season.* Yet Adam couldn't deny the evidence before him. This tree apparently had a prolonged season unlike all the other trees of the garden.

Adam was aware, of course, that he had already varied from his plan. He had planned not to stop and he had planned to circle widely around the tree, and had done neither. He remembered from his first visit how the tree had exuded a feeling of sentience that he had only perceived when he had stepped beneath its canopy. And not only sentience, but desire as well. He didn't have that sense now, but he also wasn't under its canopy.

Perhaps it had only been his imagination on his first visit, and he wondered if he was being over-cautious. Maybe the characteristics he had ascribed to the tree had existed only in his mind.

Adam took a few steps toward the tree — not really because he had decided to, or because he intended to approach the tree, but doing it nonetheless. It was almost like he was intentionally doing something he was intentionally not thinking about.

A tingle of excitement scurried through him, centered somewhere between his stomach and his chest.

Adam stopped. Intentionally. Here he was, doing exactly what he had purposed not to do. He turned to leave, took three steps away, and then stopped again as a new thought crossed his mind.

This is the tree of knowledge of good and evil. Receiving my female is surely a good thing. Perhaps all of my questions about her would be answered if I were to eat ….

The excitement remained, but it was instantly pierced by a hardened stab of fear. It was a logical thought, but Adam was still shocked that he had thought it. Some of Asah's words came back to him: "… *unless you have lost all desire for what the tree offers, you will eventually find yourself standing before the tree when you didn't intend to go there, and you will have to choose again the next time you pass by it.*"

Adam felt a surge of anger push the fear and excitement aside. This tree was not going to assert power over him! And he most certainly wouldn't be so rash as to approach the tree any closer, no matter how intriguing its appearance or how great his curiosity or how many answers he might gain. He was sovereign in the garden and he would not be enticed into doing something he didn't choose to do.

Adam stared at the tree defiantly. "I am the master of the garden," he yelled on impulse. "You are the master of nothing! You are only a strange tree that doesn't know what season it is. You have nothing I want."

Adam resumed his jog but didn't circle like he had originally planned. Instead he doggedly followed the path as it skirted close around the tree toward the other side of the clearing, glaring at the tree as he went by, refusing to divert even one step outward in deference to the tree's presence.

THIRTY-SIX

Revile not ... for a bird of the heavens shall carry the voice, and that which hath wings shall tell the matter.
— Ecclesiastes 10:20b ASV

It was the closest Ptha had ever been to the man-creature, and he watched him in silent fascination, his corpus fully tucked inside the tree trunk in case Asah or any other angels were around. Ptha had concluded his last meeting of the season with the serpent that morning. The serpent had invited Ptha to cohabit with him through the winter hibernation, but Ptha had declined, pleading the need to be on standby should Asah take a turn for the worse and pre-emptive actions become necessary for Adam's protection. Unlike so many hibernating mammals that slept though the winter, the serpent would spend the winter physically torpid but mentally awake. Ptha had promised to visit if circumstances allowed, though in truth he was inclined to limit these to the minimum necessary to maintain the serpent's pliability and emotional dependency. The serpent had fed heavily a month earlier to accumulate fat reserves, and during that time Ptha had cohabited more frequently because he so enjoyed the feeding experience. But as winter approached the serpent had abruptly stopped feeding, saying it needed to empty its gut before retiring for the winter, leaving Ptha with no incentive to share its body.

There were always watchers posted in the tree, and the shadowy passage between the tree and Satan's dominion had become a busy thoroughfare. Ptha spent a great deal of time in the tree, the corruption of

Adam now being his one and only assigned duty. The tree offered Ptha a safe and central location from where he could easily slip out and prowl the garden if he so desired. When Ptha was there, he always dismissed the other Daimónia, preferring to think and plan in solitude. But as soon as he left, there were always several demons that slid into the vacated trunk area to take up watch. Throughout all the watching and exchanging of places the demons had been careful to never reveal their presence to any of the angelic patrols.

When Adam first yelled out, Ptha had streaked down the passage, fearful that the man-creature had discerned Ptha's presence and was about to pronounce judgment. *Ptha* was not going to be the one to test whether the tree offered protection from the man's commands — a lesser demon would be used to establish that once their use of the tree was finally discovered.

But when Ptha heard the man refer to the tree directly, he paused and, still listening, reversed his direction. Making his way back to the trunk, Ptha arrived just as Adam ran past but still in time to study the man's facial expression. As Adam disappeared into the woods at the far side of the clearing, Ptha made himself comfortable and settled down to think about the man's words.

I am the master of the garden … you are the master of nothing … you have nothing I want.

Ptha mentally replayed the phrases over and over again, searching for the meaning behind the words. The words themselves were rich in content and, if correctly interpreted, could offer valuable insights into the man's thought processes. But there was more to be explored here than just *what* was said.

Why would Adam speak to the tree? Ptha asked himself. *This tree has many unusual properties, but speech isn't one of them.*

Ptha had spent a great deal of time in the tree or in close proximity to it, and there had never been any indication of any sentience associated with the tree. No words … no whispered thoughts … no feelings. The tree was anomalous in a biological sense, and it had the strange features of the surrounding exclusion zone and the shadow passage beneath it, but Ptha never thought the tree had *caused* either. Features of the spiritual realm were sometimes juxtaposed with features of the material realm, and on occasions the spiritual realm exerted influence on the material realm, but not the other way around. Non-sentient material objects never *created* spiritual phenomena. If there was any linkage, it would have been that the tree was what it was because the shadow passage was already there.

Ptha had always been a keen student of the mind, even before leaving heaven. He learned long ago that words were windows into the inner thoughts of other beings. When he joined Satan's league, he refined this knowledge through countless conversations with angels who were in the process of choosing sides. Because words almost always conveyed more than their obvious content, a careful listener could learn not only what the speaker's surficial thoughts were, but also the speaker's fears, insecurities, desires, and dreams. When it came to turning a person aside onto a path they wouldn't choose without outside influence, these deeper insights were invariably the most useful type of information.

Adam's words had briefly opened a window to his soul. It wasn't one Ptha could enter, but it *was* one he could look through.

Ptha began his mental dissection, phrase by phrase.

I am the master of the garden.

That was a statement of fact, a fact so obvious it hardly needed to be said. But Adam *had* said it, presumably because he felt a need to re-affirm his mastery by declaration. And if he felt such a need, then the clear implication was that he wasn't completely secure in his mastery, that he felt the tree represented some threat to that mastery.

You are the master of nothing.

Another statement of the obvious, but equally full of meaning. By comparing his dominion with that of the tree, Adam was acknowledging that in his mind a competition existed — or at least the potential for competition.

You are only a strange tree that doesn't know what season it is.

Adam's third phrase strengthened Ptha's belief that Adam believed himself to be in competition. By adding the word only, Adam had belittled the tree, something one does to adversaries but not to inanimate objects. Adam also attributed ignorance to the tree, a second belittling, perhaps suggesting that Adam believed the tree to be sentient in some way.

Ptha re-ordered and amplified Adam's words, a technique that often uncovered additional insights into a speaker's mental landscape.

227

As long as I am the master of the garden, you are the master of nothing.
I am the master of the garden as long as you are the master of nothing.
When you become the master of something, I am no longer the master
of the garden.

And because, in the final analysis, there can only be one sovereign over anything:

When you become the master of something, you become master over me.

Ptha clacked his toeclaws together in glee. Adam had shown his vulnerability!

They already knew, of course, that Adam had been forbidden to eat from the tree of knowledge. Up until now Ptha had assumed the man had no reason and no desire to disobey, and that the Daimónia would have to contrive some plausible reason to entice him to do so. But apparently, Adam did have a desire ... and even now was in contest with that desire.

Ptha smiled. *Adam, you are not being truthful with yourself. The tree does have something you want. You just aren't willing to admit it.*

It was too bad the serpent had already retired for the season. There was really no other way to discover what Adam wanted other than through the serpent. Ptha and the Archon could speculate and theorize, but confirmation of Adam's desires would have to wait for the serpent's emergence in the spring.

We want what we do not have, Ptha reflected. *So, my little man-creature, the question is obvious ... What do you lack?*

THIRTY-SEVEN

It is not good that man should be alone ...
— Genesis 2:18b NKJV

Adam ran hard, partly to hasten his journey but mostly to burn off the tension that was lodged in his gut. Every time he approached the tree it ended up affecting him in disturbing ways. In fact, nothing seemed to have the ability to disquiet him the way the tree did. It seemed to crawl inside his mind and spawn thoughts and feelings that were not *him*. Adam knew he had not been alive that long, yet he felt confident he knew himself well enough to know when he was thinking in ways that were unlike him.

Where, exactly, do these thoughts come from? From the tree? From somewhere within me?

During his first encounter with the tree, Adam thought the tree was sentient in some primal, elemental way. More precisely, he felt the tree exuded a desire for him, though he had been at a loss to put a name on that desire.

But this time Adam was the one that had felt desire — desire for what the tree could offer him.

Maybe the tree isn't sentient at all. Maybe all the unusual thoughts and feelings are springing from somewhere inside of me. Maybe my reactions are not to the tree, but to what the tree represents and to what it offers. Although Adam had never given even passing consideration to actually eating of the tree, or for that matter touching it, he *had* thought about the tree's properties, albeit in an abstract, intellectually curious way.

There was no disputing the tree aroused his curiosity and, in realizing that, Adam recognized the common thread between the two encounters. *Desire. Both times the tree evoked desire.*

His first interaction was driven by curiosity — the desire for knowledge about something unknown and the desire to explore the strange feelings he felt as he stood beneath the tree's canopy. Adam knew his curiosity bordered on insatiable at times, but he never considered it a vulnerability. He now realized this would require some re-thinking on his part.

Adam's latest encounter with the tree had again started with his curiosity being whetted, but the curiosity had been rapidly pushed aside when it occurred to him that the tree might provide specific knowledge about something he wanted more than anything else — his female.

Adam understood he had been tempted; and, even though he had successfully withstood the temptation, he was shaken by the realization that the temptation may have in fact arisen from within him rather than from the tree. He never imagined such a strong pull could be loosed by just a few wandering thoughts. It made him change how he regarded himself. It also forced him to broaden his understanding of temptation — allowing for the possibility that the desire for the forbidden could arise from within and not just be evoked from without. While he could avoid external sources of temptation by distancing himself from them, as he had done for months with the tree, he couldn't distance himself from himself.

Asah had told him that as long as he desired what the tree had to offer, he would have to choose every time he encountered it. At the time, Adam thought that the solution to that phenomenon was simply to not desire what the tree offered.

But what if I can't dismiss the desire out of hand? What if the desire is a good one; even one that is allowable in YHWH's eyes?

Obviously in such cases he couldn't just stop desiring.

But he could refuse to fulfill such desires in ways that were not allowable.

He could refuse to fulfill his desire for *her* in any way that was not allowable.

Adam understood that receiving his female rested in God's hands. Even if he gained some knowledge about her from the tree, it wouldn't change the fundamental fact that YHWH would bring her to him when He chose to do so. And had Adam succumbed to the temptation, YHWH might have deemed Adam unworthy and he might never have received her at all.

Not to mention the fact that his disobedience would have brought about his death.

Temptation is no simple adversary. I would be wise not to underestimate it in the future. Henceforth, he would treat temptation with the same guarded respect as he would any demonic enemy.

It is a good lesson. It is not just what I do or don't do. The way I think — the thoughts I allow -have the power to secure my safety or deliver me to death.

Somehow that realization brought some closure to the matter.

THIRTY-EIGHT

*Ask, and it shall be given you; seek, and ye shall find; knock, and
it shall be opened unto you.*
— Matthew 7:7 KJV

This holy place was one of the quiet, serene ones. In the middle
of a dense grove of towering pines was a place where the ground abruptly
dropped away into a wide, roughly circular sinkhole. The grove was thick
enough that it hid the sinkhole from view until one was very close. The
sides were vertical and weathered for most of the sinkhole's circumference,
stained with seepage lines and spotted with tufts of moss and fern-lines
sprouting along the cracks. The only passable descent was a strand of five
gently mounded platforms that stairstepped all the way down to the deep
central pool. The upper and middle platforms supported pines as massive
as those of the surrounding forest, many of them leaning precariously out
over the pool. But the lowermost platform contained only a lush carpet of
moss and grass that mounded on top and crept down over its edges. This
platform was low enough that it was occasionally inundated by high water
levels during wet periods, and these intermittent submersions prevented
the successful establishment of the trees.

Adam paused at the edge of the sinkhole.

"Are you here?" Adam didn't really call out — he just spoke the
question in a voice slightly louder than normal, as if he were speaking to
someone on the closest platform.

"I am here Adam; come down and let's talk," YHWH answered. Adam hadn't seen YHWH before that moment, but now He was sitting in plain sight on the lowest platform, smiling at Adam and waving for him to come down.

Adam scrambled down and as he crossed the next to lowest platform, he was surprised to find Asah, leaning against one of the trees in a spot not visible from above.

"Been here long?" Adam quipped as he passed Asah with a grin but without slowing down. Asah raised an eyebrow but said nothing.

Adam stopped as soon as he dropped onto the lowest platform. He was always beset with conflicting desires when he first met with YHWH in a holy place. On the one hand, he wanted to jump into God's arms with reckless abandon, yet he also wanted to prostrate himself in the reverent worship as was only fitting for one coming into His presence.

YHWH motioned Adam over and patted the ground next to him, dispelling all uncertainty as to what he should do.

Adam sat down next to God. When YHWH was present in physical form, Adam loved to nestle against His side or lean against His strong, muscular arm. But this time, Adam had important questions to ask, so he sat close enough to touch Him but where he could still see His face.

"Do you know why I came?" Adam asked.

"To see Me of course. Isn't that why you always come?" YHWH teased, His eyes brimming with merriment.

"Of course. But this is a special meeting. I have something very important to ask you."

"Wait, let me guess ...." God laid His forefinger against His cheek and angled His eyes upward, still teasing. "Perhaps you need to give Me a hint ...."

Adam was trying to be serious but couldn't keep from laughing. God could be so incredibly funny. The thought of the all-knowing One lifting His eyes toward heaven for a hint from someone above — the angels must be rolling in laughter over that one.

Adam decided to play along. "OK ... winter is coming, and based on what I've been told, the days will be cold and the nights will be colder."

"You want I should make the cave's vents warmer? That's not too difficult for me; I'm fairly sure I can handle that one," God said, laughing at His own joke.

"No, the vents are fine; at least, I think they are. But I'll be spending a lot of time in the cave and it would be nice to have a companion to stay warm with. And to talk to …."

YHWH inclined an open hand toward where Asah was standing.

"Asah's not the most available companion."

"I have to admit that's true," God said. "I do keep him rather busy. And while I am always glad to speak with you Adam, I do understand what you mean when you say you want someone to talk to. You need a different type of companion than you have had up until now, and there is no need for further delay. In fact, it would not be good for you to face this winter alone."

"Really?" Adam's reply was weak, his heart pounding. God was still smiling, but His earnest expression made it clear that He was no longer joking.

"So?" God asked.

Adam sensed a profound difference in how YHWH was looking at him — as if He were seeing more of Adam than Adam himself could perceive.

"If you are willing, I would like her to be with me. I don't want to wait any longer."

"Your life will never be the same again Adam. It will never be like it is now. It will be better, much better, but it will also be different. In receiving her, you will lose part of yourself."

"I am willing; whatever I need to do. She is worth whatever price I have to pay."

"Then I am willing also," YHWH said, pleased with Adam's response. "That is exactly the answer I would expect from a son."

THIRTY-NINE

*The LORD God fashioned into a woman the rib which He had
taken from the man ...*
> — Genesis 2:22a NASB

*For the word of God is quick, and powerful, and sharper than any
two-edged sword, piercing even to the dividing asunder of soul and
spirit, and of the joints and marrow ...*
> — Hebrews 4:12a KJV

E xcept for his deep, even breathing, Adam lay completely still
on the mound of grass. His face was composed and peaceful; his hands
open and lax. It reminded Asah of Adam's body on the day of his awakening, just before YHWH had blown upon Adam and he had received his
first breath. But this time Adam's body was not lifeless, not awaiting *the*
breath that Adam spoke of so often. This time Adam was fully alive.

All of heaven was watching, of course. But none had the vantage
point that Asah did, who now moved down to the edge of the lowest platform. YHWH had afforded Asah special honor by allowing him to remain
so close, allowing him to not only see what He was about to do, but also
to see how He did it. There was no envy in heaven, and although his fellow
Anhailas celebrated the privilege being given to Asah, there was not an
angel watching that didn't yearn to be standing next to Asah. Angels lived
for revelation; and the greater the mystery being revealed, the more
delirious their delight. The weight of the honor being afforded Asah made

him want to prostrate himself. But this wasn't the time for worship, or even for speaking; this was a time for Asah to contain his awe and watch in silence.

YHWH, the Creator of the material universe, the One who constantly gazed upon all realms seen and unseen, was once again about to do a new thing.

Asah watched as YHWH bent over Adam's body, singing softly to Himself. YHWH paused for a moment, still singing, and then assumed a position that covered Adam from the view of any distant observers while still leaving Asah a clear, unobstructed view.

YHWH stopped singing and spoke, but so quietly that His words were not discernible. Asah strained to hear what He was saying, but it was below the threshold of even his acute hearing, and Asah would never be so rash as to approach closer than where YHWH had positioned him. Asah could see the embodied energy of YHWH's words each time they left His lips, so he knew He was speaking and not just singing quietly. Occasionally, Asah could hear some fragment of a delicate whisper, but it wasn't enough for Asah to even determine the language being spoken.

Asah's focus had been on YHWH, but his attention shifted to Adam when a deep, bloody incision suddenly appeared across Adam's lower ribcage. YHWH was not touching Adam, and Asah realized that one of YHWH's spoken words had caused the flesh to part. The cut was parallel to and slightly higher than Adam's right twelfth rib, and extended from the front of Adam's abdomen to more than half of the way back around his ribcage, stopping just short of the large muscles of Adam's back. The wound had cleanly severed all the various tendons and ligaments that joined the twelfth rib to the rib above it, as well as the tendons connecting the rib to the vertebral column and the pelvis.

There were two curious aspects of the wound which Asah noticed right away. No blood was flowing out of the wound. The incised tissue surfaces were all covered with blood, but the blood, once it appeared, seemed to be held in place. Asah knew enough about bodies of flesh to understand that this was not normal. He also knew that YHWH attached special significance to the blood of flesh creatures, though why this should be so was a mystery to all of the Anhailas

The second remarkable feature was the precision of the cut. If a physical sword had cut Adam's side, there would have been stubs of ligaments and the splayed ends of tendons still attached to the rib. But the rib, other than a thin a film of blood, was completely clean. Asah focused his vision on the surface of the rib and saw that the ligaments and tendons had actually parted completely free of the bone's surface, as if they had never been attached there to begin with.

YHWH spoke a word and the subcutaneous fatty tissue on either side of the wound retracted, making the opening larger. He then extended one finger and touched the free, anterior end of the rib, and immediately withdrew His hand. As He did so, the rib traveled with it, disarticulating from the spine with a soft pop, the end of the rib adhering to the finger of God.

Asah stared in fascination and growing confusion as YHWH looked intently at the rib, now in the palm of His left hand. He couldn't fathom what YHWH was doing. Asah thought he was there to witness the creation of the female, but now it looked as if YHWH was going to disassemble Adam. That made no sense whatsoever. Asah, perhaps more than any of the angels, understood just how deeply YHWH loved Adam.

YHWH finally turned his attention back to Adam, who was still breathing regularly, his body showing no indication of being under duress. In rapid succession YHWH touched the unattached ends of the severed tendons and reattached them to new locations, the tendons momentarily adhering to his finger just as the rib had. In some cases the fascia covering the muscles remained intact, in other cases Asah could see the fascia dissolve as one muscle was realigned contiguous with another muscle. When YHWH touched the severed ligaments and cartilage that dangled from the rib above the extraction site, the connective tissues were instantly consumed in a tiny wisp of smoke. When there were no more loose ends to be attached, YHWH spoke, and the retracted tissues fell back to their previous, loosely gaping position. YHWH traced the length of the wound with His finger, and as He did so, the flesh joined seamlessly back together.

YHWH stood erect and looked at Asah and smiled. "Come, stand by his side," He said.

Asah stepped up to stand next to Adam. YHWH walked a few paces away, still holding the rib in His open palm. Then YHWH tipped His hand. The rib slid into a vertical position but didn't fall; it simply hung suspended in midair. God spoke another inaudible word and the rib split open along its length, revealing the dark red marrow that filled the interior of the bone shaft.

After a short pause, YHWH spoke again. The marrow within the bone began to swell and spill out of the open crack, flowing out around the shaft and both ends of the bone. At first the living mass retained the color and consistency of marrow, but as it grew in size it wasn't long before Asah could see different colors and shapes starting to appear within the mass. When Asah focused his vision and looked more closely he saw that the cells from inside the shaft of the bone were differentiating into new types of tissue, all of which were multiplying at an unnaturally rapid rate.

YHWH didn't speak again after uttering the word that had started the growth process, but He did resume His quiet singing. Asah thought that YHWH seemed especially pleased with what He was doing, though Asah knew this was a subjective judgment; YHWH was almost always abounding with joy and very pleased with whatever He was doing.

When the mass of living tissues reached a certain size, it simultaneously budded in four directions. The extremities slowly elongated, the hands and feet forming only once the proximal portions of the arms and legs were complete. By the time the fingers and toes were formed, the rest of the body had stopped expanding in size, though frenetic cell growth still continued over the surface of the body. Then, in the space of two of Adam's breaths, the body's surface went from wet to dry as skin suddenly materialized. The body had no hair, and its overall form was clearly different than Adam's.

Asah looked down at Adam, who was still sleeping peacefully. *How marvelous are His ways,* Asah thought, *you will soon have your female!*

Her body was upright and motionless; her feet resting lightly on the ground. Asah could see that she wasn't standing of her own accord because there was no tension in her muscles. She was being held in place by the power of YHWH. All tissue growth appeared to have ceased with the exception of her hair, which appeared as dark silky stubble. Her hair was growing at a faster rate than was normal, but it was still slow compared to how quickly the rest of her body had formed.

She resembled Adam in many, but not all respects. Her skin tone was a rich olive-brown, darker than Adam's and without any red undertones. Adam often had a ruddy appearance, especially when he exerted himself, or when he was moderately cold. But she looked like her color would remain constant no matter what her activity level.

She was perhaps half a head shorter than Adam, less wide across the shoulders, but wider across the hips. Although her body had a softer, more rounded appearance, Asah could see that she was strong, with an underlying musculature that was comparable to Adam's. Her breasts were well-developed and substantially larger than Asah would have expected, given that she was not in a lactating condition. In Asah's observations of other mammals, the mammary glands were always reduced and obscure except during periods of nursing. But Adam's female looked like she was already capable of nursing even though she had no young.

By the time her hair had reached a half-finger in length, Asah noticed another difference. No hair was growing on her face. Unlike Adam, who had hair more places than he didn't, the female's body was mostly free of hair. Even though her eyes were closed and her face was unanimated, Asah thought her face was strikingly beautiful. He imagined what she might look like with Adam's beard and decided that her lack of facial hair definitely made her more pleasant to look at. *Of course,* Asah thought to himself, *I have been looking at hairless faces for virtually all of my existence. My opinion may simply be a preference for that which is familiar.*

She looked like she was complete, and Asah expected the next event to be YHWH bestowing the breath of life upon her. But YHWH wasn't quite finished. He placed one hand on the smooth surface of her lower stomach and began speaking a blessing over her. As usual, His spoken words were visible as they went forth, being full of vibrant light. But this was a most unusual blessing, because as each word left His lips, it burst into countless tiny orbs of pulsating light. These streaked toward her abdomen, flowed around and between the fingers of God, and submerged out of sight into her belly.

When the blessing was finished, YHWH stood in front of her, lifted her head slightly with one finger, blew a single puff into her face, and spoke her name.